The Calamari Kleptocracy

Nicolas Sansone

The Calamari Kleptocracy

ISBN: 978-0-9850066-6-2

Library of Congress Control Number: 2012939224

Cover art by Eric Portis

Published in 2012 by All Things That Matter Press

FOR MY FATHER

Acknowledgments

While we often think about a work of fiction as the result of solitary creativity, there are dozens of people without whom this book would never have come into existence.

First, I would like to thank Chris Bachelder, Melvin Bukiet, Noy Holland, Rosemary Laughlin, Elizabeth Majerus, Brian Morton, and Sabina Murray for helping me even to see myself as a writer in the first place. Their gracious, consistent support has been instrumental in my development of both technical skill and artistic confidence.

Second, I must thank Phil and Deb Harris at All Things that Matter Press for their professional support and Marvin D. Wilson for his thorough editing job. Further, I would like to thank Chris Bachelder, Jensen Beach, Adam Cogbill, Chris Connelly, Christy Crutchfield, Madeline ffitch, Rachel B. Glaser, Luke Goebel, Andrea Lawlor, Gustavo Llarull, John Maradik, Robin McLean, Jess Miele, Sabina Murray, Andrew Pisansky, Eric Portis, David Sansone, Megan Turner, Ian Wang, Matt Weingast, and anybody else who looked at early versions of this book. Without their generous feedback, *The Calamari Kleptocracy* would be 800 pages long and quite unreadable.

Special thanks goes to Eric Portis, both for his offer to do the cover art for *The Calamari Kleptocracy* and for his many years of friendship and encouragement.

Finally, thank you to all the many young men and women who have joined me in watching years of their lives disappear into the exploitative jaws of the food service industry. Fight back however you can.

THE CALAMARI KLEPTOCRACY

Alan gathers the four of us together in the break-room before the lunch shift. "I want to make a change," he says, looking right at me with his greenish-gold eyes. My throat goes dry and I run my thumb along a big knife gash on the table in front of me. Alan's a smart guy, thoughtful most always, but he's never just up and said, "I want to make a change." I don't like change. "Change" is how Mom and Dad call it when we have to trade our nice car for a worse car, due to The Money Situation. Alan says, "I want to make a change," and I see myself sitting under a bridge somewhere, hungry.

Mandy-Mandy pulls a long string of pink gum out of her mouth and twists it tight around her finger. She's angry all the time. Sure, she's chipper and pretty and all those good waitressy things, but even when she's chipper, she's angry. Most of the knife scars on the break-room table came from her.

"What kind of change?" Mandy-Mandy growls at Alan. She puts a new stick of gum in her mouth and mashes up and down on it with her jaws. Mandy-Mandy likes gum; she can beat up on it and it won't complain or fight back. "Change makes Mandy-Mandy's blood pressure increase, which makes Mandy-Mandy's fight increase, which increase it does not behoove you to instigate, and etcetera," she says. She takes her corkscrew out of her pocket, flips it open, and starts twisting it into a coffee stain on the table, warning Alan not to increase her fight.

"Can it. The restaurant business is a den of backstabbing crooks and wayfarers," Alan says, pounding his fist on the marinara-splattered wall. "It's capitalism in its finest form, people: eat or get eaten. And right now, we've got a hungry pack of wolves on the loose in Gruff Valley, eagerly licking their chops at the prospect of getting a nibble of our market share."

Remus and Romulus, our twin line cooks, sit and stare at Alan with their little mouths hanging open. Alan got them from the Gruff Valley Orphan Asylum five years ago, named them, and raised them. They don't talk much, but they get along with each other and can slap a monster panini together in twenty seconds flat. "If a couple of twelve year olds can work that fast," Alan sometimes says to me, "why can't you?" It's not fair to compare us. They've got their ways and I've got mine.

"I'm talking about the fiendish maw of competition, guys!" Alan says, searching our faces, like he's looking for gold but is afraid he's not going to find it. Sometimes Alan uses such big words none of us understand what he's trying to say. I want to sit down with him and explain it'd probably be better for everybody if he'd just use words that are sharp and simple like daggers, instead of blasting us with giant bazookas of words, but Alan doesn't like feedback. "We've got Ethiopian food moving in across the street, Mister Danjoohar just opened up a new Curry in a Hurry on Blithe Street, and Churros con Burros is gaining momentum."

"Churros con Burros will never get off the ground," Mandy-Mandy says, shredding her gum with her long, pink fingernail.

"All I'm saying," Alan says, "is that we've got to stop thinking like restaurateurs and start thinking like Viet-Cong. First employee to fetch me a pint of Danjoohar's blood gets a meaty Christmas bonus."

Remus and Romulus crack their knuckles before making for the exit. They're halfway out the door when Alan yells at them to get their butts back in the break room.

"Jesus Christ, my Lord and Savior," Alan says, raising his hands up to heaven, "not a damn soul in this room understands the gentle touches of irony. I wish I were back in college, where they have safeguards against morons like you. That was a joke. I don't want to hurt Danjoohar unless it comes to that and, even then, there's no way in hell that any of you are getting a Christmas bonus this year. There's just no money in the coffers."

Remus clambers back to his place at the table, but Romulus must be disappointed because he stays in the doorway, all cowed, watching a crowd of ants carry breadcrumbs across the floor. Alan taught the twins all kinds of things about making sandwiches quickly, but I don't know if he taught them about good and bad. That's my job; I always try to teach them the right thing to do, when I know it. Romulus stomps on the ants, which isn't fair. The ants just wanted some food.

"It isn't nice to mash up bugs," I say to Romulus. He runs to his brother and burrows his head into Remus's lap. I don't know if he heard me. Maybe.

"Thor," Alan says. "Would you please, for the love of God's only begotten son, clam it, and allow me to continue talking business?"

I mime stitching my lips together. I don't mind it when Alan zings me, because that's his way. He's got dramatic Italian blood in him, so I let him say what he wants and don't take it personally.

"I think the best offense," Alan continues, "is a good defense. There's a lot of cleaning up to be done around here, in terms of getting our customers to walk out the door happy that they blew a wad of dough at A Panini for Your Thoughts. Thor," he says and points at me. I jump to smooth out my rumpled T-shirt. "You're nice and people like you, but holy crap are you slow."

"I'm not slow," I say, then remember I was supposed to have my lips sewed up. "Oops," I say, and re-stitch my lips together.

"I mean, you've got a smile that's impossible to hate," he continues, "but if a customer is waiting on a Byzantium Baguette for twenty minutes, that's just simply too long. I'm talking about sales per minute, guys. Churros con Burros is making one hundred sixty transactions every hour."

"Yeah, but their chalupas taste like road-kill sautéed in its own barf," Mandy-Mandy says. She pushes out her chest like surviving a meal at Churros con Burros should get her some kind of medal.

"Let's not forget, Mandy, that you could be doing more for the business as well," Alan says, turning to her. Alan absolutely refuses to refer to Mandy-Mandy as anything but "Mandy." He said once the name "Mandy" is tacky enough without being doubled and having a hyphen jammed up the middle, but Mandy-Mandy claims she's gotten better tips ever since she started going by Mandy-Mandy because customers think it's cute.

"Your acerb," Alan continues, "is the corrosive evil that eats holes into our Customer Satisfaction Ratings. If we could just marry your efficiency with Thor's humane decency, we might be looking at the gateway to good word of mouth and, with it, economic solvency."

"I'm plenty decent," Mandy-Mandy says, flicking her gum at Remus. The gum lands on Remus's face; he picks the gum off and glares at her. He flips Romulus's head off his lap, smears the gum on the wall, and blitzes off to the washroom. "Drama queen," Mandy-Mandy says under her breath. Romulus angrily follows his brother out of the room. The twins move as a pair most of the time, and they both hate Mandy-Mandy.

"Mandy," Alan says, "it's fine for you to muscle with Remus and Romulus, but the paying public cannot see that sort of behavior, or else we'll all be out on our asses, playing accordion in the street and pretending to be amputees. The time has come for us to step up our staff and open the doors for a new hire. I want someone nice, someone quick, and someone who is willing to subjugate all sense of individuality to the collective identity of the Panini for Your Thoughts restaurant-nation." Alan double-majored in history and restaurant management. He is a Fascist, which means he likes for things to happen on time.

"New hire?" Mandy-Mandy's eyes go tiger-ish. "If any new girl comes snuffling around here looking for work, I'll skewer her slutty tonsils with a carving knife."

Well, I don't want to skewer anybody's slutty tonsils, but I also do not like this "change" idea. I take a deep breath in and smell the focaccia just about ready to come out of the oven. I can hear the dishwasher clattering and banging in the kitchen. Sure, this place is dirty and messy and Mandy-Mandy gives me a headache and a half, but I love it here. I've been working at A Panini for Your Thoughts for three years now, and I can't imagine anybody coming in to do this job better than I do. The Gruff Valley diners know me and I know the Gruff Valley diners. If I didn't work here, I just don't know what I'd do all day. Besides, how would I tell Mom and Dad they wouldn't be seeing my tip money anymore? Dad would get fretful and pull out his calculator and start talking about "making do." He'd smile fake, how he does when he doesn't want me to know he's gotten fretful, and tell me we'll be fine without the money. I grab a paper napkin off the table and start to rip it into confetti pieces.

"Oh, holy Abraham, father of Isaac!" Alan cries. "I'm not going to *replace* either of you. I'm going to *supplement* you. You'll still get paid the same you always have, you mercenary Shylocks. You are expressly forbidden to gut or otherwise physically assault any applicants."

Mandy-Mandy yanks her corkscrew out of the table. She's about to say something, but Remus and Romulus hustle back in. They're both tying on their aprons and we all look at the clock. It's almost eleven. Time to open shop.

"Looks like we'll need to cut this forum short," Alan says. "Remus, you unlock. Romulus, get back to the kitchen and make sure we're stocked. And you two," he continues, glaring at Mandy-Mandy and me, "get your asses prepared to start peddling some serious panini."

***

A Panini for Your Thoughts isn't the biggest restaurant-nation in Gruff Valley. We've got ten tables, ten booths, and a takeaway counter. Mostly, everything is painted red. This is because we spill a lot of marinara sauce all over the place, and in the lunch rush there's no time to wipe up. So we've got red tabletops, red booths, and a red tile floor. We've got laminated menus, too, that Alan's grandmother did up on her mimeograph. We've got a great business going. We serve all sorts of Italian sandwiches and pizzas. My favorite is pesto. It's basil and garlic, mashed up and delicious. I'd never had it before I started working here, but now I eat it twice a week.

My feet are killing me tonight. I've had to work straight on from lunch until dinner, and from dinner until closing. Mandy-Mandy usually gets to go home earlier than me, seeing as how I'm a better sport and Alan doesn't like to ask Mandy-Mandy to do things that Mandy-Mandy doesn't want to do, such as staying late. Tonight, though, Alan said she can't go home until the dining room is spotless, so she's busy wiping down the stools in front of the counter, all pissed off. Otherwise, it's just me and Alan and the twins, and a few tables where people are finishing up their meals and sipping on coffees.

I know the guys at Table 0-7—Bruce Billington and Ronald Harpoon. They're cops, but I can't tell which is the bad cop and which is the good cop. They work the overnight beat, so they come into A Panini for Your Thoughts around closing time most nights for coffee. Bruce is short and skinny and is always smiling. I wonder if he smiles when he's busting the bad guys. Ronald is a really cool cat. He's got shiny black hair, always slicked back, and he never takes his sunglasses off. If I were a cop, I'd want to be just like him.

The guy sitting at the next table over from them gives me the jitters. He's done up to the nines and tens in a sharp blue suit with shining gold buttons. His hair is nice and black and totally perfect and whenever I go over to refill his coffee, he smiles at me like he's starring in a milk commercial. He keeps pulling out an enormous pocket watch and checking the time. A Panini for Your Thoughts is great, but it's not the sort of place where people wear ties or come in with their shoes polished, so this fellow is very unusual. I don't think I like him. I haven't counted, but it looks like he's got more teeth than a normal guy ought to have. He's had at least eight coffees by this point and the more he drinks, the more he grins and chuckles and looks at me like I'm an old buddy of his. I keep looking over to see if Bruce and Ronald notice him; maybe he's a crazy, smooth criminal that's wanted in twenty-nine states. They don't seem to mind him, so maybe I shouldn't either. I see that the well-dressed man is out of coffee, so I walk back to the beverage station to get the coffeepot.

Alan interrupts me on my way by shoving an old broom into my hands.

"Alright, cabin boy," he says to me with his eyebrows raised up, and half his mouth smiling, "here's your mizzenmast. Now go swab the decks."

For some reason, our parking lot is where Gruff Valley's gay gentlemen go to "cruise." I say "cruising," but I don't mean big ocean liners and shiver my timbers and all that brouhaha. "Cruising" means something else entirely. The first time Alan ever sent me into the parking lot to hammer on all those steamed-up windows and try to get the gay gentlemen to clear out, I saw all different odd kinds of intimacy that did not look so great. My face went red for weeks. But I understand how important it is for us to maintain a family-friendly image, and it really won't do to have that kind of intimate business going on right under the customers' noses, so whenever it's my turn to "swab the decks," I just remember that it's all for the good of our restaurant-nation.

I step out into the parking lot. Even though it's pushing on towards eleven in the evening, it's still boiling hot outside. I like Gruff Valley — I've lived here my whole life and I can't think of anywhere better than home — but it's always too hot. We're in the middle of the desert, and I don't get along well with the sun. The sun always struck me as this kind of bully. It's a million miles across and a million degrees hot, whereas I'm five foot six and room temperature; it doesn't seem like a fair fight.

Across the street, a construction crew has set up a bunch of bright bluish lights so they can continue working during the night. They're building an Ethiopian restaurant. The builders have got all four brick walls up, but the restaurant doesn't have a roof or any windows yet. In the darkness, the building is an enormous monster with weird shadows crossing it every which way, on account of the blue lights shining through the empty window-holes. During the day, though, the building doesn't scare me at all. In fact, when it gets slow at work, I sometimes like to watch out the window while they build, even though Alan says the Ethiopians are our competition.

The construction crew's generator is grumbling, and the cicadas are chirping. The bugs and the generator are so noisy I can barely hear the groaning coming from the four bouncing vehicles parked in the back of the lot. I've got to swab the decks. I take twenty deep breaths and walk toward the cars. I grab my broom with both hands, like it's some kind of baseball bat, step up to one of the vehicles, and whack the windshield. The grunting from inside stops and a growly voice yells out at me.

"What?"

I go red. I wish they'd get the hint. Fornicating is not appropriate behavior for the parking lot.

"Well," I say, "if you please could just not express your intimacy here in our lot, it would be the tops." I stutter when I'm embarrassed, and that makes me more embarrassed, so by the time I finish talking I have a whole army of grasshoppers leapfrogging around in my stomach.

"Five minutes," says another voice.

If Alan comes out and sees that they've talked me into letting them stay for a while, then he'll yell at me about whether or not I'm really suited for this job.

"Please?" I say.

"Five minutes," comes back the first voice.

My ribcage goes icy. I look out beyond the construction crews across the street to the distant mountains, dark against the night sky, and spend a second counting the mountaintops. That always calms me down. I shudder and say, "If you just could please be out of here in five minutes? Or else I'll be in all kinds of trouble." The gay gentlemen don't answer; they just go back to doing whatever thing it was they were doing before.

I move on to the next vehicle—a pickup truck—and those guys tell me they're sorry and drive on off. Thank gracious. There's only one guy in the third car, maybe waiting for somebody else to show up. He looks sad and old. Before I can ask him if he's waiting for a friend or what, he keys the ignition up and drives away.

I come up to the last car. It's red and flashy. I take a quick glance in the windshield, hoping that there's nothing too private going on in there, but there's just a big guy sitting in the driver's seat and watching me. He's got gigantic arm muscles bulging out of a tight pink T-shirt that has "Hottie" written on the front in rhinestones. This gay gentleman is a stranger and that means maybe he is dangerous. Mom always tells me it's not nice to assume the worst about folks, but that it's also not smart to assume the best. So, I eye this gay gentleman and try to figure out what he's about. He's got nice blonde hair and watchful eyes. He's got a long, white scar running down his right jawbone. I bet he's been in lots of fights, with guys bigger than me. I should get Bruce and Ronald to take care of him.

The gay gentleman sees me standing by his car, wondering what to do. He smiles at me pleasantly, showing off his gold tooth. He waves casually, and I check behind me to make sure he's not waving at somebody else, but I am the only person standing out in the parking lot in the middle of the night. I wave back, but I'm not smiling. Maybe this gay gentleman is smiling and waving, but he's big and a stranger and those two things are usually pretty dangerous together.

He holds out his hand and makes a beckon at me, like I should come up to the car. A cicada screams past my ear, telling me not to go near that car. I hear a sudden click and a growl from behind me and I'm covered in headlights—I look over my shoulder, and see that the first car I rapped on, where the gay gentlemen asked me for five more minutes, has started up and is pulling out of the parking lot.

The stranger is still smiling, and he makes another beckon at me. I think again about those cops in the restaurant and feel silly. Bruce and Ronald face down bad guys every day and get shot at, but they just have to take it, because that's what being the good guy is all about. Here is a stranger who, sure, is big and has a scar, but is even smiling at me and hasn't done anything wrong at all except have some muscles. I hold on tight to the broomstick in my hands. If it comes down to roughhousing, at least I've got something I can hit at him with.

I tell my stomach to settle down, and I walk, shaky, over to the stranger's open window. When I get closer, I can tell he's a little bit older, maybe in his thirties, and his blonde hair is combed neatly across his head. He's got tiny crinkles around the corners of his eyes. That's a good sign. I stop ten feet from his car, hold the broomstick so tightly I think my biceps might explode, and jut out my lower lip, looking intimidating. The stranger makes his beckon at me again, but I keep my feet planted and shake my head.

"Why do you stand out in parking lot and stare at mein hotrod?" the man says. He's got a fearsome accent. My nerves are sizzling, and it's not easy for me to keep my feet solid on the ground.

I swallow hard. Sweat is pouring off my head and getting caught up in my eyebrows. "Hi there, friend," I say, trembling in my voice. "I'm just supposed to ask you—if you wouldn't mind, that is—to please …"

The big guy flicks his hand at me.

"We will not talk about 'supposed to,' mein herr," he says. "I have seen you for long time now, and I have decided that you will be mein new partner."

I have to lean on my broomstick to keep standing. Partner? This big guy with the accent wants me to be intimate with him. What if he gets out of his car? What's the best way to run? Is he faster than me? I think about dropping the broomstick and making a bolt for the light, safe, air-conditioned restaurant, but my knees are shaking so bad I don't think they'd get me too far. I should scream for help, but, then again, the man is still sitting calmly in his car, and I don't want to do anything to rile him up. If this man takes me up in his car and drives away with me, will Mom and Dad ever know what happened?

"You must get in car now," the big guy is saying. His voice isn't unfriendly, but it's firm.

"N-n-n-n …" I say. I'm trying to say, "No," but my stomach keeps flipping over on top of the word before it can get to my mouth. My eyes sting.

"Mein herr," he says, and his smile is gone. "This is not time for acting like child." I've got both my arms around the broomstick now, like somehow if I hold onto it hard enough, I'll be safe.

Now this guy is out of his car and coming toward me. I try to call out, but I can't. I'm crying for sure. This isn't fair. I tried all my life to live right and be nice. I make one last wish that Bruce and Ronald will come out of the restaurant, and then this guy's hands are on my shoulders.

"You must pull yourself together, mein herr," he says, looking right in my eyes. Smelling his overpowering cologne makes me light-headed. The air is heavy and humid and it's hard to breathe. "We are going to be best of friends."

His hands are holding me steady, which helps me not shake so much. I breathe five times, deep, and try to get some words out of my mouth. "L-l-l-listen, friend," I say. My voice won't get above a whisper. "I d-don't know if, if … th-this is about getting p-p-p-p-private and intimate, b-b-but …" I can't get any further.

The stranger throws his head back and laughs. His laughter seems to live somewhere in his belly, and the pink fabric of his shirt chuckles along with him. I try to laugh too, but I can't. Every time my heart beats, I hear my blood whooshing in my ears.

"Get private and intimate, mein herr?" the man says as he struggles to stop laughing. He slams a hand on my back, like we're old friends. The blow makes me cough. I try to scramble out of his grip, but my legs, which have always been there for me in the past, are not where they're supposed to be when it really matters. "You is not mein 'type,' mein herr. You is scrawny and no real man. I would break you!"

The stranger looks at me with curiosity.

"No, mein herr. When I say I want for you to be mein 'partner,' I do not mean mein 'sexual-partner.' I mean mein 'business-partner.' How would you like to go on journey with me and earn two million of dollars?"

Two million dollars? I gulp.

"Two million," I say. I just want to get away from this man, and now he's talking about two million dollars. I wonder where he got his scar.

The stranger smiles at me again. His gold tooth shines like a little sun. Across the street, I hear a loud power saw running.

"Two million," I say.

"Mein herr," says the stranger, and he shakes me a bit. "You must focus on things I am telling to you. Think hard. Two million of dollars."

The gay gentleman's cologne and the heat and the noise from the construction crews across the way make me dreamy. Two million. How much money is two million dollars? I could get my own place, so I wouldn't have to live with Mom and Dad. I could live in an apartment building with a swimming pool and air conditioning. Mom and Dad would never have to think about The Money Situation again. I could get the best Christmas presents for everybody at work. I could surprise Alan by getting some new menus made up by professionals to replace our mimeographs. That would make his day. Two million dollars.

"Two million," I say.

"Yes. Two million of dollars," the stranger says, getting a little growly.

"I don't know," I say.

The stranger nods. "Mein name is Hans Hess," he says, "and I come from Berlin. I have come to this parking lot often and I have seen you. I have had property, very valuable, taken from mein family, and I need most trustworthy herr to come with me to get it back. I am in search of paintings, done by Italian master Tintoretto, all one hundred percent authentic. They are of value over ten million of dollars—and for your help, mein young friend, I would give you most healthy share of mein profits. Two million of dollars. I believe that you are right man for such a job; you are blameless and most able to be trusted. I have seen you and I have decided: it will be you."

I take a step away from Mr. Hans, and my feet are back where they're supposed to be. This gay gentleman's offer sounds exciting, like something I might see in an old black and white movie—some sort of a caper, or a heist. What would happen if I drove away with him? Of course, that's silly. Mom always says to me, "Thor, don't believe everything they tell you." I don't know who "they" is, but I'm sure it includes a muscular German who asks me to join him on an adventure to look for stolen treasure.

"I don't know, Mister Hans. That's a lot of money, but, well, it's all pretty much out of nowhere ..."

Bruce and Ronald are loading back up into their squad car. They're probably going back on their beat, to round up bad guys and keep the streets safe. What would they say if they heard Mr. Hans's offer? Probably they've heard it all before from hustlers and rascals. They'd be cool and skeptical and look over their sunglasses at one another like they were in on some big secret.

Mr. Hans has also noticed the cops getting into their vehicle and he looks back to his own car. He smiles peacefully.

"I will not make you decide tonight, mein herr," Mr. Hans says to me. He looks again at the cops. "It is big decision to make in one evening. However, I will promise you that I am speaking with full honesty. I will continue coming to this parking lot every night until you will decide to join me in my quest. When you decide that you want these two millions of dollars—and you will—you will come to me and say, 'Hans, I have decide to undertake adventure-quest.' And you will become a rich man and a blessing to me. Now," he says, waving, and climbing back into his car, "I must go away, and so you too must go as well."

Mr. Hans revs up his engine, waves one more time, and disappears in a cloud of exhaust. I look out at the mountaintops and count them until I get to twenty-five. Did this whole Mr. Hans thing really happen? I can still smell his pine tree cologne. Gracious, what a night.

Ronald Harpoon's voice startles me: "Have a good night, Thor!"

The cops are pulling out of the parking lot. Ronald is leaning out of the window and waving at me, his sunglasses dark and characterless in the night. Bruce pulls the car up next to me and rolls his window down.

"Make a friend out here tonight, Thor?"

"Yeah, some German," I say. My shirt is stuck to me with sweat, so I pluck at it. "He said he wants me to go on an adventure-quest."

"Thor, Thor, Thor." Ronald shakes his head. "I wouldn't be going on any adventure-quests with strange Germans—at least not in this parking lot. This place is a hotbed for thieves, fornicators, and swindlers, and the men in this neck of the woods will be feeding you so much honey that you won't even notice how stuck they've got you."

"I wasn't going to go or anything," I say. My ears heat up like pizza ovens. I wish I could be smooth and brave like Bruce and Ronald. "We were just talking, that's all. I didn't want to be rude."

"It's not rude to call a spade a spade, my friend," Ronald continues. "It's just honest. When you smell a rat, it's rude if you *don't* cry foul ball. Otherwise, the stench lingers on to clog up other fellows' nostrils."

"Sorry," I say. I try to dig a chunk out of the asphalt with my toe.

"We'd better get back on the beat, and you'd better get back to help Alan close shop," Bruce says. "You did a good job swabbing the decks tonight. Sure makes our job easier—right, Ronald?"

Bruce turns to Ronald, but Ronald just nods coldly, his eyes hidden behind his sunglasses. I wave at the cops as they drive away, and they wave back.

I wipe some sweat off my forehead and walk back into the restaurant. Mandy-Mandy is bussing off the tables, and Alan is sitting at the table with that smiley, well-dressed guy that was drinking all the coffees. Alan and the man are laughing like old buddies. Something doesn't seem right about that. I walk back to help Remus and Romulus degrease the kitchen, but Alan makes a beckon that I should go over to him. I approach Alan and the dodgy customer, feeling the whole time like a hummingbird is trapped in my heart and is just itching to bust out.

"Thor, don't look like such a namby-pamby nasturtium," Alan says to me. "I want you to meet my business associate, Tony Rigatoni."

Mr. Rigatoni looks me over with his dark eyes and I notice his hands just won't stay still. He picks at the cuff of his suit, lets go, rubs his hands together, digs out some dirt from under his fingernail, and then starts all over again. I can't stop watching his twitchy hands.

"It's-a-pleasure!" Tony Rigatoni says, running his words together, grabbing my hand and shaking it. "Thor, is it?"

"Crafthor—but you can just call me Thor, sir. It's shorter that way."

"Crafthor," says Tony Rigatoni, looking me up and down admiringly. He claps his hands together, loud, and then again, soft. "Are you ready for some changes around this restaurant, Crafthor?" Mr. Rigatoni says. He nods at me, and my heart just slumps.

"Yes, sir," I say, without meaning it. "Some changes would be nice." I catch Mandy-Mandy's eye as I say this. She's moved over to the front counter and is busy mating ketchup bottles. She snarls at me.

"Priceless as a Botticelli!" Mr. Rigatoni says to Alan.

"He's a little slow," Alan says to Mr. Rigatoni.

"I'm not slow," I say. I feel hot blood swim into my face. I know Alan is quick and smart and great, but when he says things like that, I feel like he doesn't like me as much as I like him. "I'm really actually just fine."

"*Bene! Bene!*" says Mr. Rigatoni, taking a yellow silk handkerchief out of his breast pocket and unfolding it like he's got all the time in the world. "What does it matter to Tony Rigatoni if this handsome slice of *carpaccio* is a little *lento*? He's got plenty of time to flourish. He can't be older than twenty-five, can he?" He dabs at his forehead exactly twice and then folds his handkerchief back up, being careful to crease it just so.

"I'm twenty-two, sir," I say.

"I am *charmed*," Mr. Rigatoni says to Alan. "Our little *tortellino* is the very embodiment of *spirito dell'Italia*."

"He has a good heart. It's true," Alan says. I look over at Mandy-Mandy, who is now rolling sets of silverware up in napkins. I sort of want to be doing that, too. "If we can find more like him, who are willing to subsume their personal identities in favor of shares in the collective Panini for Your Thoughts restaurant-nation, our staff-army will prove indivisible. We've got those Ethiopians to think about."

"Oh," I say. "The Ethiopians."

"It's true," Mr. Rigatoni says. "Crafthor has the aura of a potential *marionetta di Fascismo* about him."

I see half of an old dinner roll on the floor, pick it up, and toss it toward the trashcan like I'm a basketball star. It goes past the trashcan by a couple feet.

"The other," Alan says, "Mandy, will prove valuable if we strategize correctly."

"Mandy-Mandy's rage," Mr. Rigatoni says, "cannot be general and undirected, as it is now." I look to the counter to see if Mandy-Mandy knows she's being talked about, but she's not there. She must have gone in back. "Her fire is *il incendio di Fascismo*, but we must focus it." Both men nod thoughtfully, and the pause looks like a good opportunity for me to get out of here.

"Has Mandy-Mandy already mopped?" I ask.

"*Agnus dei!*" Mr. Rigatoni cries out, and he grabs my shoulder. He squeezes hard, and I think he's on a pressure point or something, because it feels like he's shooting two million volts of electricity through me. "Our sweet young *biscotti* here is tired, and we are keeping him from his duties with our machinating. Crafthor," he says, with me trying to pry his fingers off me, and him just squeezing harder, "we will be seeing much of one another in the future. I am going to be helping your friend Alan bring *la vita* back into this venerable organization. Think of me as a friend. Now, you may help the others with cleanup so that you can get home and get some rest." He lets go of me, and I realize that I've been holding all my breath in. I exhale.

"Thank you, Mister Rigatoni."

"Please," Mr. Rigatoni says, touching his heart with both hands, "call me 'Tony.'"

I rub my shoulder, and Mr. Tony smiles at me. Alan smiles at both of us. I don't like all this smiling, so I head back into the kitchen to see if Remus, Romulus, and Mandy-Mandy need any help. As soon as I get out of the dining room, though, I see Mandy-Mandy standing at one of the kitchen's stainless steel counters, cutting apart a potato with a carving knife. She has a savage scowl on and I wish I hadn't come back here. I'm too tired to get yelled at.

"So?" she says to me. "Did you meet our new neighborhood greaseball?"

"Mister Tony?" I say. "Sure. He seems okay."

Mandy-Mandy growls and stabs at the potato again. "Everyone seems okay to you, Thor, because you're a moron."

I feel like telling her that *she* sure doesn't seem okay to me, but she's got a knife, so I don't.

"It's fine, though," she continues, flashing a fake, mean smile at me. "Don't defend yourself or anything. But when Alan sends in his pack of bloodsucking Italians to take our jobs away, I'm not giving you any sort of shoulder to weep on."

"Mister Tony doesn't want our jobs. He's our friend. He was just saying about you and restaurant-nations and your rage being like a Fascism. He likes you."

"You're a chump if you think that, Thor," Mandy-Mandy says, as she grabs the mutilated potato, crushes it in her fist, and throws it into the garbage can. "Someday you'll get tired of being a chump, but until abovementioned moment of realization and whatnot, please just keep your dopey platitudes to yourself." She turns around, flips her blonde hair like it's some kind of awful whip, and marches out of the kitchen.

"I'm not a chump," I yell after her.

I see a quick motion behind the deep fat fryer, and I know that Remus and Romulus must be darting around, playing. Remus and Romulus are small but quick and adept at being invisible. If you came into the kitchen one night and didn't know that the twins stayed there, you'd swear the place had spooks.

"Remus!" I call out, and the kid's head pops up from behind our industrial mixer. His face is tense and watchful, unsmiling as always. "What are you playing?" I say.

"Hunting," Remus says. He and his brother usually only speak one word at a time before they're waiting for you to speak again.

"What are you hunting?"

Remus doesn't answer my question but instead holds up an enormous steel meat cleaver in response. He grins, sick and crazy, and pops back behind the mixer. A minute later, I hear the pitter-patter of his feet moving across the kitchen.

I look over and see that Romulus is already crawling into his sleeping bag at the foot of the walk-in freezer. Alan has the kids stay at the restaurant overnight because his landlord will up the rent if he thinks Alan's hiding orphans in his apartment. Remus and Romulus don't seem to mind. I've got no idea what sort of life they had before A Panini for Your Thoughts, but at least here they've got a nice place to set up camp, plenty of space to play, and all the pesto they can eat.

I hear a mouse squeak and a little grunt of pleasure somewhere over near the salad station. "Gotcha!" Remus says, and then I hear him bounding out to the dining room. A small dribble of blood is on the kitchen floor. It makes me sad to see it. Alan sometimes has the twins go hunting, to catch all the little vermin that run around. If somebody has to do it, I'm glad it's the twins. They kill quick, but I think Mandy-Mandy would kill slow.

I wipe up the blood with a little paper napkin and look over the kitchen. It all seems pretty clean, so I'm ready to go. Thank gracious. My back feels like two million chainsaws. Bed is going to feel like a beautiful cloud.

***

"Thor, you lazy crazy, let's see some hustle!" Dad calls. I snap up and look at my clock. It's already eight—wake-up time.

I get out of bed, and the carpet is nice and soft on my toes. When my feet complain at work, I think about how good my carpet will feel on them. Mom and Dad have warned me, though, that if things don't get better with The Money Situation, I'm going to have to move into their room so we can rent out my room. I do not like that thought at all. I am too old to live in the same room with Mom and Dad and, besides, their carpet is red—which reminds me too much of work.

I smell Mom's breakfast coming up through the vent. I hate to say it, but Mom is not a very good cook. I will always eat whatever she makes, because it would make her so sad if she thought I didn't like her food— but sometimes I have to battle with myself to choke down every last bite. Today it smells like she's burning bacon and something plastic. We used to have meat with breakfast all the time, because Mom said I needed protein. Now we only eat it once a week, because Mom says it's too much sodium.

I get dressed and go downstairs. Mom is fiddling with the dial on her skillet and Dad is sitting at our old wooden table, drinking coffee from his "Number One Dad" mug I gave him for his fiftieth birthday. He's got the newspaper open in front of him and is hunting for coupons.

"I just can't get this skillet down. Too hot or too cold, but never right," Mom says. She used to have a pretty nice skillet, but she traded it in last week for a used one. She keeps saying the old owners must have beat up on it, because it never heats the way she tells it to. The smell of plastic is really strong; she has accidentally melted her spatula to the skillet.

"It's okay, Mom," I say. "The bacon smells really good."

Mom brings the plate of bacon to the table and kisses me on the forehead. "You're a good boy, Crafthor," she says.

"Don't lie to your mother, son," Dad says. "That bacon's as burnt as a jilted prom date."

"I love Mom's food," I say. It's a lie, but I love Mom, which is almost the same thing.

"It's a little burnt, I guess," Mom says, as she sits down next to Dad.

"That's three dollars and forty-nine cents that you just turned into carbon," Dad grumbles to her.

"No," Mom says. "I bought it on sale."

"We don't have money to burn," he says, and frowns. I bite off a big hunk of bacon. It tastes gross and ashy.

"It's too much sodium, anyway," Mom says under her breath, sounding like she might cry. It's always a bad sign when Mom can't make it through breakfast without crying. She runs her hand over the tabletop, sweeping the crumbs into a tidy little pile.

"It's delicious," I say, and quickly take another bite. The faster I eat it, the less I have to taste it.

"Don't lean on the table, baby," Mom says to me.

Dad looks at me, looks at Mom, and sighs. He puts his hand on Mom's head and pats her brownish-silvery hair. "You may be a train wreck in the kitchen, but, good gracious, are you the most beautiful living creature."

Mom smiles, but I can still see little sparkles of tears in her eyes. She's pretty when she smiles, so I wish she wouldn't take The Money Situation so hard. Most of the time, Mom and Dad go together like basil and olive oil. He likes to joke and she likes to take it. She likes to cook bad food and he likes to complain about it. Dad is bald and loud, with a big belly that Mom likes to call his "girth." Mom is small and pale; Dad is always saying she needs some meat on her bones, but I think he likes her fine just the way she is.

"How is work going, Thorrie?" Mom asks me. She picks up a strip of bacon and nibbles on the end like she's maybe a little scared of it.

"Oh, *great*," I say, taking a big chomp of my toast. "I met one of

Alan's friends. He's going to help us with the restaurant. I think he's a Fascist, just like Alan."

"Leave it to the Italians," Dad says, ripping out a coupon for apple juice and handing it to Mom. "They've got all that mania for Fascism and pasta and gracious knows what else. I don't like you working with Fascists, son."

"Mister Tony seems okay, though," I say. "And Alan's my buddy." Mom pours me a cup of milk. I pick it up with both hands and drink half of it in one gulp.

"Don't drink your milk so fast, sweetie," Mom says. "Once you've finished it, you don't get more until tomorrow. Make it last."

"Sorry, Mom," I say. "Oh, and I met a *German*, too." What would Mom and Dad say if I came home from work one day with two million dollars in my back pocket?

Dad's forehead wrinkles up. "Germans and Fascists, hey? I've got some misgivings about that restaurant of yours, Crafthor."

"But Mister Hans seems like he's nice," I say, before gulping down the rest of my milk. "He's pretty watchful, though. I like him, a little." I look at my empty milk glass and wish I hadn't drunk it all already. "Can I have just a little more milk, please, Mom?"

Sad frown wrinkles show up on Mom's face. "Tomorrow, Thorrie," she says. She takes my empty glass, sweeps the pile of crumbs into it, gets up and puts my glass into the sink.

"I don't give a barrel of beans how watchful this German is or isn't," Dad says. "Germans are good for building efficient aircraft and hosting sadomasochistic cabaret performances, but otherwise it's all sauerkraut and self-loathing to me."

Mom puts a hand on Dad's hand. "Are you done with your coffee?" she asks him, already taking his mug away from him. Dad grunts, not taking his eyes off the coupon section. "We're glad you're having a good time at work, Thorrie," Mom says. "Dad just wants you to be safe, that's all; there's definitely people out there that have tricks up their sleeves."

"Don't worry, Dad. If there's any trouble, Bruce and Ronald will take care of it, with handcuffs flying every which way."

Dad looks up from the paper and grins. "Alright, mister," he says to me, rubbing the top of my head with his fist. "You'll be late for work if you don't get a move on. Say hi to Alan for me."

"Hi to Alan for me," I say. It's an old joke, but we do it every morning.

"That's my boy," Dad says, and punches me on the arm. Mom sighs and starts washing the dishes, but I hope she's at least smiling a little.

***

When I get to work, I see that Alan's posted a sign with big red words in the window that looks out on the parking lot: "Join the Panini family! HELP WANTED!"

Even from outside, I can hear Mandy-Mandy raging in the kitchen. When she is annoyed, which is most always, she likes to grind up breadsticks in our industrial food processor. I can hear the machine whining and the familiar sound of Mandy-Mandy being "vociferously profane," as Alan likes to call it.

I catch her mid-vocifery as I enter the dining room.

"… goddamned swooning bitches with bouillabaisse for brains!" I hear Mandy-Mandy say. I hear a quick whirring and a muddy splatter and know that another handful of breadsticks has come to its end.

Alan is in the dining room, refilling the salt and pepper shakers on each table. He looks up at me with a sad kind of smile. He's got droopy black wrinkles under his eyes and his hair is sticking up in all directions. Alan cares so much about our restaurant-nation and so whenever things start to go sour, like when Mandy-Mandy starts vociferacating, he gets strung out. Even though Alan looks like he hasn't slept, he's dressed sharp, like always. His suit's got silver pinstripes running all over it, and I can't find a single wrinkle on his butter-colored dress shirt. That's part of being a Fascist—dressing up to the nines and tens.

"Mandy-Mandy isn't too happy about hiring some new friends, is she?" I say.

"No," says Alan. "She does not believe me that I have no intention of making any staff cuts and, as best as I can gather, she thinks she's making an excellent case for her indispensability by brutalizing our kitchen stock." As Alan refills the salt shaker on Table 0-1, a spider runs by his hand. He swats at it, but misses, and accidentally knocks over the salt shaker. Little white salt crystals fall all over. "God damn it!" Alan says, shaking off his hand. "I had a cut on that hand."

"Oh," I say, glad the spider got away from him.

"Damn, that burns."

"Alan?" I say. He looks at me, irritated. "You're *not* going to fire us, are you?"

Alan rolls his eyes. "Oh, my sweet Jesus, Thor, please don't tell me that you are losing sleep over this."

"Bread-headed bitches!" Mandy-Mandy screams over the grinding food processor. "Foccacia fuckers!"

I scoop the spilled salt off the table and into my hand. "I guess I'm not as worried as Mandy-Mandy is," I say. I grab a sanitized rag and start wiping down the tables.

"Ah," says Alan, "she's a whirling harpy, but she's a great asset to have on board. Her thug tactics are going to serve us well, if I can only figure out how best to harness them."

"Really, Alan," I say. I look down at the red and white checkered tabletop I'm scrubbing. "I know we need to make sure our restaurant-nation is the tops, but I think we can do it without being thugs."

A roar of Mandy-Mandy's awful laughter comes from the kitchen, followed by a high whining noise. The bread splatter is enormous this time, and even Alan looks up in surprise. He peeks into the kitchen and then looks back at me, shaking his head.

"She has just jammed an entire baking sheet full of rosemary flatbread down there. Thor, what good is a thug army you can't control?" Alan looks at me like he wants an answer. I start to sweat under my shirt collar, because I have no idea. At least Mandy-Mandy is nice to look at, when she isn't being ferocious.

"At least Mandy-Mandy is nice to look at, when she isn't being ferocious," I say. It seemed good in my head, but when I said it out loud it sounded weird, like I am in some sort of attraction with Mandy-Mandy.

"I'll never understand you, Thor," Alan says, like I'm quantum mechanics or something else that's just numbers and graphs. He frowns and packs up his salt and his pepper. "Hey, Thor," he says, "if you didn't work here, what would you do with yourself?"

I stop wiping off tables and straighten up, my sanitized rag hanging off my hand wet and heavy. My heart is pumping. Alan's saying danger words.

"Well, Mom and Dad would be sad, for one, and I'd be upset, I guess." My rag is dripping all over my sneakers. "I'd miss you a whole lot."

"Thor," Alan says, and I drop my rag on the ground. He is going to tell me I'm fired, after three years of being buddies. "Business is an ugly, ugly thing."

Mom will cry. Dad will smile and tell me it's alright and that we'll make do somehow, but he won't mean it. We'll find some renter to stay in my room, who will maybe be big and not very clean, and I'll have to ask his permission if I want to go in and walk on my blue carpet. Maybe he'll be rude to Mom, and make her cry. I'll have to go back to looking all over town for jobs, and having everybody tell me, all over again, that they're sorry but that I'm just not the guy they're looking for.

Mandy-Mandy cackles in the kitchen. "Die, *ciabatta*, die!" she screams.

Alan puts his hand on mine and pats it. "I don't know, Thor," he says. "As long as I'm in charge, you're not going anywhere." He picks up my rag and hands it to me.

I smile, nervous. "Well, but you're the boss," I say. "You're always in charge."

Alan goes up to the takeout counter and squares up our stack of menus. "Why don't you go wake up the twins?" he says.

I nod, feeling queasy, and head into the kitchen. Even with Mandy-Mandy and all her raging vociferications, Remus and Romulus are still snuggled in their sleeping bags, fast asleep like little Fascist angels. Remus is cuddling a meat cleaver like it's his grade-school sweetheart.

"Wake up, boys!" I shout. Remus wiggles a little and I worry about how close that cleaver is getting to his face. I tap Romulus on the shoulder, and he is immediately sitting straight up, awake, and with a sort of panic all over his face while he figures out he is just in the kitchen, being woken up for work, and not in the middle of the jungle or wherever, being torn up by hostile bears and wolves.

I smile at Romulus, even though my heart's not really in it, and point at Remus, who is still asleep. Remus is sort of the leader of the duo, and so whenever I see a chance to give Romulus some responsibility, I always take it. Sure, Remus is stealthy at hunting varmints and grilling up panini, but I want Romulus to have the chance to take responsibility for his brother; maybe, deep down, Romulus is a nurturer.

Romulus sees what I am indicating, so he grabs a spatula off the nearest counter and brings it down on Remus's head, full force. The impact makes a cracking sound that makes me flinch, but it does the trick—Remus is on his feet quick as lightning with his cleaver raised above his head and his eyes scanning the kitchen. He sees me and nods good morning; he sees his brother and his eyes narrow into mean little slits. Romulus copies back Remus's facial expression and they stare at each other, looking like they're going to have a fight any minute. However, like always, they stare at each other and stare at each other and, just when I think they're actually going to kill each other this time, they burst into this creepy sort of silent laughter like they've had this joke between just the two of them since the beginning of time. Whenever the twins laugh, they shake their shoulders and frown less severely; it's not like they smile or make any sort of noise.

I don't need to tell them to get started with prepping the kitchen for the workday. They work well when they've got a routine, and they've been doing the same pre-shift tasks in the same order since the day they were adopted—they cut the veggies, defrost the meat, make up the soups and salads, and do two million other small things. We leave all the kitchen duties to Remus and Romulus. Alan and I take care of getting the dining room ready. Mandy-Mandy is pretty much allowed to do whatever she wants, which usually consists of making a mess I have to clean up later.

Now that Remus and Romulus are working, I need to make sure Mandy-Mandy is presentable. I approach her carefully. Even though she's upset, her hair is perfect. Mandy-Mandy is the blondest person I've ever seen; she likes her hair to be just so—a ponytail in back, enormous bangs, and a smiley face barrette clipped just to the right of center. Mandy-Mandy calls this her "maximum tip-getting configuration."

"Hey, Mandy-Mandy," I say, being polite. She's mashing on a stick of gum like keeping her jaws moving is the only thing that's keeping her from completely and totally losing it. "We've got fifteen minutes until we open, so maybe we could clean up all this bread." The whole wall behind the food processor is flecked with destroyed focaccia.

"Then I still got me fifteen minutes to bash bread," Mandy-Mandy says before jamming a whole loaf of Harvest Wheat into the jaws of the machine. I am sprayed with crumbs.

"Yuck," I say. I grab a dishtowel off the counter and brush myself off. "Why are you so mad today? Is it the changes Alan wants to make?"

Mandy-Mandy rolls her eyes. "Know what, Thor? I'd eviscerate you right now, but blood on my uniform would not maximize my tip-getting potential. You are happy to just sit around like some complacent fuckwit while Help Wanted signs go up all around you? You are just going to go on whistling while Alan hires your replacement and sends you out to live on the street, scrapping with wolves and bums to even get enough food to keep on with your miserable life?"

"Alan told me he's not going to fire us," I say, but I think about what Alan just asked me out in the dining room and my stomach does a somersault.

"Alan is a Fascist," Mandy-Mandy says. "You cannot trust a Fascist."

"I do not know what sorts of Fascists you have been hanging around, but I think that Fascists are reliable, as a rule." I hand Mandy-Mandy the towel that I used to wipe myself off. She hurls it back at my face with considerable force. I peel the towel off my face, chuck it on the ground, and just let loose. "No offense," I say, "but if you are so concerned about your job, maybe not making a mess or being all full of rage would be useful." I turn pink in the ears. Mandy-Mandy glares me. I've never really talked back to her before, and for a second I worry that she's going to jam me face-first down the food processor and that I will leave such an enormous stain on the kitchen walls that Alan will shake his head, sad and angry all at the same time, and never be able to scrub me out.

Mandy-Mandy looks me in the eye, makes a fist, and then, suddenly, she exhales. All the tension zooms out of her body. She shakes her head, almost sad, and astonishes me: "You're a nice guy, Thor," she says.

If she had started beating me up, I would have known to stick my hands in front of my face and try to protect my eyes. If she had started yelling at me, I would have known to just stand there and take it. But I do not know what to do when she pays me a compliment, so I take a big mixing spoon off a nearby countertop and look at my reflection in it. My nose is huge. I turn the spoon the other way, so that Mandy-Mandy can see her reflection.

"Check it out," I say, and grin into the spoon. My teeth take up two thirds of my face, and my eyes are scrunched up into my forehead. Mandy-Mandy doesn't smile.

"Thor," she says, and snatches the spoon out of my hand, "you are a nice guy, but you are the most infuriating idiot I have ever encountered."

"I am not an idiot, in fact, and it is not nice for you to say that."

"Thor," she says, and jabs my breastbone with her pointy pink fingernails, "I am trying to issue you some pearls of goddamned wisdom here, so would you just stop flailing your tongue around like you're a clownish butt monster, and appreciate the fact that I am not shattering your skull right now? I hate to see the path you're going down. Do you know what I mean when I say, 'the economy'?"

"Yes."

"What do you know about the economy?"

I shrug. "It's bad."

"How bad is it?" she says, staring at me like she has laser eyes and is hoping to sizzle my skin.

"It is bad enough," she answers herself, "that being nice and passive is a one-way ticket to a life of misery and destitution. If Alan fired you today, Thor, you'd just walk right out the door, all weepy. If he tried to give *me* the axe, trust me, I'd burn down the restaurant with his stupid orphan twins inside—and he knows it, too. A scientific question, then, Thor: which of us will be happier in the long run?"

I reckon that Mandy-Mandy does not think that it will be me.

Before I can answer, I hear a jingle from out in the dining room. Some customer has come.

"God damn it," Mandy-Mandy exclaims. She looks down at her uniform, annoyed. "I've got bread dust all over me. You take the first table, Thor."

Mandy-Mandy goes to get a dishrag and I head into the dining room. The minute I see who has come in, my jaw drops slack.

The most beautiful person I have ever seen is standing in the doorway, crying and looking lost.

The strange woman does not look like a supermodel, with enormousness in her chest, but she's got shiny red hair and skin that's got more freckles splattered over it than the sky has stars. I can tell she's athletic, like maybe she runs or something, because her arms and legs seem strong. Her eyes are dark brown and shiny from crying. Her cheeks are red and just a little chubby. I don't know what it is about this woman that makes her the most beautiful person I have ever seen, but it might just be how sad she is. She is just crying and crying and when she sees me, she looks at me like I am the only person in this entire world who can help her.

And, right now, the only thing I want is to be able to help her, so she will never stop looking at me like I am her hero.

"Can I help you out, friend?" I say.

"Well, Christ, I sure hope so."

"Would you like to sit down and maybe drink a glass of water?" I pull out a chair at the nearest table. She sits, but she looks far away in her eyes; her mind is still on whatever thing is making her cry. I take a fistful of paper napkins from the dispenser on the table and dab at her cheeks with them. The napkins are thin and soak through quickly, so I ball them up, get a fresh fistful, and keep on letting her cry.

"I am not usually what one would call a crier," she says, like she's talking to herself.

"Do you want a glass of water?" I offer again.

"I do not take charity," she says. She looks at me and something changes in her eyes, like suddenly she sees me for the first time. I see a tiny smile flicker at the corner of her mouth. If I never accomplish another thing in my life, that smile will be enough to keep me happy forever.

"It's no trouble," I say, "and water is free for anyone."

"Do you realize that I walked here from Kansas?"

"You walked here from Kansas? That's a long ways, and I hope you will not think I am being rude if I ask you why you did that."

"I am a young woman what is capable of being sublimely independent. Look at me."

I look at her. Now that she is talking, her crying has died down.

"Do I strike you as a young woman what is capable of being sublimely independent?"

"Yes."

"Well, I agree." She leans in close, like what she is about to say is top secret and will maybe cost me my life if I let it fall into the wrong ears. "And I do *not* need Parker. So, one day, I realized that what the hell am I doing out in the middle of nowhere in Kansas, when I am a young woman what is capable of being sublimely independent, what does not need Parker, nor any other asshole. So, I decided that I would walk west and that I would not stop until I found Opportunity. And do you know what sort of Opportunity I found?"

The beautiful woman squeezes the wad of wet napkins I've balled up on the table. Tears leak out from the pulpy bundle and run through her fingers.

"Dung!" the woman says. "I've walked and walked halfway across the country, every single damn place saying they're not hiring, times are tough and money is tight, and there's just nothing they can do for me. And today …" She sniffs deeply and I get a fresh handful of napkins together because I am afraid she will start crying again. "Today, I was thinking that another day or so of walking would get me to the Pacific Ocean, and, well, so much for Opportunity, so maybe I should just throw myself into the water and get drowned up. But, as I was passing by, I saw that sign in your window, saying you are looking for help, and it was like God or whoever was telling me that maybe miracles happen, and …" She sniffs again and takes the napkins out of my hands. "And, well, I am not usually what one would call a crier, but, but, but, I mean, do you think I could help it, when I saw that sign, and thought maybe …?"

She's crying too hard to keep talking, and the napkins are going to soggy shreds in her hands. I wonder if I should put my hand on hers, but I don't know if she'd like that, so I pluck a ketchup bottle out of the table setting and roll it from hand to hand. The gorgeous stranger peeks up at me through her hands, her eyes like little fishponds.

"Maybe this is the place where I'm meant to be," she says, looking at me like I am the Opportunity she was talking about. I roll the ketchup bottle to her; she catches it and rolls it back at me.

"I'll get you some water," I say. I head to the beverage station and take a small water glass from the rack. I fill her glass to the top with ice, because she must be hot from walking outside so long, and then pour in cold water up to the brim. I set the glass down in front of her, fighting with my shuddery hands to keep them from spilling.

"Well," she says, taking the water from me and gulping down a big mouthful. "Let's just cut through these tears and boo-hoos and get right to the meat of what-all I'm talking about here." She wipes her mouth with the back of her hand. Her wrist has freckles all over it. "Your sign said, 'Help Wanted.' You are in need of help. I am also in need of help. Jesus, aren't we all?" She rolls her eyes up to the sky, and I think maybe she's done talking, but just as I'm about to go ahead and be brave and touch that freckly hand of hers, she looks at me again. "Well, what do you say we help each other? You need a worker, I need a job, and it seems to me that maybe today is the day that's going to make us both happy."

How would it be to work with this woman? When I am busy with tables, maybe she will get salads ready for me. When she is busy, maybe I will go refill the water glasses at her tables. Mandy-Mandy and I do not help each other out on the floor. Mandy-Mandy looks out for her tables, and I look out for mine. Maybe with this new woman, everything will be different. Maybe I will save up enough money so I could ask her to go out for a milkshake after work, and we will talk about what happened that day, and laugh at the funny parts and frown at the sad parts, and we will just go on helping each other more and more every day.

"Friend," I say. It's hard for me to keep from blasting off in my head into the future, so I look around to remind myself where I am right now. The restaurant is still clean, because we haven't started slinging food around yet today. The red floor is mopped, and I can see our fluorescent track lighting reflected in it. All the tabletops are scrubbed off, the glass door that leads out to the parking lot is fresh with Windex, and the takeout counter has its ketchup bottles, salt shakers, pepper shakers, and dessert menus arranged perfectly. I think of the table settings as little families that get broken up and scattered around during the shift but that always get brought back to their normal, happy order at the end of every day.

"Friend," I say again. "This restaurant is just about the tops." The front door opens and Little Greta walks in like she owns the place, sits down at Table 0-5, which is her favorite, owing to it's right under the air conditioning vent, and slides on a pair of enormous green sunglasses. She looks over at me and holds up her crooked index finger.

Little Greta is a nice old woman who comes in sometimes. Maybe she's crazy. She likes to pretend she's famous and so she is always hiding her face behind sunglasses or tabloid newspapers. Of course, maybe she actually is someone famous and is doing such a good job of keeping her true identity hidden that everyone just *thinks* she's a crazy old lady.

"I guess you gotta go, huh?" says my pretty new friend. She even looks a little disappointed.

"Well," I say. I wave to Little Greta, and she waves back. She pulls a paperback spy novel out of her humongous alligator-skin purse and buries her face in it. She always holds her books so close to her face that I don't think she can actually be reading them. I think they're just all part of the disguise. "I think you're a friendly woman that got dealt a bad hand, and I would love to know you better, like about how it was to walk across the country. So if you will just hold onto your horses, I will see what I can do about getting you a job."

My friend smiles at me and grabs my hand. "Thank you," she says, quietly, and I get strangled by happiness. Her hand is soft and her eyes are happy. When I think about how sad she was when she walked in here, and how happy she is now, I know I have just done the most important work of my life in cheering her up.

"I'm Thor," I say. "What's your name?"

"Barbara Hackbush."

"Well, Miss Barbara," I say, "I am going to go get my boss, Alan, and I'm sure he will be so happy to meet you."

Ms. Barbara starts crying again, but I'm pretty sure they're happy tears. I'd better see what I can do for Little Greta.

"What's the news these days, Miss Greta?" I ask as I step up to her table. Little Greta looks up at me. We call her "Little Greta" around the restaurant because she's tiny. Everything she carries around with her is huge, by comparison. She is so short that her teeny legs don't reach the floor.

"Oh, Thor," she says, and smiles at me. Her teeth are grey and snaggly, but she got braces recently, so maybe that will help them settle down and move over to where they're supposed to be. "Thor the floor." Little Greta likes me.

"How is school, Thor?" Little Greta asks.

"School is great, Miss," I say. One time I told Little Greta that I wasn't in school, but that just made her confused, so I play along.

"How are the girls?" She pokes me with her elbow, and I laugh. Little Greta always asks about the girls.

"The girls are very polite," I say. I look over at Ms. Barbara and a whole aquarium-full of guppies are swimming around inside my guts. I laugh again, because the guppies tickle.

"Nice as rice and pretty as a city," Little Greta agrees. She reaches into her purse and pulls out a fuzzy purple billfold with gold stars all over it. Her fingers wobble as she takes out exactly three dollars and hands them to me. She yells, "Soup's on," and laughs secretly, like she made a dirty joke.

"The soup's good today, Miss Greta." I don't remember what the soup is, but the soup's always good. "Do you want some bread, too?"

"Oh, no, Thor." Little Greta pulls an orange cylinder out of her purse and taps it with a wrinkled finger. "I have pills today."

"Okay." The door jingles behind me and I turn around. A young couple comes in. The woman is tan all over and fans herself with a handful of concert flyers. The man is wearing khaki shorts and sandals and a half-unbuttoned cotton shirt with the collar popped up. I bet they're on their way to the beach. "You can just sit wherever you like," I call out to them, smiling big. I like Beach People. They're never in a hurry. "I'll be back with your soup," I say to Little Greta.

As I head back to the kitchen, I brush by Ms. Barbara and give her a squeeze on the shoulder. She's gathered up a little Mt. Everest of wet paper napkins at this point, and she's still crying and crying. Her water glass is empty, so I fill it back up and drop it off at her table. She mouths, "Thank you," and looks at me like I'm some hero.

"Mandy-Mandy!" I scream, as I push through the swinging double doors that lead back to the kitchen. "You've got some Beach People out there." I hear the front door again as I head to the soup station, and I know that it's my turn again. Mandy-Mandy pushes by me and heads into the dining room, straightening out her nametag as she goes. No matter how busy it gets out there, Mandy-Mandy always seems to stay on top of it.

I take a deep breath as I scoop out a big ladle of soup—white bean today, which I will have to remember—into a pink bowl. I start a list in my head of what I have to do. Find Alan and get him to hire Ms. Barbara. Soup and water for Little Greta. Go say hi to my new table.

Steam from the soup hits my face as I put the bowl on a tray and wipe off the sides of the bowl with my thumb. "Alan!" I call out. I hear another jingle from out in the dining room. A new table—Mandy-Mandy's this time.

Alan is back behind the food processor, sweeping up Mandy-Mandy's massacred bread. He looks exhausted.

"Need help out there, Thor?" Alan asks.

"Alan!" I say again. I hear another jingle. Another table for me. I feel my heart start pumping and thumping, and tell myself to just stick to my to-do list. I'll get to my table when I can. "We've got some kind of woman out there, Miss Barbara, and she's looking to come and work for us."

"Great," Alan says, without really making it sound like he thinks it's great. "Tell her to come back tomorrow around two."

"No!" I say, before I can think about it. I can't take time to be as polite as I want to be. I've got two tables out there I've got to say hi to, and Little Greta's soup is getting cold. "I mean, she walked across the country, and she's looking for Opportunity."

Alan raises his eyebrows at me. I am afraid he will yell at me, so I start talking before he can. "She is super and I know how much you will want to tell Mister Tony Rigatoni this afternoon that we have a new friend and colleague." I frown and try to maybe even glower. "It's not like I care, or anything. She's just some woman." I shrug so big that I almost spill Little Greta's soup.

Alan turns to me and holds out his hands, which are covered with little mushy pieces of bread. He sighs sadly. "Okay, Thor," he says and walks over to our hand-wash station. He undoes his cufflinks, careful not to get any crumbs on them, folds up the sleeves of his shirt like he's doing some origami project, and turns on the water. "But I'm not making any promises. If she's not right, she's not right."

"Oh," I say. "It's all one to me."

Alan looks at me like of course he doesn't believe me. I hear another group of customers come in—Mandy-Mandy's turn.

The swinging door into the kitchen almost knocks me over as Mandy-Mandy pushes her way in, back first, hefting a huge tray of water glasses.

"There you are," Mandy-Mandy says to me. She balances her tray on one hand as she whips an order pad out of her apron, rips off the top sheet with her teeth, and clips it to the order bar above Remus and Romulus's fry station. "You've got two tables you haven't even been to yet. People are hungry. It's like the siege of Stalingrad out there. They're going to start gnawing off each other's arms and we'll all drown in the ensuing bloodbath." She grabs two breadbaskets, wedges them onto a free spot on her tray, and checks her bangs in the stainless steel counter.

"Could you run a water to Miss Greta?"

"No. Time management, Thor," she says, and pushes back through the double doors to the dining room.

"Thor," Alan says, "for the love of Baby Jesus, swaddled in the manger, the object of mankind's ultimate adoration, would you please just get moving?"

I hear another jingle—my turn—and my heart skyrockets into my head.

"Sorry, Alan," I say, and go back into the dining room, afraid of what I'm going to see. My three tables are all four-tops. I brush by Ms. Barbara and tell her Alan will be right out to her, drop Ms. Greta's soup off, and go to my first table—all Business People, probably on tight schedules—to get their order. I realize I don't have an order pad in my apron and so I try to put all their orders right into my memory. I get back to the beverage station and realize I don't remember their orders at all, so I grab an order pad and waters for all of my tables. Meanwhile, Mandy-Mandy is buzzing around, Ms. Speedy Time Management, shooting food out to table after table, clearing dishes, and printing out bills. I try to speed myself up by pretending I'm racing her, but I get frustrated by how much faster she is, so I forget about my game.

I go back to the table of Business People and try to get their order again, but when I tell them I forgot what they ordered, they all stand up and leave. *My job. My tip.* Alan's here in the dining room, talking to Ms.

Barbara, so there's no way he missed it.

I take a deep breath and get the orders from my other tables—Beach People, thank gracious. One super-tan fellow with hair that's almost as blonde as Mandy-Mandy's orders a chicken pesto panini, and I say, "Pesto is the best-o," which is an old joke, and everyone laughs, so I know I'm okay at that table. Another jingle—some more Business People for Mandy-Mandy.

On my way back to the kitchen to drop off my orders for Remus and Romulus, I glance to the table where Alan and Ms. Barbara are still talking. Ms. Barbara doesn't look sad anymore—she looks determined, like she is going to get this job if it is the last thing she does. I can also tell that Alan likes her. He's trying to make it look like he is stern and bored, but I know he's been won over.

I drop off my orders in the kitchen and grab some bread and olive oil. When I come back into the dining room, Ms. Barbara and Alan are standing up and shaking hands. Ms. Barbara's face shines with gratitude. I'm startled by another chime from the front door, and a crew of four high school kids comes in with one middle-aged woman, and I know they're going to give me a headache and a half—but I don't even care, because I think I might be in love with Ms. Barbara.

"*Basta*!" Remus hollers from the kitchen. That means my food is ready.

"Have a seat wherever," I call out to the woman with the high school kids. I am on my way back to the beverage station to get them water, when Ms. Barbara comes up to me, excited and happy-faced. She grabs my hands, looks me right in the eye, smiles an angel's smile, and says, "Thor, I do not forget when a guy's been good to me—and you've been good to me. I will not forget that you are a good soul. We will have high times working together, and we will not even talk about Parker a singular once." Then, she leans in, moves closer, and *kisses me on the cheek* right there in the middle of the restaurant, with people eating their soup and waiting for water refills!

High times … *I'd* say!

"*Basta—Basta—Basta*!" Remus's holler is up to a screech.

I don't try to hide the enormous blush I get on my face; every customer in the entire place must be staring at me and thinking how lucky I am. I know for sure Mandy-Mandy sees me because she stomps hard on my toes as she heads back to the kitchen. She does not like to see other people be happy, because she feels like there is only a limited amount of happiness out there—so if I am happy and in love, that is happiness that will not be around for her.

Ms. Barbara skips out the front door and, for a minute, I stare after her, lost.

"*Basta! Basta!*" Remus is beside himself, yelping like a lunatic. *My food.* Oh no! I leave the water glasses for later and head back to the kitchen.

Mandy-Mandy is standing at the dessert station, drizzling raspberry sauce in the shape of a heart onto a Chocolate Mousse-olini. I snag my trays of food, sprinkle parmesan onto the pastas, and garnish the paninis with pickles and giardiniera.

Mandy-Mandy pauses in her decorating. Mandy-Mandy never pauses when the lunch rush is going hot and heavy.

"You know, Thor," she says. "You are an idiot."

"Why did you squash my foot earlier?" I hear the front door— Mandy-Mandy's turn—and expect she will rocket out into the dining room, but she stays right where she is, looking at me without blinking.

Mandy-Mandy laughs and laughs, but not in a nice way. "You, Thor, just got Alan to hire your replacement." She grabs up her dessert in one hand and a coffee cup in the other and winks at me as she scurries back into the dining room, still laughing.

Even with the steam from a full plate of baked ziti blowing up into my face, I feel chilly.

"*Basta!*" Remus screams and nudges me. I move out of his way and he puts up a tray full of food for one of Mandy-Mandy's tables. Another jingle—my turn. Another jingle—Mandy-Mandy's turn. I can hear my heart beating in my ears. Another jingle—my turn. Mandy-Mandy is back in the kitchen, seizing her tray of food.

"Get a move on, you *dope*," she says, and claps right next to my ear. "Your food is getting cold, and those high school kids are going to mutiny in a minute. And you've got another table."

I want to knock Mandy-Mandy's tray out of her hands and watch all the food clatter to the floor. I want to smash a plate against the wall. I am hot and cold and hungry and not hungry at all. No more weekly chocolate for Mom. No more weekly beer for Dad. Dinners will get smaller. No more cheese. We'll drop to four hours of electricity a day.

"Thor," Mandy-Mandy says again. She swats my face with her palm, almost gently. "This is why it doesn't pay to be nice. This is why you are the world's number one idiot." She sounds almost sad. "I'll get your new tables set up with water." She's back out to the dining room, and I'm standing by the fry station with a tray full of food that is already going cold.

***

After lunch, the staff meets together in the break room, waiting for Alan to come in and start our pre-dinner meeting. I've still got Ms. Barbara on my mind. She will start tomorrow. Mandy-Mandy is going to train her. This is because I will be fired by then. I just know it.

I drum my fists on the break room table. I'm wearing my Super Waiter Face, which is a big smile, but a slight squint in my eyes, so I look like I'm thinking hard about Great Things. After the shift, I scrubbed my hands and made sure my hair was lying down just right—polished my corkscrew, too.

Mandy-Mandy is chomping on her gum and counting through a stack of dollar bills. She is in an alright mood because she made a lot of money during our lunch shift. If Mandy-Mandy is smiling, I know she has a wad of cash in her hands.

"Fifty-four dollars and thirteen cents," Mandy-Mandy says to nobody in particular, as she folds up her money and stuffs it into the pocket of her apron. "I blitzkrieged the cute factor today. I'm always cute, but, man oh man, I was like an A-bomb of cute today, blasting cute little shrapnel all over this disgusting world."

"That's good news, Mandy-Mandy," I say. I've been too worried to count out my tips yet. I feel the cash in my pocket. There isn't much of it. Remus is staring at Mandy-Mandy with the most burning anger I have ever seen. His little teeth are bared. Poor guy. He's too young to be full of that much hate. If he knew Mandy-Mandy helped me out with my tables today, would that soften him up? Romulus puts a hand on Remus's and that seems to settle the kid down a bit; I knew Romulus was a nurturer.

"Thanks for helping with my tables," I say to Mandy-Mandy. I feel around on the underside of the table, and my fingers catch on a sticky wad of gum. I start picking it free from the wood.

"You're a nincompoop," says Mandy-Mandy.

"Actually, I'm not a nincompoop," I say. The gum comes off the table bottom. Now that it's in my hand, I don't know what to do with it, so I stick it back where it came from. "I'm a professional."

"Well," says Mandy-Mandy. She pulls a long string of gum out of her mouth, sticks it on the bottom of the table, and pops a fresh piece between her jaws. "I have fifty-four dollars and thirteen cents in my pocket right now. What about you?"

I take out my corkscrew. It's got a little flip-out knife that I can use to cut off the foil from wine bottles. I'm suddenly curious how many teeth the knife has.

"Why don't you count your money?" Mandy-Mandy says. She leans her elbows onto the table, which is bad manners, and stares at me. I pretend not to notice. One tooth. Two teeth. Three teeth.

"I bet you don't even have twenty dollars," she says. "What are Mom and Dad gonna say to *that*, huh?" I lose count of the teeth and start over from the beginning.

"Pathetic," Mandy-Mandy says. Remus slams a fist into the wall, and small cracks show up in the drywall. "Oh, take a chill pill, kid," Mandy-Mandy says to Remus. "I would not necessarily recommend giving yourself an aneurysm over Crafthor 'Yesterday's News' Gunderson. He's not going to be working here much longer."

I lose count again and just sort of stare at the knife. I notice a splotch of rust I've never seen before. I try to scrape it off with my fingernail, but it doesn't work.

"You," says Remus, staring hard at Mandy-Mandy. He punches the air in front of him quickly, about twenty or thirty times, exhales loudly, and slumps back into his chair. Romulus bares his teeth at Mandy-Mandy, swipes an old vermicelli noodle off the floor, and flings it at her. I feel the money in my pocket again. Maybe twenty-five dollars and some change?

Alan comes into the break room with thin, wire-framed glasses on his face. Alan only wears his glasses when he's thinking about something or when he wants to talk about money matters. He's got a clipboard full of spreadsheets and numbers tucked under his arm. I untuck my shirt and use its hem to scrub at my knife blade, but the rust spot just won't go away.

Alan sets his clipboard on the table, straightens out the lapels of his suit jacket, and calls us all to attention in his usual dramatic way.

"Dear God, you reprobates," he says. "I would just like a little bit of attentiveness around here, if it is not too much to ask." I tuck my knife blade back into my corkscrew and look up at Alan. He sees me looking at him and turns his head away. I remember the table of Business People that walked out on me earlier and hope that Alan doesn't. "Remus," Alan says. "There is a box of T-shirts on my desk. Would you please run and get four of them?"

Remus leaps to his feet and scurries out of the break room.

I can hear water dripping from one of the faucets in the kitchen. If Alan is going to yell at me about the Business People, I hope he will just do it now and get it out of the way. Instead, he stays quiet as he pulls a silver pen out of his breast pocket and nibbles on the end of it. I look out our window to the construction across the street. The workers are crawling around on scaffolds, putting up triangular supports for the roof.

Remus comes back into the break room with a stack of brown T-shirts. He hands the shirts to Alan, and Alan starts handing them out to all of us. "These are your new uniforms, guys," he says. "Treat them with respect."

I'm getting a uniform. If I am getting a uniform, it means I am an employee here. If I am an employee here, it means I am not getting fired. If I am not getting fired, it means that Barbara is not replacing me. I take my brown shirt from Alan; it feels warm and soft and wonderful in my hands. I want to put it on right away, but nobody else is doing that, so I wait.

Alan holds out a shirt to Mandy-Mandy, but she doesn't take it. "What?" she says.

"This is your new uniform," Alan says.

"Alan," Mandy-Mandy says, in a tone of voice that implies things are soon about to get very ugly. "Bunnies are cute. Puppies are cute. Mandy-Mandy is cute. Janky-ass brown shirts that suck hardcore are not cute."

Alan does not immediately reply and this irritates Mandy-Mandy. "Do you understand what all I am currently communicating, or shall I draw you a picture, using your vital juices as my goddamn Tempera paints?"

"*Kyrie eleison!*" Alan screams, rolling his eyes up to the break room's crumbly ceiling. "Fascism is not meant to be cute, Mandy-Mandy. It is about power and structure, and nothing says power and structure like a utilitarian piece of uninspiring garb."

An opportunity to keep Alan liking me. Still dizzy from happiness, I pull on my new uniform shirt over my regular shirt. I imagine my uniform T-shirt is like a superhero's cape—it radiates energy at me. I look down at my chest so I can see the shirt's design. The shirt says "A Panini for Your Thoughts" in plain black letters. The shirt is perfect—dark enough that it won't stain too badly if I spill on it.

"I love it!" I say. Mandy-Mandy kicks my knee under the table.

"That's absolutely the correct spirit, Thor," Alan says. He drops a shirt in Mandy-Mandy's lap, and she flings it against the wall.

"We are all," Alan says, glaring at her, "going to put on these damn shirts, because we are all a part of this restaurant-nation. If you do not put on one of these shirts, you are not a part of this restaurant-nation. If you are not a part of this restaurant-nation, you are an enemy."

Slowly and thoughtfully, Mandy-Mandy blows an enormous bubble with her gum. It pops with an awful crack. Mandy-Mandy sucks the gum wreckage back into her mouth and swallows it. I have never once seen Mandy-Mandy swallow her gum and it cannot be a good sign.

"Do you realize," she says, chilly, "that you are threatening me?"

Alan looks daggers at Mandy-Mandy. "You are a cruel and snarly bitch, Mandy, and—"

"Mandy-*Mandy*," she spits out at him.

"You are no longer to have your own way around here. Things are changing, and they're changing fast."

"Then it is simple," Mandy-Mandy says. She's smiling just a bit, like she is getting some good kind of feeling from being angry. For my part, I feel sick and awful and want the staff meeting to end so I can set up for the dinner shift and look up florists in the yellow pages. I have decided I will buy flowers for Ms. Barbara's first day of work.

Mandy-Mandy goes on. "I'll have to yank your guts out through your dago nostrils."

Mandy-Mandy jumps to her feet, raising up her terrible, long fingernails, and lunges toward Alan like she is going to completely obliterate him.

Remus shakes his brother's hand off, knocks a chair into Mandy-Mandy's warpath, and leaps over the chair like he's some sort of small, graceful lizard. He reaches up, grabs Mandy-Mandy's wrist, and pulls it down to his mouth. *Crunch—snap*. Remus's teeth are sunk into Mandy-Mandy's flesh. Now there's red blood all over Remus's face and between his teeth.

Alan claps one time, loud and terrifying. Two big guys I've never seen before are here now. They push Mandy-Mandy and Remus and Romulus to different corners of the room. Alan stands at the front of the room, worry lines all over his face.

"You have all been warned," he says, his voice heaped up with sadness.

Mandy-Mandy is on the ground. One of the big guys—an Italian with enormous muscles—has his foot on her neck. Mandy-Mandy has picked up her brown uniform shirt, which is stained with blood from her wrist.

Remus is thrashing his fists against another huge guy's chest, but the big man barely even seems to notice. He's not hurting Remus, just holding him back so he doesn't go kill Mandy-Mandy.

Romulus is at his brother's side, but I can't tell if he's helping Remus fight the Italian or helping the Italian restrain Remus.

I want to turn tail, but that is not the action of a brave young man, particularly a brave young man who is about to go into the courtship of a dazzling young lady.

"I would like for you all to meet," Alan says, "our new *squadristi*, Numero Uno and Numero Due. They are here to help us keep our profit margins wide and verdant like meadows. If we all cooperate and get along, we will be rich as kings, swimming in dollars and cents just as drunkards swim in the effluvia of their own damnable vices. If we do not get along, an entirely different sort of effluvia will be involved, and it will not be pretty."

"Fucking Fascist," Mandy-Mandy growls from underneath Mr. Uno's wing-tipped shoe.

Mr. Uno bends over to put his face near Mandy-Mandy's. He is dressed just the same as Mr. Due, in a brown A Panini for Your Thoughts shirt and black snakeskin pants. Quietly, he says, "You would be unwise to continue in such-like manner of caterwauling."

Mandy-Mandy doesn't say anything. Alan doesn't say anything. Mr. Uno and Mr. Due don't say anything. I wonder if maybe I shouldn't say something gutsy and sensational just to get everyone talking again. Instead, I see some alfredo sauce on my shoe and wipe it off with my thumb. If Ms. Barbara were here, I would take her hand and squeeze it so that she would know I will never let any of this ugliness touch her.

"Mandy-Mandy, this is not the way to conduct ourselves," comes a sad, disappointed voice from the door to the kitchen. I look over and see Mr. Tony Rigatoni, looking sharp in a brand new suit. I didn't notice him before, but he seems sure and smooth, like he's been watching all along. His hands, I notice, are still as twitchy as they were last night. He reaches up to his head to flatten down a cowlick, then picks an invisible piece of scuzz off the cuff of his suit jacket, and then scratches his nose. He sees I'm watching him, and he winks at me.

"I think that we are all friends in this room," Mr. Tony says. "Is that correct, *amico mio*?" he says, looking at me. He winks again, and I feel spasms in my guts.

"Yeah, Mister Tony," I say. My heart pounds at my ribs. This is my chance to speak up. I close my eyes and picture Ms. Barbara looking at me. She wants me to make everything peaceful and happy. I can hear my voice wobbling, but I speak anyway: "But, Mister Tony, friends do not beat each other and hit and yell."

"Crafthor," Mr. Tony says. He walks to me and puts a hand on my shoulder, firm and fatherly. I tense up my muscles, preparing for him to squeeze too hard. "Sometimes in this sad world, friends have to hurt each other to keep one another from getting hurt by an even more *sinistro nemico*. Do you understand?"

I nod, hoping he will take his hand off my shoulder.

"I would like for us all to have a chat," Mr. Tony continues. He squeezes my shoulder a little, and tiny nibbles of pain bite into me. I squirm. "I trust that we will be more at ease if we can put all thoughts of bloodshed and other such unpleasantnesses at the rear of our brains.

Numero Uno, Numero Due, I believe we can unhand our *rivoluzionarios* and allow them to discuss our business operations like responsible adults."

Mr. Tony releases my shoulder, and I sigh in relief. Mr. Uno and Mr. Due let Mandy-Mandy, Remus, and Romulus go. Mandy-Mandy smoothes the front of her shirt, like nothing happened at all. Remus is holding on tight to his brother's hand. Alan stands motionless, trying not to make eye contact with any of us.

"Let's get this break room in order, why don't we?" Mr. Tony says, and a smile worms up on his face. I feel sick to my stomach. In silence, Mandy-Mandy, the twins, and I pick up all the chairs that have been knocked over and then sit at our usual places at the table.

"Now," Mr. Tony says, "isn't that better? Alan and I deplore violence." Mr. Tony looks at Alan, but Alan is staring out the window, frowning at the construction crews across the street. "However, what I deplore more than violence is watching my new beloved friends and associates tear one another apart when the real enemy is lying in wait to rip the last morsel of *pane* from their *boccas*." Mr. Tony slowly looks at each one of us in turn, tracing a figure eight on the table with his finger, and wiping it off with his other hand.

"Enemies?" I say, finally.

"Enemies!" Mr. Tony says, and slams the table with his fists so hard that Alan looks over, startled. Mr. Tony runs to the window and points to the construction across the street. His eyes are wide and enormous and I am terrified. "Enemies!" he says again, and he pounds the window. The glass panes shudder, and I'm surprised they don't crack. "Look!" he says. He's bouncing on the balls of his feet and is almost hopping up and down with excitement.

"Now, Tony," Alan says, and puts his hand on Mr. Tony's cuff. Mr. Tony shakes off Alan's hand, steps to the twins, and drags them out of their seats by their shirt collars. Remus claws at Mr. Tony's face, and I can see Mr. Uno and Mr. Due step forward, but Mr. Tony waves them off. Mr. Tony pulls the twins over to the window and presses their faces up against the glass.

"Mandy-Mandy, *mi bella*," Mr. Tony says, "I would like for you to please take a look out of this window."

In all the fighting, Mandy-Mandy's smiley-face barrette has gone lopsided and her hair is a mess. She looks like she's thinking of making a break for it and running off. She looks at Mr. Uno, then at Mr. Due, and … and thinks better of it. She stands up with incredible poise and, pretending like she's completely in control, walks to the window. I edge to the window as well. All the roof supports are up at the Ethiopian place, and a bunch of builders are crawling around on top of the new restaurant's walls, fitting huge pieces of plywood into place. A guy in a red hardhat is shimmying over the plywood, nailing down all the edges.

"They've got a roof," I say. Buildings should have roofs. Maybe this will make their restaurant look less like a monster at night.

"Oh my God," Mandy-Mandy says. "They're nearly done."

Mr. Tony laughs and claps Mandy-Mandy on the back. I am afraid she will use her nails to scrape up his eyes, because she hates to be touched, but she is too focused on the construction to want to dismember Mr. Tony.

"Do you see, *mi bella*?" Mr. Tony says. "While you are busy squabbling with your fellow citizens, enemy forces are silently amassing. Unless we act, these Ethiopian *puttanas* will continue to silently gain strength until, one day, they will lash out and become the puppeteers of our *catastrofe*."

Mr. Tony's words make that Ethiopian restaurant sound terrifying, even with a roof. The construction crew still hasn't put the windows in, so big, black holes stare at me from the brick walls. What sort of flower will I buy for Ms. Barbara? I could probably get a rose for a dollar, or maybe two carnations.

"Tony," Alan says, "our dinner shift awaits. Perhaps we would be best advised to discuss your plan."

Mr. Tony smiles and snaps his fingers. "Numero Uno, Numero Due, you are no longer necessary for this most ordinary business conference. Thank you for your services."

Mr. Uno and Mr. Due head out of the break room. Their snazzy wing-tip shoes clack as they walk through the dining room and out through the front door.

"Colleagues and friends," Mr. Tony says, "the enemy is close. Up to this point in time, Alan has been doing an admirable job of maintaining a viable and financially expedient non-franchised eatery. However, evildoers lurk around every corner, and they are just waiting to suck away your livelihood and force you to pledge allegiance to their vastly inferior restaurant-nations."

Mandy-Mandy is still watching the workers nail on the roof across the street. She shakes her head, slow and sad, and says, "Those damn Ethiopians."

"Here we are, a fine upstanding community of food service practitioners," Mr. Tony says, "vending our modest wares for the good people of Gruff Valley, and never making no trouble for nobody. Gruff Valley is not Los Angeles, granted, but it is big enough that there is sufficient room for people of all ages, races, and ethnic food preferences to keep to themselves without bothering each other. Well," he says, furrowing his brow and touching his heart tenderly, "it pains me to say this, but another restaurant-nation has decided it has the right to go tromping about wherever it wants and that it feels like challenging us for the economic dominance of this particular commercial zone. Can we call these Ethiopians anything other than bullies?"

Remus suddenly shudders like somebody slammed him big-time in his guts. "Ethiopians," he grunts out with an awful twist of his face, like he's going to be sick.

"Ethiopians," Romulus repeats. His jaw goes hard and his eyes get narrow. He looks at his brother and they glower and glower and glower at each other. Then, they look at Mandy-Mandy, and the glowering continues. I don't think things will end up very well for these Ethiopians.

I look at Alan. He's standing in front of the break table, polishing the lenses of his glasses with a white handkerchief and ignoring us.

Mr. Tony stabs at the window with his finger. "Our enemy," he says. He pauses and then says it again, even louder. "Our enemy. Mister Bogale Gojjam and his *digustoso* Rasta-raunt. He would like the money that you all work so hard for—and he'll get it, too, unless we organize a resistance."

"Fucking Ethiopians," says Mandy-Mandy. "How can they have a restaurant in Gruff Valley when they don't even have any food in their own goddamn country?"

Romulus pounds his fist into the table with enough force to leave a dent where his knuckles strike.

"It is simple," Mr. Tony continues. "We must invade. Their demon nation cannot be permitted to prosper."

"Alan," I say. I bite my lip and look out at the construction workers. It looks like they are all just doing their jobs. "Maybe we should wait and see—"

"Tony," Alan says, a little quivery. He lifts up his glasses to the light, looks through the lenses, and must think they're not clean enough, because he goes on polishing them. "We haven't necessarily committed to that course of action."

"At what point, *mi amico*," says Tony, "should we commit upon said course of action? When the Ethiopians already have our throats between their jaws?" Tony crosses over to Alan and whacks his right arm around Alan's shoulders. Alan puts his glasses back on and frowns. "*La economia!*" he says, waving his left arm to the rest of us, like he's showing off an amazing science project. "Our economy is a *disastro*. In good times, my friends, we must all help each other to enjoy *la dolce vita*, but when *la vita* turns *acida*, then we must look to ourselves. *Credere, obbedire, combattere.* It is the only way!"

"Tony," Alan says. Mandy-Mandy, Remus, and Romulus are still staring out the window, their eyes narrow and cruel. I put my fingers over a long marinara streak on the wall and pretend I'm feeling for a pulse. For a second, I feel a heartbeat inside the wall, but then I realize it's my own.

"Alan," says Mr. Tony. "This is not the time to turn *insicuro*." Mr. Tony's smile grows so enormous that it mushes his cheeks up into his eyes.

"But, Alan …" I say.

"Tony," says Alan.

"Alan," says Tony.

"Thor," says Alan.

Just as I think we're going to stand here saying our names over and over forever, Mandy-Mandy squeaks her fingernail loudly over the glass of the window.

"I got to just make one damn thing clear," Mandy-Mandy says. Even though she's still bleeding some from Remus's bite, she doesn't seem to feel the hurt at all. She's not taking her eyes off the construction site across the street. "I am not going to give up my tip money to some anorexic Ethiopian, and if that means I've got to invade their hoodoo restaurant, then that's just exactly what it means."

"Well," says Alan, "we haven't really—"

Mr. Tony pinches Alan's hand and Alan stops talking. Instead, Alan reaches down to pick a dirty napkin off the floor and puts it in the wastebasket.

Mr. Tony nods and grabs Mandy-Mandy by the arm. "You are going to be a hero, Mandy." Now he turns to Remus, Romulus, and me. "Are you ready to be heroes, too?"

Remus grins with two million teeth and nods. Romulus does the same.

Everybody's eyes are on me. I look at Alan, and his green-gold eyes are wet and bloodshot. He shrugs at me like he is angry—annoyed that I'm even looking at him. When Ms. Barbara came into the restaurant, she seemed so beautiful. I do not like to invade things, and I do not like to fight wars, and this whole stupid thing is going too far, too fast. Maybe I need to say the first thing that comes into my mind. But, then again, if I say something stupid, maybe I will not be able to take it back later. Well, one thing is certain; I have got to say something brilliant and wonderful that is going to turn all this around. I know I can.

"Thor, you are a good-hearted man, yes?" Mr. Tony is talking to me, but I can't quite take in what he's saying.

"Sure."

"Well, this is a difficult thing for me to say, *mi amico*, but this is the way the business is going. Mandy-Mandy wants *invasione*. Remus wants *invasione*. Romulus wants *invasione*. Alan indisputably wants *invasione*. Do you want to remain a part of *nostra famiglia*?"

Alan again scrunches up his eyebrows at me, again, fed up with me, and that's not fair, because I am the only one wanting to be reasonable and not hot-headed. I've got lots of words crowding into my belly and, all of a sudden, the words are crunched so tight together they start flooding out of my mouth.

"I don't like all this fighting and maybe we should just cool our jets," I hear myself saying. "You see, I don't know anything about an

Ethiopian, except that he probably does not have all the food and money that we would have in our own bellies and whatnot and in light of such statistics, then maybe it's not silly to think that an Ethiopian is not going to come threaten us and burn down our restaurant." My words are sinking in. I feel myself blushing, but I keep on going. "And if you were an Ethiopian, Mister Tony, or some other such person who just wanted to make an honest living, then you would not want yourself invaded. Maybe you would want somebody to shake your hand and be respectful of your crazy restaurant-nation. And, well, I don't like to make waves, but—"

Something soft and warm hits my face. Mandy-Mandy's thrown a dinner roll at my head.

"Someone shut this boob up before I decapitate the hell out of him!" Mandy-Mandy says.

Remus snaps his angry jaws at Mandy-Mandy. Mandy-Mandy snaps her jaws right back at Remus, and for a minute I'm afraid they're going to sink their teeth into each other's necks and rip each other to shreds in the middle of the break room like they were enraged cannibal dogs.

Alan is picking pieces of lint off his suit, like nothing matters. I want to yell at him, but it's Alan, so I don't want to yell at him, but Mandy-Mandy grabs Remus by the wrist and twists hard, and it's like instead of twisting his hand she's twisting my stomach, because here come the words out of my mouth:

"Alan, I am upset at all this, because you are supposed to be the boss, and how are you—"

"Crafthor," Alan says, whipping his red, furious face around to me. "Why don't you shut your goddamn mouth, okay? If you're going to obstruct the progress of our restaurant-nation, I simply do not see you working for us anymore. So, instead of telling me how to do my job, perhaps you should start setting up the dining room for dinner and we can talk about this when you're acting more reasonably."

Mandy-Mandy's dinner roll didn't hurt my face when it smashed into it. However, what Alan is saying to me is like an enormous cannonball to the chest. I do not want anyone to know how much I'm hurt, so, thinking about Ms. Barbara, and how she is the most beautiful woman, and also the nicest, I just smile and mime like I'm zipping up my lips. Everybody's watching me as I back off into the dining room, my face blazing with shame and anger.

***

It is hot out in the parking lot tonight and the bugs are screaming so loud I can't hear myself think. I walk to the edge of our asphalt lot, where all the lighting ends, so I can stare off into the black desert of Gruff Valley. If I squint, I can see the flat outline of a mesa Mom calls The Big, Big Anvil, due to a little rock horn that juts out on the western side. It points right toward the Pacific Ocean. The Big, Big Anvil is a sort of friend of mine; I know Gruff Valley inside and out, but if I ever get lost, I know the mesa will always be pointing me in the right direction.

I'm holding on to my broomstick, like always, but there haven't been any gay gentlemen to disrupt tonight. A couple drops of sweat drip off my forehead into my eyes, so I wipe out the sweat with the back of my wrist. I squint, trying to get the outline of the mesa back in focus, but my vision is bleary with heat and sweat and dark.

I've got to think about my future. Alan was nice to me all through the dinner rush and even took a bunch of tables for me. I bet he feels bad for yelling at me, because I feel bad for yelling at him. But if Mr. Tony is going to make me go invading new restaurant-nations, I'm not sure I can keep going in to work every day and stay happy. Of course, if I quit, then it's goodbye to my blue carpet. If I quit, then Mom will cry and cry and cry. If I quit, then Dad will go into the fridge for his weekly beer and then remember we don't have any beer, and he'll know it's my fault because I quit my job, and he will pretend he doesn't want a beer this week after all, and I'll know that he's lying.

Then there's Ms. Barbara.

If I quit, then I will not get to see Ms. Barbara every day and make her fall in love with me by being wonderful to her. Even worse, what will she do if Mandy-Mandy is cruel and murderous, and I am not there to protect her? What if Alan tries to make Ms. Barbara go invade some Ethiopian restaurant and she doesn't want to?

Invade. Guns and soldiers and all kinds of crazy pain.

I stare at the construction crews. They're putting in one of the front windows, lining up the corners just so. Alan says they're going to be done with the Ethiopian restaurant in about a week. I look back at A Panini for Your Thoughts. Our walls are black and white checked tile. There's a soft, red light shining down just over the entryway, and it makes the tiles look pink. The light always makes me feel warm. The roof is shingled and a little droopy, but it doesn't leak at all. To advertise, we've got a big orange sign with our name on it sticking out of the roof. Alan had the twins paint the sign during my second year at the restaurant. When I look at it closely, I can see where Romulus accidentally kicked over a pail of black paint. There used to be a huge stain, but Alan painted over it so carefully I'd never know it was there if I weren't looking for it. There are still repairs Alan wants to make, like he wants to put in a drive-thru window and maybe put in some supports for the roof, but it's a fine building and I'm proud to know I work there. I don't know much about Ethiopia, but I know I don't want that Rasta-Raunt to take over or hurt us or anything else. I don't see why we can't have our restaurant, and they can have theirs.

A car horn blares and my thoughts scatter every which way.

I turn around and see Mr. Hans's flashy red car parked in our lot. Mr. Hans is in the driver's seat, and he waves big at me. He's wearing a tight black shirt that makes his arms seem like enormous baseball bats. Maybe he will listen to me. I wave back. He smiles at me and then makes his beckon for me to come over to the car.

I walk to it, glad not to be caught up in thinking anymore. When I get to thinking about serious things, I sometimes fall into my thinking like it's an enormous spider web. The more I try and think, hoping I'll get some incredible answer that will solve everything, the worse I get stuck in more and more problems and possibilities.

When I get to the car, Mr. Hans powers his window down. I stand at a little distance so Mr. Hans can't see how sweated through my brown work shirt is.

"How are you, mein herr?" asks Mr. Hans. He's got a huge gold ring on his right index finger, and while he waits for me to answer, he taps the ring on the steering wheel.

"Well, Mister Hans, I don't want to sound down, but I have been better."

Tap. Tap. Tap.

Mr. Hans seems to be waiting for me to go on talking, so I do. "I might lose my job, maybe."

He smiles, big and golden, and says, "Well, you have opportunity for adventure-quest and so money is not any sort of problem, mein herr."

"I don't want to lose my job," I say. "I think that I'm in love."

Mr. Hans laughs big. "Ach! You have not learned that love is an illusion, mein herr. In this world, every man must have for himself self-love, and that is the only kind of true love. All else is just pleasuresome sex-romp. You are wonderful trusting-and-senseless-herr."

I don't know why I thought a German gay gentleman would understand my problems. A breeze runs over me. I smell like panini grease.

"If you love a woman, best way is with two millions of dollars to woo her. Have you given thought to invitation of partake in frolicsome adventure-quest?"

"Again, I think it's polite of you, friend," I say. "But, ahm …"

Mr. Hans bangs his ring again on the steering wheel. He frowns heavily, and two million small wrinkles appear just above his eyebrows, like suddenly there was an earthquake there. However, he doesn't seem like he's about to say anything. He just keeps staring through his windshield, frowning and biting his lip. My neck starts sweating; I wipe at it with my hand, but that makes my hand slimy, so I wipe my hand on my pants.

Tap. Tap. Tap.

Finally, he looks at me and his eyes are different. I can't see too well, what with all the darkness, and Mr. Hans's face is shadowy because the parking lot lights beam almost straight down. All the same, I can tell that he is looking at me, and seeing me. I suddenly feel like Mr. Hans is understanding me, like I can say anything and he will want to hear it.

"You is sad, mein herr, and I laughed at that," he says. "I am no good friend, after all. You must accept mein apologies, if you can."

"Of course, Mister Hans."

"I am lonely herr, you see?" Mr. Hans says. "And I think I am not much caring about feelings of other herren. I want for you to tell me many problems you are having, and maybe we then go on adventure-quest, yes?"

I tell it all to him, about Ms. Barbara, and about Ethiopia, and how Remus bit Mandy-Mandy, and how I felt so awful, and how I'm afraid things will get more and more vicious, and how Ms. Barbara is still upset at this Parker fellow, which fellow was mean to her, but how she is the nicest ever. The more I talk, the heavier all that humid desert air feels on my face, and all I can do is just keep talking. If I stop telling my thoughts, all the words are going to collect up in my head and cram in on one another until there is no room left in my skull, and I will explode. I go red in the face, talking and talking, and sweating all the while. Suddenly, I hit a word in the middle of a sentence and realize I've got no more air in my lungs to say the next word—and so I stop to breathe, and this pause is just long enough for me to feel how hot I am, and tired, and exhausted, and how long I've been spouting up my guts for Mr. Hans to hear, who is such a nice listener, and who is probably not too interested.

Now that there's silence again, I can hear all those whirring parking lot bugs talking to each other all at once in their different languages.

Tap. Tap. Tap.

"Oh, mein herr," Mr. Hans says, slowly, like he is talking to me, but to himself, too. "World is full of viciousness and fighting. So if you have found woman that you are true-loving, you must keep in love with her no matter what else is happens."

I'm tired of talking.

"Well, mein herr, you is not in good mood to make big decisions tonight, but I will hope for you to continue thinking about go on adventure-quest. With two millions of dollars, I know that you could help to be provider for Miss Barbara. Maybe she would not have to work in restaurant-nation, and you could have free time to travel and do things of young newlyweds."

I look at the broomstick I am still holding in my hands. Alan will be wondering where I am. I look out at the Big, Big Anvil, strong and sturdy and always pointing out the way to the Pacific. I've got nothing to say anymore.

***

When I get home, Mom is still awake. She's sitting in her favorite chair with the red poppies printed all over the cushions, mending the collar of one of Dad's dress shirts. The house is dark, except for one bare bulb burning over Mom's head. She has always told me the most awful thing in the world is waste, but it still strikes me as sad to see her sitting all alone with no light, this tiny woman in this big, dark house.

"G'night, Mom," I whisper, as I tiptoe over to the stairs.

Mom looks up at me and, even though all she can probably see of me is my outline, somehow she knows I've got a lot on my mind.

"Sweetie, what's wrong?" she says, setting the shirt down in her lap.

I think maybe I'll tell her the whole story, but I already told Mr. Hans, and that confused me enough. Anyway, I'm tired and I don't want Mom to worry.

"Nothing," I say.

This line appears on Mom's forehead and she looks five years older. She starts to say something, but then she stops and frowns.

"Do you want some warm milk?"

"No, thanks," I say. Mom always scalds the milk when she tries to heat it. Plus, if I drink milk tonight, that means no milk tomorrow.

"I don't want any milk tomorrow," Mom says, "so if you want some now, you can still have some with breakfast."

"No, thanks."

"Do you want me to tell you a secret?"

"Okay," I say. It's always the same secret.

"You are the sweetest boy in the whole entire world, Thorrie, and your father and I love you so much."

And now, for whatever dumb reason, I'm fighting to keep tears from building up in my eyes.

***

Before I get into bed, I lay my tip money out on my soft blue carpet. There's enough light coming through the window from the streetlamp outside that I can count easily without turning on my light. It's bad— twenty-two dollars and eighteen cents. I count again, just to make sure I've got it right. I fish into the pockets of my work pants to see if maybe I missed a couple bucks, but no luck. I can hear Mom walking around in the kitchen, still up. She's been staying up later and later every night, and waking up earlier and earlier.

Even in the dark I can see my cardboard rectangles all over my wall. We don't have money to throw around on posters, which is too bad, because I'd love to have a big picture of a jetliner or rocket ship above my bed. Instead, I do what Dad likes to call "improvise." Every time we finish a box of cereal, I cut off the front picture and put it on my wall. Cereal boxes are better than posters anyway, because posters are made out of flimsy paper, but cereal boxes are durable and cardboard, and sometimes even smell a little like the cereal that used to be inside.

I've got all sorts of boxes on my wall. I've got one that's an enormous field of wheat, stretching off miles and miles and miles into the sunset. I've got another that shows a family wrestling together on a fuzzy orange couch. One of my favorites shows a muscled guy throwing out this Cheerio as a life preserver to save a redheaded kid that's drowning in a swimming pool full of milk. Even though he's drowning, the kid smiles away, happy, I guess, to have his picture taken and to have all that milk around him. My favorite picture, though, is a woman with dark hair and a red flower behind her ear. She's standing in front of some mountains, smiling like she's got the most amazing secret, but isn't going to tell you unless you find exactly the way to ask. I call her Francesca, on account of she looks sort of foreign and exotic. I hung Francesca right over the milk crates where I keep my clothes, so that as I get out of bed in the morning and get ready to start the day, I can ask her for whatever foreign advice she has. Of course, she's just cardboard, so it's not like she can tell me anything useful, but sometimes pretending what her answer might be gets me thinking constructively. I don't like to bother Francesca too much, so I usually ask her for advice only in the mornings and not really at night, but tonight is different. Tonight, I'm facing what Mom would call a "conscience crunch."

I listen for a second. Mom is still thumping around. It sounds like she's taking the dishes out of the drying rack and putting them away in their proper cupboards. Dad's snoring across the hall. So, I crawl over to my milk crates and, making my voice into something really small, start asking Francesca for advice:

"Hi, Francesca," I whisper. "I know it's late, but can you help me?"

Even with the light from the streetlamp, Francesca's picture is just a dark rectangle on my wall. I can't make out her outline, but I know she's listening away, just waiting to shed some light on my dilemmas.

"Today I got twenty-two dollars and eighteen cents, which is not so good." Francesca waits for me to go on, so I do. "And so I need to put that money in the ashtray." Mom has a little green glass ashtray that she keeps on the kitchen counter. None of us smoke—Dad used to have a pipe now and then, but he's given that up since The Money Situation—but Mom got the ashtray from her mom and so she doesn't like to pawn it off. Every day after work, I put my tip money in the ashtray. Mom takes the money and puts it in the "Family Fund," which goes toward food and bills.

"But," I say to Francesca, "what if I only put in twenty-*one* dollars and eighteen cents?" The words sound ugly coming out of my mouth. I almost expect Francesca to come to life and start yelling at me all about how selfish it would be to take a dollar for myself, what with Mom and Dad being so nice and trusting.

I hear a big clatter from the kitchen, like maybe Mom dropped a pot. Dad stops snoring for a second, but then goes right on back to it. I wait until I hear Mom pick up the pot and put it in its cupboard before I keep talking.

"You see," I say to Francesca, "there is a beautiful woman I'm going to be working with now, and she's in hard times, too. So it would just be the tops if I could get her a flower, like what you've got behind your ear."

Now I've got to think through what Francesca would say if she were real.

"You're taking money from Mom and Dad, and that's very bad," is the first thing she'd say, in her nutty Spanish accent.

"But I am beautiful lady," she says, "and so I know that other beautiful lady would like flower."

Francesca has it good. She stands in front of mountains every day, looking enchanting in her nice red dress. I bet it's pretty up in the mountains in Spain or wherever she lives, with snow all over and young people skiing. I wonder if Ms. Barbara has ever been to the mountains, and I guess she probably hasn't. Wouldn't it be great if we could go up into the mountains and live some day, and bring Mom and Dad and Alan and the twins, and maybe even Mandy-Mandy—if she agreed to be nice? We could hike around and pick wildflowers and drink all the milk we wanted to.

"Thor," says Francesca, "you must stay in focus and all."

"Sorry."

"A dollar is much money," she says, "and so you must not take from Mom and Dad. But, if you take from yourself and all, then it is not stealing, you know?"

I hear Mom's heavy footsteps as she comes on down the hall. She opens the door to her bedroom and shuts it behind her. Her saggy floor creaks as she walks across her bedroom to the bathroom. It used to be that Mom and Dad would go to bed at the same time, but that was before the Money Situation. A couple weeks after I first started hearing about our finances, when Dad would be ready for bed, Mom would tell him she'd follow him up. Then she'd start finding things to do late at night. Now, I'd be surprised to hear it if she said she got even five hours of sleep a night.

"Thor," says Francesca. "Go to bed." In my head, she sounds tired, which must mean I'm tired, since I'm the one doing the talking for her.

"Thanks, Francesca. It's been real helpful."

I pick one of the dollar bills from the stack on my carpet and stuff it into the pocket of my uniform pants. Francesca is right. I shouldn't take the money from the Family Fund, but if I take it from myself, it's all okay. So, if I take a dollar today and then don't drink milk or use electricity for the rest of the week, then it's fair. Still and all, I feel jumbled-up as I climb in to bed. I want to be nice to Ms. Barbara. I want to be honest to my parents. For some reason, life's made it so it's not possible to do both.

I hear some water running and then Mom's brushing her teeth in the bathroom. I pull my sheets up over my head to block out the sound, but I can still hear her scrub and spit, and scrub and spit, and scrub and spit over and over and over and over.

***

The flower I got for Ms. Barbara is pretty and it makes me happy to look at it. I don't know what kind she likes, so I got her a sunflower, because everybody likes sunflowers. It's two feet tall, with petals sprouting all over it like feathers made of butter. In the middle, there's an enormous black eye that looks at first like it's just one solid lump, but it's actually made up of tiny black hairs that are soft and bendy. The best part of all is that I'm going to give it to Ms. Barbara and so I know whenever she looks at it and thinks how pretty it is, she will think about me.

As I wake up Remus and Romulus for their day's shift, I feel a little better than I did last night. Alan's been so nice to me since last night that I think he wants for us to be buddies again. I'm not keen about invading this Ethiopian place, but Alan knows me and is not going to make me do anything despicable. The dollar, too, isn't such a big deal today. I'm going to pay Mom and Dad back, in my way. I didn't have any juice with breakfast at all, and even though my belly felt slightly empty when I got to work, it isn't any kind of matter, because I'm in love with Ms. Barbara and I've got a flower for her, which is colorful and nice to look at.

I put the sunflower in a cup of water in the refrigerator to keep it looking spruced and healthy, and then start getting the restaurant ready for the lunch shift. As I'm checking to make sure each table has enough olive oil, I hear the bell on the front door, and so I look up to see Ms. Barbara enter the store. She looks maybe even more beautiful than yesterday, because she has done herself up for work. She's wound up her red hair into a tight little bun, held in place with a shiny blue chopstick. Her face is pale, but she's made her eyes dark and her lips red. Alan must have given her a brown uniform T-shirt yesterday, because she's wearing it, and I can still see the creases where it used to be folded up. When she sees me, she smiles, and I spill olive oil all over my hand.

"Morning, Thor," she says to me.

"Morning," I say, wiping my hand on the rag I keep tucked into the side of my pants when I'm working. "How are you today?"

"I'm okay, except my ailment is acting up."

"Your ailment?" I say. I make another try at filling up the olive oil bottle on the table, being careful to keep my hand steady.

"I got tons of ailments, like you wouldn't even believe. I got everything from flaccid spine to adult-onset brain pox. The doctor says." She sucks in a snatch of air and bends over a bit. A frown shows up on her eyebrows, and then it disappears and she straightens back up. "Yuck," she says, and smiles.

"Wow. That must be rough."

"Damn right, it's rough," says Ms. Barbara. Even though she is talking about something serious, she looks proud of herself. I guess she should. If I had a million and a half germs running around inside me, and I still looked attractive, I'd be pretty proud, too. "Today I've got a stomachache, on account of my obstinate uterus."

"Obstinate uterus?" I ask. I feel like I should know what that is, so I try to make it sound like I'm asking to make sure I heard her right.

"Yeah. See, when a uterus gets all angsty, it starts to devour the rest of your body."

"That sounds serious." I pick up a set of salt and pepper shakers and eyeball them to see if they're full enough. "You must be taking two million pills, huh?"

"Nah," she says. "I can't afford meds." A rumble of pain gives her a shudder, and she grabs onto the edge of the table next to her. "Jeez," she says. "I guess walking all the way across this whole country ain't good for a gal's uterus."

"What's your doctor say?"

"My doc don't say much." She laughs a little, and the laugh comes through her nose like a snort. "He's a real hands-off sort of fellow."

"Sheesh," I say. I see a salt shaker that's only about half full, so I unscrew the top and fill it the rest of the way. "Who's your doctor?"

"The internet."

"How does that work?" I screw the top back on the salt shaker and give it a satisfied shake.

"It's Doctor Dirk," she says. "He's on the internet. I mail him about whatever my ailments are doing, and he gives me all sorts of advice. Like today, for my uterus. All you have to do for an obstinate uterus is just drink some seltzer mixed with curry powder. It's disgusting, but it also makes your guts taste awful, so your uterus isn't interested in chowing down on them anymore."

"I don't know, but … I guess you should get a real doctor."

"Nah. With so many ailments as I got, a real doctor would just take all my cash and leave me hungry. Doctor Dirk only charges five bucks for a consultation, and he's the real deal."

"Is that a fact?" I think about Mr. Hans and his two million dollars. With that kind of money, I bet Ms. Barbara's uterus could be taught to keep quiet and not make trouble. She could go to the best doctor there is, and get cured of everything and anything.

"Besides," Ms. Barbara says, "I don't want some strange guy poking at me with all sorts of ice-cold implements and fingers and such." She smoothes out the front of her brown uniform shirt, like she is done talking about ailments. "But you don't have to worry. I am a hard worker, and no ailment on Earth can stop Barbara Hackbush from putting her back into her business, as my old man used to say."

"Well, you'll do well here, then." I start picking up salt and pepper shakers again, though I've forgot which ones I already checked. "Alan's motto is 'Work makes you free.'"

"That's real pretty," Ms. Barbara Hackbush says, holding up her index finger to her red lips, like she just tasted something delicious. "Is that from the Bible or something?"

"I guess so." Suddenly, I remember about her flower. "I got a flower keeping cool for you in the walk-in fridge. I didn't know what kind you like, so I just got you something that's got some color to it."

Ms. Barbara makes her lips into an unhappy little 'o.' "Are you trying to court me, or something?"

I had not imagined Ms. Barbara would not like for me to be in love with her, and I try to think of something to say that will make it look like I am not in love with her at all. Maybe I should be gutsy and say that, yes, I am trying to court her, and she might not know it at this moment, but she is going to fall in love with me and we will be the happiest people in Gruff Valley.

"Thor," she says, "it's sweet of you and all. It's just … the last man what bought me flowers was trying to court me, which man was Parker, which relationship, as you well know, I am not eager to bring back up via conversation or via reliving of past mistakes or via any other damn thing." Ms. Barbara reaches out and squeezes my hand, which is still sort of slimy from the olive oil, and I know I did the right thing not to say anything.

I hear an awful slam. Ms. Barbara and I look up and see the source of the noise is Mandy-Mandy, who has just come in and flung her purse on the ground. Mandy-Mandy looks way less cute today than she ever has before. She is actually wearing her brown uniform shirt, which has a big black streak all over the front—where she bled on it yesterday. The shirt hides her womanly areas, too, without which she sort of looks ordinary. Her pants are camouflage and not tight at all, and she's wearing some kind of combat boots. There's no smiley barrette on her head today—her blonde hair is pulled back extremely tight in a plain old ponytail. Still, she's got that demon look in her awful green eyes, and I can tell that she is ready to make some money, cute or not cute.

"Quit your canoodling," Mandy-Mandy says, yanking Ms. Barbara away from me by the arm. "You're training with me today, woman, so I hope you brought a notebook, 'cause I know how to play this business inside and out. First lesson is that true go-getters which have their eyes on the prize do not go about playing lovebirds with Crafthor 'Trouble' Gundersen, which is *not* a true go-getter, which does *not* have his eyes on aforementioned prize."

Ms. Barbara is giving Mandy-Mandy too much attention.

"Second lesson is that we've got a battle plan to devise, because we are going to invade some Ethiopians' sucky restaurant."

Ms. Barbara makes that unhappy 'o' with her lips again when she hears the word "invade."

"I have to admit," Ms. Barbara says, polite as you please, "that I am not much in the business of invasions. I prefer the quiet life, you know."

I swear that, for a moment, Mandy-Mandy's eyes turn red and shot through with lightning bolts. She rips five pieces of gum out of her pants pocket and jams them into her mouth before she can do anything worse. Immediately, her jaws start munching frantically up and down.

"You cannot," Mandy-Mandy says, through a mouthful of bubble gum, "come in here all boo-hoo and needing money, and then turn right around and tell us how to run a business. Either you need money, in which case you damn well cannot let Ethiopians run around free, hoping to eat up our profits like they eat up their own children during those nutty African famines you hear about, or you do not need money, in which case you can exit this restaurant-nation, ensuring that you kiss my ass on your way out, and fling your filthy cash around to whichever bloodsucking charity you goddamn choose."

Ms. Barbara looks like she is about to cry; her eyes go wet, and little wrinkles show up around the corners of her mouth. This poor woman, who is capable of being sublimely independent, has walked across the entire country, looking for Opportunity, and is now being roughhoused by a woman not half her worth! This is the perfect time for me to step in and save her and stand up to Mandy-Mandy and to this whole Fascist idea about invading other restaurant-nations.

"Well, I don't like it," says Ms. Barbara, "but maybe it'll all make more sense once you show me the ropes."

Mandy-Mandy smiles in that smug way she always does when someone comes around to her point of view, or compliments her outfit.

"Don't be mean with Miss Barbara," I say to Mandy-Mandy. She ignores me.

"Hackbush," Mandy-Mandy says, "maybe there's some kind of hope for you. Now," she says, leading Ms. Barbara away to the kitchen, "first thing we've got to do is get your hair out of that bun and scrub off your makeup, because no way are you going to out-cute me today. Cute is for the past. We're gone guerilla now."

Ms. Barbara gives me a sad little wave as she disappears with Mandy-Mandy into the kitchen. I head back to Table 0-1 and start checking salt and pepper shakers all over again. I don't know what to do. I don't want to be gone guerilla, but I cannot leave Ms. Barbara alone to face this awful Ethiopian invasion and to be the only one looking to avoid all this nastiness. Together, we could be partners in peace—but when I think about how set Alan is on invasion, my lips feel dry. I try to swallow my nerves, trusting to gracious the right path will come clear to me some way or the other.

***

The lunch shift is quiet, but I'm happy to see Bruce and Ronald come in and sit in my section. Sometimes they'll come in for lunch, but I usually don't see them until closing time.

Bruce beams when he sees me coming up to the table. "How's the good life treating you, partner?" he asks me.

"Well, friend, we've got a new lady working for us. She's in back with Mandy-Mandy right now, learning to make salads. You want to meet her?"

Bruce laughs. "That's okay, Thor. Better not interrupt her training, you know. I like the new shirt."

My brown uniform shirt is small on me, but it's comfy enough. "What brings you in so early today?" I ask.

"We're off the rest of the day," Ronald says. Even inside, he's wearing his sunglasses so you can't tell what he's thinking. When he speaks, he barely moves his mouth; he's the most discreet guy I've ever seen. "We were up all night."

"We stopped a robbery in progress at the Tequila Mockingbird," Bruce says, grinning from ear to ear. "Wild night, I'd say."

"Wow," I exclaim, digging an order pad and a pen from my pocket. "Did they shoot at you?" No matter how many times I hear from Bruce and Ronald about all the heists and capers they see, I can't get over the fact that I am talking to real, actual cops.

"There was some crossfire, sure," Ronald says, like "crossfire" is just the same as sass or something else that is mildly obnoxious but not really going to tear holes in your chest and make you die in a bloody pool.

"Jeez," I say, and whistle. "We sure don't see that kind of excitement around here." Suddenly, I think about Ethiopia and what Bruce and Ronald would think if they knew about Mr. Tony Rigatoni or Misters Uno and Due. Is it illegal to invade somebody else's restaurant-nation? When Alan talked about invasion, he made it sound normal, like it is just some way to do business, like cutting costs or cooking the books.

"In our line of work," Bruce says, "excitement is about the worst thing you can hope for; it means people aren't doing what they should be doing. No, sir, when you're a cop, you hope for a quiet night, when you can just sit around at your favorite restaurant and eat some tiramisu." He drums his hands on the table. "Speaking of which, I am hungry as all holy hell. An Octavian omelet would hit the spot, Thor, and an iced tea—extra sweet, if you would."

I write down Bruce's order, still thinking about Ethiopia, and turn to Ronald. Ronald lowers his sunglasses a bit and points to "Rubicon Reuben" on the menu. He glances quickly side-to-side, to make sure nobody but me saw him order, and pushes his sunglasses back up onto his nose.

"Anything to drink?" I whisper. For some reason, whenever I talk to Ronald, I feel the need to keep my voice down so nobody else hears.

Ronald shakes his head a fraction of an inch, and I know that means he just wants water, with only a tiny bit of ice and some cucumber slices in it for flavor.

"Alright, fellows," I say, "Remus and Romulus will have your order up in no time." I put my order pad back into my pocket and head into the kitchen. Remus and Romulus are busy flinging handfuls of flour at one another. Their new brown T-shirts are already streaked with white and discoloration.

"Hey boys," I say, "I sure could use an Octavian omelet and a Rubicon Reuben, toasted extra dark and crispy."

The boys cut out their horseplay and jump to work. I can never get over how fast their hands fly when they're set to work—they shred, dice, chop, fry, and flip like nobody's business.

"Thor," a voice says behind me. I turn to see Alan, looking serious. "We need to talk. Do you have a minute?"

"Well, sure, but Bruce and Ronald are out in the dining room, pretty hungry."

"I'll have Barbara bring them their food and beverages," Alan says. "Hey, Barbara!" he hollers out toward the salad station, where Ms. Barbara and Mandy-Mandy are putting together an Augustus Caesar salad.

Ms. Barbara wipes her hands on her slacks and comes over to us. Her hair is down, and she's wiped her makeup all off, except for a little smudge of dark that's hanging on just under her right eye. A bit of Gallic dressing is smeared on the tip of her nose.

I hand her my order slip. "This all goes out to Bruce Billingon and Ronald Harpoon, the two cops sitting at table nine. They're super nice and you'll love to meet them."

"Okay, Thor," she says, and smiles.

"How are you feeling with your ailments?"

"Oh, *bomber*," she says, and laugh-snorts like the happiest woman in the universe. I wipe the dressing off her nose with my thumb. "Thanks," she says, and hustles out to the beverage station to get the cops' drinks ready.

Alan watches Ms. Barbara go off. She's tied her apron strings in back in this flourishy, wonderful bow. The bow bounces as she walks, like she's wagging some sort of tail. "She's good," Alan says. "She's a real workhorse. Even Mandy likes her as well as she'd like anybody."

I feel pride glowing all over my body.

"Anyway, Thor," Alan says, "why don't you come into my office?"

Icy spears of fear shoot through all the good feelings I was just having. I tell myself to nod and look sly like Ronald would do, but if I push the fear out of my chest, it swims around in my bladder; if I push it up out of my bladder, then it starts gobbling my guts. I grab a fistful of my shirt and start twisting it around in my hands. When I pull on the shirt, its black letters get distorted. I pull the letters out wide and then scrunch them up tight together.

"Thor," says Alan.

I pull on my shirt harder. I can hear Remus call out that Bruce and Ronald's order is ready. "I should show Ms. Barbara how to garnish," I say, and start to walk away.

"Thor," Alan says, louder. "Mandy-Mandy will sufficiently demonstrate our panini artistry to our new hire. You need to come with me."

Heat from Remus and Romulus's grill pulses out at me. I think about Ms. Barbara's sunflower, cool in the refrigerator, and wish I were there, or maybe in the mountains with Francesca.

"Thor," Alan says, and grabs my wrist. His hands are soft and his fingernails are trimmed just so, with a smidgeon of white nail coming out from the pink in clean little crescents. The cuff of his purple dress shirt is dangling into a smear of blue cheese dressing that I've got on the back of my hand.

"You've got goop," I say, and wipe the dressing off the edge of his sleeve with my free thumb.

"Thanks," Alan says. "Thor, you're not in any trouble, but I need you to please cooperate with me." I don't say anything, but Alan starts leading me back to his office, and what can I do? He's already got me by the wrist and, if Alan wants to talk, he's the boss, and so it's going to happen sooner or later, so, sweating and balling my free hand into a fist and stuffing it in my pants pocket, I go with Alan past the clattering dishwashing unit, past the corkboard where he posts our work schedules and any announcements, and through the red doorway that guards his office.

I look around as I follow Alan inside. I don't come in here often; Alan only brings people here when he's angry with them, and he's never been angry with me before. There are papers all over the entire room—they're stacked on Alan's desk, scattered over the cement floor, and overflowing out of the trash can. Alan has a large adding machine in the center of his desk, and a big, long roll of paper is coming out of the top and running over the edge of the desk and on to the floor. Alan's taped up a lot of posters on his wall. Mostly, they're old World War II recruitment posters, but there is one enormous map of the Roman Empire that stretches over the whole back wall.

"Have a seat," Alan says, moving a stack of carbon paper off the chair across from his desk. I sit. My nerves are twitching in my fingers and I can't keep my hands still.

"You're a good kid, Thor," Alan says.

"Thanks," I say, hoping he'll stop there and let me get back to the dining room. I pick up a paper clip from on top of his desk and start unbending it.

"You are just so foundational to this restaurant-nation," he says.

"Thanks," I say. Alan's going to say "but" in just a minute.

"In fact, I really don't know what we would do without your enthusiastic commitment to A Panini for Your Thoughts and all its great ideals."

"Thanks." The paper clip is totally unbent into a straight line. Now I don't know what to do with it, so I start bending it back into its original shape. "The food is great."

Alan smiles like I've said something wise. "Yes," he says, looking off at the ceiling. A bunch of the ceiling tiles are cracked and some are missing. "Yes, the food is great."

I give up on the paper clip and toss it, mangled and bent out of shape, back onto Alan's desk. I look at my hands. If I flex my hands, little tendons pop out; then, when I relax, my tendons disappear. Flex. Relax.

Flex. Relax.

"I don't want you to have to leave us, Crafthor," Alan says. I do not look up at him, but I can tell that he is staring at me. I'm sweating on my neck and under my arms. I can't tell if my eyes are watering, but there's an awful metal taste in my mouth. I keep flexing my hands. My tendons pop up, and then they melt back into my knuckles. Pop. Melt. Up. Down.

"I don't want you to leave," Alan says again. "What do you think, Thor?"

If I stay quiet and don't answer his question, maybe he'll leave me alone. I can smell fresh bread out in the kitchen and it makes me hungry. I wonder how long I'm going to have to go without juice in the mornings before I've paid Mom and Dad back for the dollar I took.

"You're not going to talk to me?" Alan says.

With my right thumbnail, I trace the big blue veins on the back of my left hand. I feel like I'm sitting in an enormous oven, hot enough to make me feel awful, but not hot enough to scorch me through and through. I only want the silence to end, so I can get out of this office, so I get up all my strength and shake my head.

"Let me ask you a question, then," Alan says. He puts his hand under my chin and gently brings my head up so I'm looking right at him. His eyelids are dark and droopy. He's got black stubble poking out all over his chin. I never noticed all the little wrinkles running along his forehead before, but they seem obvious now. I hardly see any of my friendly boss in his face—the teeny bit of friendship that I still see looks tired, like it's been fighting an awful war with some dark kind of enemy.

"Do you think it's easy for me?" Alan goes on. "You, kid, make me smile on the worst of days. Do you think I am eager about the prospect of sending you off into the bottomless abyss of joblessness? We have had some good times together."

Joblessness. No tip money. No Barbara. No pesto.

"However," Alan says, "I firmly believe that our restaurant-nation is the cradle of opportunity and bonhomie. If we give ourselves over to others, all those good things you love about A Panini for Your Thoughts will be done and gone. Not only will we lose our money and our jobs, but we will lose our joy and our livelihood. We will be rootless. The principles of Fascism, Thor," he says, leaning so close I can smell the garlic and mouthwash on his breath, "dictate that, in order to have worth, a person must belong to a state that is larger than himself. If you can't identify as part of something, then what are you? Nothing, Thor." He swats his hand onto his desk. The bang makes me jump in my seat. *"Nothing."*

Something seems wrong with what Alan's saying, but he's telling the truth. Without this restaurant-nation, I can't imagine what I'd do all day. I work at A Panini for Your Thoughts. That's what I do. I'd sit at home with Mom, wondering how Ms. Barbara was getting on. Maybe I'd help with the cooking or little chores around the house, or learn to mend and do what Mom calls "freelancing." I'd try to get another job, but even if I got someone to hire me in spite of the economy, it'd be someplace without pesto and without Ronald and Bruce, where nobody knows me and I don't know a thing about the rules, or the food, or the people.

"Thor," says Alan. He's talking fast and crazy. "I love this place and I know that it has the power to elevate people into better versions of themselves. Christ's blood, Christ's nails, Christ's passion, Thor. Remember when you first came to work here? For the love of the holy almighty and ever-living God, your mother came to your *interview* with you. It took you six weeks before you had enough gumption to go out into the dining room and approach a customer. Let's think about that, why don't we? And now, look at you. Sure you're as slow as a fat man on a treadmill, but … *your confidence.* You like the customers and the customers like you. You can carry four plates at a time without spilling. You know the menu inside and out, and I've even seen you look after Remus and Romulus's moral education. Would you have been capable of any of this without this restaurant?"

I shake my head. The fluorescent lights in Alan's office are like little mini-suns, burning and burning and shooting down rays of heat at me. "But, I—"

"But nothing, Crafthor. Without a nurturing restaurant-nation, you could not have been built up as a man—and, now that you've reaped the benefits of your motherland, you're ready to give it over to savages and scoundrels and thereby burn the bridge to enlightenment behind you, ensuring that the other young men and women of Gruff Valley have no opportunity to grasp the advantages that you have had? What about this

Barbara Hackbush you claim to care so much about? She has walked halfway across the country just to be a member of our collective, and you will leave her shrouded in spiritual and material destitution, to be ravaged at the hands of entrepreneurial Africans?"

Is Alan right? If I could only have some time to sort all this out in my mind. A baking pan clatters out in the kitchen.

Alan grabs my cheeks between his hands and squeezes the sides of my face together. "I. Love. This. Place," he says, nodding so hard after each word that I think he's determined to whip his head clear off his neck. His eyes are so dark I can't tell where the pupil ends and the colored part starts; they're twitching all over as Alan can't decide what part of my face he wants to look at.

"And you should love this place, too," Alan says, blasting me with the smell of minty garlic. He's smiling now, but it's a crazy smile that I've never seen from him before. "I know this is all new for you, Thor. I've never done business this way. If it were up to me, I'd be a pacifist, just like you—but that's just not an option right now. If I seem a little high-strung, it's only because I care about this place, and I do not want to see it go bankrupt. Running a restaurant is the only thing I have ever wanted to do."

Alan relaxes the pressure on my face, and I wiggle out from between his hands. My heart's beating too fast. I start breathing deep and counting to myself in my head. One, two, three.

Alan leans back in his chair, looking worn out and disappointed. "I'm sorry, Thor," he says. A look, concerned and sad, slides onto his face. Four, five, six.

"It's complicated for me," he says in a thick voice. "I want things to keep going like they've been going, but there are just so many threats from outside in this day and age. I want you to stay with us, Thor, because I care about you—I really do—and I want you to have every possible advantage you can." He sighs and picks a pen off his desk. He tries balancing it on his fingertips as he talks. "It's your decision, though. I don't want to drag you along with us if you're concerned about the direction our business is taking. So, I want you to stay in the family, but, more than anything, I want you to make the choice that you like best."

Seven, eight, nine, and it's my turn to say something. Uh-oh.

"Well," I say. "I don't know." Barbara's red hair is so beautiful and she's so confident and sure of herself. "The thing is," I say. Mandy-Mandy scares me, and I know she doesn't like me, but what would the world look like without her in it? "I just don't know." I look at Alan and hope this will be good enough for him, but he's still looking at me like he's waiting for me to make up my mind.

Ms. Barbara suddenly pops her head into the office, and she's smiling with her perfect white teeth that all gleam like sunshine. "Here, Crafthor," she says, and holds out something gold and shiny for me. I take it from her and my hand brushes against hers, which is warm and soft and covered in ketchup and pesto.

"It's from them cops," she says. Her voice is full of wonder, like she's giving me some amazing relic, like an Amazon harpoon or something else that a real, live archaeologist would pee all over himself thinking about. I look over to Alan to see if he's okay with this interruption, but he nods to me like I should stop worrying and see what this woman just gave me.

My new treasure is cool and heavy in my hand. I look at it, and it's shaped like a shield, with all sorts of letters and numbers along the bottom. Once I recognize it, even in spite of all the tough decisions weighing down on me, I can't help this million-mile smile from blazing across my face.

"It's a genuine cop badge from, like, old days," Ms. Barbara says, but she sees I already figured that.

I immediately bring the badge up to my chest, ready to pin it on my shirt, right over my heart, but I pause after I unclasp the pin. "Is it okay to put it on?" I ask. Alan is nuts about his uniforms.

Alan nods, smiling. "It'll look great on you, Thor," he says. I pin on the badge, and it is heavier than I thought it would be, but I feel like a powerful guy wearing it, like I am capable of doing whatever it is I want to do. "Tell you what, even," Alan continues, as he watches me fill up with pride. "If you stay on with us, Crafthor, I would like to appoint you to be the Moral Authority of our restaurant nation. If we start to go at all off track with this invasion, I'm going to count on you to bring all our heads back around to reason and rationality. How does that sound?"

Ms. Barbara gasps a little and brings her hand to her chest. "You're leaving, Thor? We didn't even get to know each other, beyond just a little." She's got a bit of frown on the edges of her mouth, and I know I put that frown there. If I stay, the frown will go away. If I go, the frown will get bigger. I put my fingers on my badge.

"Don't you worry, Miss Barbara," I say. Then, not even knowing where I get up all this nerve, I grab her hand, squeeze it hard, and look right into her chocolaty eyes.

"For God's sake, just call me Barbara," she says, blushing.

I grin at her, she grins at me, and Alan grins at us both. Just for the moment I realize that, whatever crazy plans Alan has for the restaurant-nation, they don't matter even a singular bit to me. People really are good at heart—they just want to be loved and happy. That's why everything is going to work out in the end.

***

The next few days are happy and scary, all at the same time. The happy parts are seeing Barbara at work and getting to be the Moral Authority. I keep speaking up and saying maybe we should live and let live, as concerns those Ethiopians. Even if Mandy-Mandy calls me Deputy Doofbag, Barbara looks at me happily whenever I speak up about the right thing to do, and Alan always tells me I'm keeping us all honest, even though he doesn't show any signs of wanting to give up this crazy invasion.

I never get to see Barbara outside of work; she is secretive about how she is living. She will not tell me where she is staying or how she gets to a computer to talk to Doctor Dirk. I'm afraid she's staying in some women's shelter and is too proud to accept Alan's offer to stay in the restaurant overnight with Remus and Romulus. Some days, she is sunshine and happy words, but some days she is cranky and teary-eyed. When she's upset, though, it is always on account of one or the other of her ailments and she is always careful to apologize to me if she says anything to hurt my feelings. Sometimes I ask her to go out for a walk after work, but she always says something about Parker and how if she went out with me outside of work, she'd see me in a "different" way; I guess that different way would be bad somehow.

The scary part is the invasion. Alan says we're going to do it on the night the Ethiopian restaurant-nation opens and, as the date crawls nearer and nearer, I see more and more of Mr. Tony Rigatoni. He is always friendly, and he listens carefully when I talk about maybe not destroying the Ethiopians' restaurant, but he usually ends up chuckling and calling me something loud and happy in Italian. Mr. Uno and Mr. Due hang out a lot near the Dumpster in back of the restaurant. They don't say much, but they always salute me when they see me coming. I tried to talk to them once, to see where they come from and what kind of gelato they like. They answered all my questions politely but didn't give me any more information than I asked for. Finally, I felt too much like some nosy newspaper reporter and stopped asking them questions. I did manage to find out Mr. Uno likes lemon sorbet and doesn't own a dog. Mr. Due plays the cello. I asked him if he'd play something for me sometime, and he said maybe after the invasion.

As days go on, I get the feeling I'm not going to be able to stop this invasion from happening. Alan Xeroxed off this big battle plan and threatened to feed us to wolves if we let anybody outside the restaurant-nation see it. I keep all this quiet from Mom and Dad, which feels sort of bad, but I know they'd be worried sick if they knew what Alan was planning. They can tell something is wrong, but I don't tell what's bothering me and by now they've stopped asking.

I see Mr. Hans every day in the parking lot, but I always shoo him off without talking to him. I'm afraid if I stop to chat I will want to tell him all our awful plans. Part of me wants to let it all spill, so somebody can step in to stop the invasion, but I can't even figure out what would happen if anybody found out about the plan. The restaurant would get shut down, that's for sure, and maybe Alan would go to jail. Maybe Barbara would lose her job and have to walk back across the country to Parker. Mom and Dad would be so scared they'd never let me leave the house again. It seems the best thing to do is to go along with Alan, even though I don't like his plan, and maybe try to soften things from the inside.

As if that isn't enough to worry about, we've also got this big Rasta-Raunt right next door. It's finally got all the windows in, and the construction crews have been painting it and doing finishing work on the inside. The Rasta-Raunt looks chipper and green, yellow, and red on the outside, but Alan says the folks who run it are out for blood. It must be true—I think about how vicious we are, and we're the good guys, so the bad guys must be much worse. Alan has Mr. Uno and Mr. Due escort me to the bus stop every night after we close; he says the Ethiopians have hired people to hide out in the parking lot and jump me, so we have to be careful. One day before the lunch shift, I went over to talk to the construction crew and to watch them install all the booth seating. Alan said it was lucky I didn't get a machete in my head—that's just one of their "unseemly business practices," he says.

Some nights, I have trouble sleeping. I'm afraid there are Ethiopians in the hall with bazookas—waiting for me to go to the bathroom so they can use them, *bambambambambambam*, and shoot me so full of bullets there wouldn't be any of me left. I know it's just a silly superstition, but I told Mr. Tony about it, and he went wide-eyed and said that it's not superstition at all. He said one time, long ago, he came into his house and it was dark, but he felt like he was being watched. All of a sudden there was this knife up against his neck and he thought he was going to die! Well, he let loose with his Italian fists and, after he'd floored the bad guy, he took a look at who it was who had just tried to kill him and it was the ambassador from Addis-Ababa, which is in Ethiopia. After I heard that story, I thought my heart would never slow down to beat at a normal pace. I dropped six plates during lunch shift that day, because every time I saw Remus or Romulus out of the corner of my eye, I thought maybe they were enemy spies, and my heart decided it was going to save itself by blasting out of my throat and into the sky. Mr. Tony saw how upset I was and tried to calm me down. He pointed at the cop badge on my chest and told me not to worry. He said Ethiopians are scared of justice and so they won't come near me if I'm wearing my badge. I was still scared at first but, after a few days, I stopped getting the feeling the Ethiopians were following me everywhere, so I guess I'm going to be safe, just like Mr. Tony says.

All the same, I am not looking forward to this invasion. At first, I was thinking about how I didn't want anything bad to happen to the Ethiopians, but I hadn't even thought about how dangerous it is going to be. What if they have guns? What if they kidnap Barbara and try to get rough with her? No wonder Alan has been going so crazy lately—he's worried sick about our safety. I still try to talk him out of the invasion, but thinking about what will happen if we *don't* go attack the Ethiopians is awful, too—they will come after us, and maybe we won't be ready for them. I want to go to Bruce and Ronald for help, but Alan told me about what Ethiopians do to people who go to the police.

So, every day when I wake up, I hope I've dreamed all this up, but then I feel for my cop badge under my pillow and realize the invasion is one day closer. And after day after day of hoping and hoping and trying to talk Alan out of all this, but also knowing that we have to go through with it, time has done what it does best—kept on going forward—and the Rasta-Raunt is set to open tomorrow.

***

"Let's sing something," I say, after we've downed as much of Mom's rubbery asparagus as it's possible to down. When I was little, Mom and Dad, but mostly Dad, would teach me songs and jokes and after dinner we'd all sing together or tell each other knee-slappers. We never eat dessert in our family, because sweet things cost a lot and nourish not at all, as Dad says, and so the family time would give me something to look forward to at the end of a meal. We don't sing anymore, now that I'm older, but on special days like Christmas or the Super Bowl, Dad will have us remember our old tunes and belt 'em as loud as we can. Mom can't sing loud, but her voice is pretty; Dad sings worse, but much louder; I sing worst of any of us, but loudest of all.

Dad and Mom exchange a worried look, but I don't care how weird my request comes off; for some reason, I feel like this is the last night I'm going to get to spend with my folks before everything changes, and so I want us to be happy, like old times.

"Thor," Mom says. "Your father and I have been very worried about you lately." She gets up from the dinner table to start clearing away our empty dishes.

"Don't worry, be happy," I say. I grin nervously and pour myself another glass of lemonade from our chipped porcelain pitcher.

"If you drink too much sugar, you won't be able to sleep," says Dad, leaning back in his chair and looking at me, frowning, like I'm some piece of modern art nobody can understand.

The lemonade's already in my glass and there's nothing I can do about it, so I pretend Dad didn't say anything and say, "You don't need to worry, because tonight is a celebration."

"Oh?" Mom says, taking the pitcher off the table and putting it back into the fridge. "Why is it a celebration?"

"Because we are all together and happy, right?"

Mom and Dad trade that look again. I do not want them creasing their foreheads up like they're unhappy. I want them to be happy and festive and for them to want to sing and drink lemonade until late. I want for Dad to tease Mom and for Mom to pretend she doesn't think it's funny, and then for them to kiss and tell each other how lucky they are to be part of this great family.

"Crafthor," says Dad, "what has been going on lately?"

"Nothing."

"Have things been going okay at work?" Mom asks. She starts washing the dinner dishes, still not looking at me.

"I don't see why you are asking all these questions," I say. I am mad at myself for sounding testy. "I just would like to sing and be all happy as a family."

"Don't raise your voice, Thorrie," Mom says, as she scrubs hard at a baking sheet. She sounds like I just hurt her feelings.

If I say anything, I will start crying and the whole awful story will spill out of me. So, I clam up. Water whooshes in the sink as Mom rinses off our dinner plates, and Dad's stomach gurgles as it digests its asparagus and potatoes. I look at my glass of lemonade, and I don't want it anymore—too sweet and sticky.

Finally, Dad claps his hands down on his knees, straightens up, and says, "Alright, Thor. What should we sing?"

I'm not in the mood to sing anymore. I want to be somewhere else.

"Let's sing the one about the postman."

"Ah," says Dad, fighting to smile. "Your mother's favorite. Right, honey?"

Mom nods tensely without saying anything.

Dad starts singing first, louder than usual, and I join in, louder than I ever did before, and Mom sings a little bit with us for the first verse, but her voice sounds flat and quiet like she doesn't want to be singing at all. In fact, I don't think any of us want to be singing—but we all do anyway, at least until the chorus, when Mom just trails off and stops, and Dad and I continue on without her. Mom's back is to me, so I can't tell if she's crying, but I sort of feel like maybe she is.

***

I come up to bed straight after dinner, but it's too early to sleep, so I pull out the paper where Alan has typed out the instructions for tomorrow's invasion. I read it over to make sure I've got it all right:

"Regarding the operation which will be herein referred to as the Orechiette Offensive. This information is of the highest level of classification. Offensive to be undertaken at 2300 hours, after close of business. It is not expected that The Enemy or his operatives will be present at that time, but precautions must be taken in case of unexpected defensive retaliation. M, B, Re, and Ro to be equipped with pepper spray. #1 and #2 each to carry devices of a traditional assault nature. Violent action to be taken only in a Mayday situation. Following timetable must be adhered to if success is to be guaranteed:

"2200- Pre-invasion logistics meeting. Location as discussed.

"2230- Outfit for battle.

"2300- Re and Ro to gain entry. By 2305, all personnel must be inside. Th to remain as lookout. Must station himself at entry to kitchen quarters. In case of emergency, retreat signal is to be issued: four short whistle blasts. In case of police intervention or severe compromise of staff safety, Mayday signal is to be issued: one long whistle blast. Re and Ro to destroy fryers, dishwashing station, refrigeration apparatus. M to upturn dining area, with aid of B. #1 and #2 to oversee refrigerated and dry goods dispersal. Aim at 75% super-saturation of vital strategic areas.

"2330- All personnel to retreat severally to pre-designated staging area.

"2335- Departure from scene of #1.

"2340- Departure from scene of M.

"2345- Departure from scene of B.

"2350- Departure from scene of #2.

"2355- Re and Ro to situate themselves for bedtime.

"0000- Departure from scene of Th.

"0030- Postmortem and celebratory drinks at the Daiquiri Factory.

"COMMIT TO MEMORY AND DESTROY."

My job is easy enough. Alan knows I'm nervous, so he isn't going to make me carry weapons; all I need is a whistle. I know I'm supposed to destroy the instructions, but I'm afraid I'll just forget everything when I get panicky.

"I hate this," I whisper to Francesca, and hold up my instructions. "What can I do?" Francesca stands still in her mountain paradise, staring out at me, pouty. I try to think of how she would answer me.

"You are in very bad situation," I can hear her say. "You should not have got involved in such situation."

"I know," I whisper. I hear Mom and Dad walking around in the hall and I quiet down. I don't want them to know I talk to Francesca, because they might think it's silly, and I do enough to worry them. I wait until I can't hear their footsteps anymore and then go on. "Do you think Barbara and me will be safe?"

"I do not predict future, Thor."

I try to come up with a different answer—one that maybe I like a little bit better—but there isn't any other answer sensible enough to come out of Francesca's mouth.

"You know," she says, "I have some idea."

"Great. Tell me."

There's a knock on my door. I scramble into my bed and bundle my white cotton sheets around me.

"Thor!" Dad's voice comes from outside my door.

"Come on in," I say, and yawn loudly so he'll think he's waking me up. Just as my door is opening, I realize that I left my Orechiette Offensive instructions sitting out in the middle of my carpet. I think about jumping out of bed to snatch them and hide them somewhere, but it's too late—Dad's already coming into the room. I start to sweat.

"It's hot in here," Dad says as he sits near my feet. "Do you want the window open?"

"I'll get it," I say, sitting up and cracking open my window. A dry desert wind breezes in, smelling like barbecue. The wind rattles the instructions on the floor. I tell myself not to look at the paper, because maybe Dad won't notice it if I don't bring any attention to it, but my eyes are these magnets that keep getting pulled toward the paper, no matter what my brain tells me is the smartest thing to do.

"Smells good out there," Dad says. He looks out the window. The instructions are close enough for me to reach them if I lean out of bed and stretch. "Check out the moon," he says.

I look up at the sky. The moon is huge tonight, burning bright orange, and close to the horizon. A couple of small, dark clouds float along in front of it, but the sky is otherwise clear, so I can see stars glittering all over, like little drops of water shining on the feathers of a big, black duck. Tomorrow, right around this time, I'm going to be standing watch outside the Rasta-Raunt. I'll be listening as Remus, Romulus, and the others smash up the place: metal screaming out as it scrapes on other metal, thundery booms of expensive fry stations getting bashed in, thuds and heavy creaking as Mr. Uno and Mr. Due throw themselves against the windows, and watery, high-pitched tinkles as they finally smash through the glass.

"Thor, what's been going on?" Dad says. "Whatever it is, you just need to bare your belly, and Mom and I will do what we can."

"Nothing," I say, but I bet Dad can hear my teeth chattering.

"Why've you stopped drinking your milk with breakfast?"

I try to think of some answer that won't give too much away. He might not mind too much about me taking the dollar to buy Barbara a flower, but if I told him about that, then I'd probably start telling him about the Offensive, and Mr. Hans, and everything else, and then he'd be telling me to quit the job, and there goes the money, and there goes Barbara, and there goes being the Moral Authority, and there goes everything else.

Dad looks over my cereal box posters. "That's a good one," he says, and points at a picture of a bear running around with a beehive stuck on its paw. Dad's eyes keep moving around and I can tell he's looking for something to talk about. Suddenly, he sees my instructions, which are lying face-up, open to any set of roaming eyes. He leans over to pick the paper up off the carpet.

"Is this your schedule?" he says, pulling the paper toward him.

Well, I heard somewhere that folks who are facing these big crisis moments sometimes have weird slow-downs of time, where they're completely aware of every tiny thing about the world around them. I guess that's what happens to me when I see Dad taking up the instructions, about to discover about our invasion and about all the secrets I've been keeping from him and Mom. There's this moment where I don't even care—I *want* him to find out all about it, and get mad and call the cops and say he'll never let me set foot at A Panini for Your Thoughts again. But then I hear Mom washing her face in the bathroom, and I think about her going to bed later and later, and getting up earlier and earlier, just so worn down, but not able to get any sleep all the same. If she knew about the Offensive ...

I hear a hungry dog barking far off somewhere in the night, and I know I've got to keep Dad from finding out what's on that paper, so I open my mouth, and, trusting to gracious, blurt out in one breath,

"Hey, Dad, tell me about when you first knew you were in love with Mom."

Dad pulls down on his lower lip, confused, but at least his eyes are on me, his mind is back in some past time when he and Mom were courting and, even though he's still got his hand on my instructions, he's got something else to think about.

"Why do you ask?" he says, looking down at the paper.

"Because I like to hear about it," I say. Dad taps the paper on the carpet, and I know I need to give him a bigger distraction. "And because there's somebody that I'm maybe in love with, myself."

Dad lets go of the paper entirely and sits straight up, looking at me with this crazy, happy smile. "Is that what all this is about?" he says, like he's some scientist who's just solved an enormous chemistry problem he's been working on for years.

I laugh. I haven't seen Dad this happy in months and months, and it makes me feel good to know I caused it. "Well," I say, whacking Dad on the shoulder with my pillow, "how about let's just never mind about me, but talk about you and Mom and when you fell in love."

Dad chuckles, red in the face with relief, and pushes me back down on my bed, grabs my pillow out of my hands, and starts whacking me all over with it. "Thor," he says, "you had your mother so worried." He pretends like he's angry, but he's laughing, and as he keeps hitting me with the pillow, I'm laughing so hard I can hardly catch my breath. Finally, Dad tosses the pillow back down on me and leans back against the wall, glowing with sweat and happiness.

"Tell … Mom," I gasp out, as I try to get the oxygen pumping back into my lungs, "don't … worry … be … happy." I let out a laugh as I give my pillow a big hug and close my eyes.

"Well," Dad says, "I know I've told you this one before."

"Tell it again," I say. I sound sleepy, even though I'm not tired at all. I want to stay up all night and have Dad tell me stories from when he was my age.

"I don't know if you know this, Thor, but your old man was quite the heartbreaker in his day," Dad says, jutting out his chest. He looks over my cereal boxes again and his eyes fall on Francesca. He blows a little kiss at her, and I just about die from laughing. "Back in dinosaur times, women liked a little bit of heft on their hubbies." Dad grabs his belly and jiggles it around with both hands. "Well, all through high school, I was spoiled for choice. Every month we had some kind of dance, and every month I would get to pick what lovely female friend to go with. I would walk around with all this pride, like I was king of the universe and, tell you what, the better I thought of myself, the better everyone else seemed to think of me, too. One Valentine's Day, I had twelve lovely ladies asking to come to the formal on my arm."

"Twelve!" I say. Last time he told the story, I think it was ten.

"Hard to believe your old man was such a Casanova, eh, Thor?" says Dad, thumping his chest with his fist. "But I'll tell you what: even with all those females, each one nice and fun and pretty, I just wasn't in love. Little Julie Harbor, for one. Tiniest young lady in Gruff Valley, but always with more energy than a bullfrog on pep pills. She wore these enormous glasses and was president of our Women's Athletic Society. Whenever she was with her girlfriends, she was a riot—but whenever it was only the two of us, she would clam right up and let me do the talking. What's the fun in that?"

"Yeah," I say, cuddling up into my sheets. Dad's story is like a magic spell for my eyelids, making them droop down. "That's no fun at all."

"So," says Dad, "I knew I was looking for something different. Well, I met your mother completely out of the blue, like a gift from good gracious. Back in those days, I was still with Gunter the Butcher. Every day, I'd clock out at school at four and then clock in with Gunter at four-oh-five on the money."

"Did it smell at the butchery?" I say. I think about how awful my uniform gets by the end of work sometimes, reeking like garlic and sweat and frying oil. I bury my nose in my sheets, which smell like Mom's lemon laundry detergent.

"Thor, I can't even tell you what that place smelled like. Every day, Marv would pull up in his old clunker and unload these huge coolers full of ice and bloody beef shanks and plucked chickens. Marv lived all the way up in Righteous Plains, so even though he'd speed on down to get his meat to us fresh, his coolers always smelled just a little bit sharp and rotten. And the flies. Swarms of huge, black horseflies puffing around like enormous clouds of smoke. We'd burn incense, hang up strips and strips of flypaper, and run electric fans in every direction, but nothing helped. Gunter used to say, 'You kill a fly and four will grow back in its place.' By the time I clocked out at eight o'clock, my arms and legs would look like mountain ranges of fly bites, with crusty rivers of pig blood flowing all through the valleys. Disgusting."

I crunch up my face to show Dad how gross I think that is, but he can't see me in the dark. A big yawn makes me stretch my face back out, and I feel like I could easily pass out into sleep. Some realization creeps up on me—I'm happy. Even with tomorrow's schedule sitting on my carpet, even with Alan and Mr. Tony plotting wrongness, even with the Ethiopians ready to open this awful Rasta-Raunt, right now, in my white cotton sheets, listening to my Dad go on about his old story, knowing that Mom's right across the hall, I feel happy. But, it's the weirdest thing—as soon as I realize I'm happy, I get to thinking about how Dad's going to finish his story and go to bed, and I'll be all by myself, and then I'll get to thinking about the Ethiopians and what's coming tomorrow, and this little moment of happiness is not going to last. Soon, it'll be a memory and then, after a few months, I'll even forget it happened at all, and then what? Is happiness just some moment-to-moment thing? Is it possible to be happy all the time, or do you just have to look for these tiny specks of happiness randomly scattered at little moments in your life?

I yank the sheets up to my nose again, but the lemon smell is too strong, and the cotton is itching my legs. Somewhere outside the window, a hungry dog keeps screaming out for its dinner, and I can feel my lips start shaking how they do before I start to cry.

"Every Friday after work," Dad goes on, "I'd go out for tonics with Max and Hunter at Coleman's Bar. Well, old man Coleman was no fun at all, and he'd clear out the high school crowd at ten on the weekends, so I never had time to clean up proper before meeting the boys. The first time I saw your mother, it was a particularly boiling Friday in early November. I was a sight to see, sure. My shirt was stained up and down with yellow and red and I smelled like a slaughterhouse. I never minded too much about how I looked or smelled after work, but the minute I saw your Mom, I felt … well, humiliated. She was even tinier in those days than she is now, with these blue eyes the size of the Pacific Ocean and blonde hair like you read about in fairy tales."

I think about how Mom looks now. Her hair is getting gray, and her big blue eyes are always full up with tears. I try to imagine how Mom must have looked, way back in olden days, but I can't see the picture.

"She was wearing this cheesy barmaid dress," Dad says. I can't quite tell in the dark, but I don't even think he's facing me anymore. He's lost in his happy memories. "And I'll never forget her red plastic nametag with the prettiest name I'd ever heard: 'Gracie.' Well, Max and Hunter weren't around yet, so I went up to the bar, plopped myself down, and said to your mother, 'Anyone ever tell you that you ought to be on a movie poster somewhere?' And do you want to know what your mom said to me?"

"What'd she say?" I look out my window. The dog's stopped howling, and everything's quiet outside. Only a few lights are on in our neighborhood; everyone's asleep, I guess.

Dad's sat on one of my milk crates, and I can't see him moving around at all. I wonder if he's going to keep telling his story, so I repeat my question: "What'd Mom say when you gave her that compliment?"

"Ah." I can see Dad's shadow's head jerk up. He laughs. "Sorry, Thor. Guess I lost track of myself there for a minute."

"It's okay."

"Well, Thor, your mother looked me straight in the eye and said, 'What sort of woman do you think I am?'" Dad stands up again. "You hear that, Thor? 'What sort of woman do you think I am?'"

I don't say anything, so Dad keeps right on going. "Let me just tell you, Thor, I guess she could tell by my face how surprised I was. I don't think in all of my seventeen years I had ever seen a woman that was not flattered by my attention. 'What sort of woman do you think I am?' she said to me. I don't remember what I said next to this young beauty in a barmaid's outfit with a nametag that said 'Gracie,' but I sure remember what she said to me:

"'You are going to barge in here, smelling like some barnyard animal, and come on to me? What caveman taught you manners?' I was just dumbfounded, Thor, completely and totally dumbfounded. No girl had ever talked to me this way before.

"'If you want to ask me out on a nice date,' she said to me, 'then how about you go home and scrub that blood off you, and put on a clean shirt, and ask me proper, like a civilized person?'"

Dad's back into his story; his shadow-hands are flailing all over the place as he tries to talk with Mom's voice. I try to imagine Mom speaking so sassy today, but I guess that's some side of her I'll never see. Either that, or Dad's making up this part of the story. He's not a liar, but sometimes he has so much fun telling a good story that he's not too worried about what's fact and what isn't.

"Well, Thor," Dad says, "I looked her right in the eye, and said, 'Okay, Gracie, say I go home and scrub up, and get all decked out to the nines and tens, and come in here to sweep you off your feet. Will you let me?' And do you want to know what she says next?"

"Sure."

"She tells me I'm getting blood all over the place, and that I shouldn't lean my elbows on the bar."

I laugh. A light breeze blows in through the window. I can't smell barbecue anymore—just hot, gritty desert. "That sounds just like Mom," I say.

Dad yawns and I can see his shadow stretch its arms up over its head. "So," he says, "that's when I knew I was going to marry Gracie and have a kid or two, and that would be enough to make me happy forever."

I want to ask if it worked—if Dad is really happy forever, just on account of marrying Mom—but I stop myself. I think the answer is probably yes, but if it's no, I don't want to hear it. All the sleepiness I was feeling before vanished off somewhere, along with the happiness. Now I don't really know how I feel. Anxious, I guess.

"Tell me about your lovely lady, then," Dad says. He yawns again. I can hear the floorboards creaking as Mom paces around in her bedroom across the hall.

"Never mind, Dad. It's bedtime. I can tell you all about her some other time." Part of me likes thinking of Barbara as some kind of secret. I don't think I could explain to Dad about how her red hair is the most wonderful thing ever, or that making her smile is more important than anything else.

"Well, okay," Dad says. He walks over to me and puts his hand on my forehead, like he's checking for a fever. He must be happy with what he feels, because he messes up my hair with his fist the way he does when I've said something he thinks is clever. "Thor, you're a grade-A kid, you know that?"

"Love you, Dad."

"Love you, too." Dad walks to the doorway and turns to me. "And Thor—no more getting your mother worried, okay? If something's on your mind, open up your guts." I close my eyes and can hear Dad step out of my room and shut the door behind him. After a minute, I hear his footsteps join Mom's in his bedroom, and then I hear him kiss Mom.

I sigh. My heart is enormous, and it's crushing me from inside. My head is some balloon that keeps floating away from my body. My skin is restless in bed, but my insides are already asleep.

The Offensive instructions are still lying on the carpet. The white paper has caught a little sliver of reddish moonlight, and so Alan's instructions are glowing pink like some alien thing in the middle of my floor. I am scared to touch them, but I don't want to forget about them again and have Mom and Dad find them by accident. I've been keeping my cop badge under my pillow at night for strength, so I reach under my head and pull out the badge. I hold it tight in my fist. Ronald and Bruce wouldn't be scared of anything at all, so I slip out of bed, still holding on to my badge, and grab the glowing sheet of paper with Alan's instructions on it. I crumple up the paper and stuff it into my pillowcase. Then, I think about sleeping all night with those terrible instructions under my head, and don't like the thought, so I pull the paper out again and stuff it under one of my milk crates.

"There," I say to Francesca. My badge flashes in the moonlight and I show it off to her a little. "No fear."

Talking to Francesca, I remember she was going to give me an idea before Dad came in to interrupt. I look up at her dark outline and think about what she might have been wanting to say.

"What was your idea?" I ask Francesca, but she doesn't say anything back. Suddenly it hits me that even though there's nothing I can do to stop the invasion, maybe there's something I can do that will make me feel better, at least here and now. I smile at Francesca through my fear, and say, "Thanks." It's too dark to tell, but I think Francesca maybe winks at me.

I climb back into bed and wait until I hear Mom and Dad's bed creak as they get into it. I wait until I stop hearing their voices and until I start hearing Dad's caveman snores. Even then, I wait a while longer to make sure Mom and Dad are asleep before I sneak into our front hall and get our big, yellow phone book. According to the Yellow Pages, Gruff Valley has two women's shelters—Home and Hearth, and The Light at the End of the Tunnel. I'm nervous about using the phone without Mom and Dad's permission. They trust me so much, and here I go, keeping even more secrets from them. What if I get caught? It'd make them worry about me even more, especially if they figure out about the dollar I took last week.

My hands shake as I dial the number for Home and Hearth. The phone rings four times before a woman picks up. She sounds older and not too friendly. I have a quick moment of panic as I think maybe I should not be calling in the middle of the night, but it's too late to turn back now.

"Hello," I say, keeping my voice down so that I don't wake up Mom and Dad. "My name is Thor. Can you tell me please if there is a Miss Barbara Hackbush with you: a redhead sort of, and very pretty?"

Maybe we got disconnected, because my new woman friend isn't saying anything. Did Mom and Dad hear me using the phone and somehow shut it off from their room?

"That information," the woman friend finally says, "is not really for public knowledge. I think you'd better just leave well enough alone, sir."

"But please," I say. "I am her friend, Thor, and I really want to talk to her."

She coughs, and when she starts speaking again she sounds mad. "Sir, I do not know anything about you, but I do know this: if you had a reason to be calling up here in the middle of the night, I would know about it. Now, if your *friend* wants you to know where she is staying, she will make that information known to you."

She is talking at me like I'm in trouble or a bad guy, and so for a minute I forget I'm trying to be quiet. "This is important!" I say.

"Please do not call this number again," she says, and, the next thing I know, I'm listening to the dial tone. I hope the people at The Light at the End of the Tunnel are not wacked-out and crazy like the last unfriendly woman friend. I listen to see if my parents are moving around, but I don't hear anything from upstairs, so I go ahead and call.

"The Light at the End of the Tunnel. This is Melody," says this young woman, bright and chipper. I know she will help me track down Ms. Barbara Hackbush.

"Hi, Miss Melody," I say, trying to be just as chipper as she is, but also trying to keep quiet. "My name is Thor, and I am looking for my friend, Ms. Barbara Hackbush."

Ms. Melody pauses, just like the first woman did.

"I know it's late," I say, figuring maybe she's worried about that, "but it's important."

"Did your friend tell you that you could reach her here?" Ms. Melody says, sounding way less chipper, but still friendly enough.

"Well, no," I say, "but she's my friend and she's new to town, because she ran off from this Parker fellow, which fellow wasn't so good to her, so I figure maybe she is staying with you. I also tried at Home and Hearth, but they were not so nice there, and would not tell me if she is there."

"Hm," Ms. Melody says. "Do you know we're not really authorized to give out the names or information of any of the women staying with us?"

"That's what they said at Home and Hearth, but you seem nicer than the phone-woman there."

Ms. Melody's voice brightens up a bit, but I don't know if it's because of my compliment. "Do you realize, Mister Thor," she says, a little too slowly, "that it doesn't have anything to do with being nice or not nice? Our policies are in place for the protection of the women who need their confidentiality honored."

Oh my gracious! She thinks I am some deadbeat guy who isn't nice to women, and that I want to find out where Barbara is so I can track her down and bust her lip. I almost laugh. That isn't like me at all. "Oh yeah," I say, "that makes good sense, why you wouldn't want to go blabbing away about young women's whereabouts to their danger. But I think women are just A-one, and I care lots about Barbara. I want to find her because she is my friend, and not because I am going to be alpha-male and victimizing."

"I think," says Melody, "that your best bet is to clear this up with your friend. We keep a database of people who are authorized to contact their friends and loved ones here, and the only way you can be put in that database is if you are put into it by Barbara herself."

"But, Miss Melody, it's important, and I swear that I am not a weirdo."

"I'm very sorry, but I can't help you right now," Ms. Melody says. "Best of luck to you." And then I hear that awful dial tone again. I try to remember how the phone book was lying when I first picked it up, but I can't. I'm so downhearted I don't even care if I get found out or not, so I set the phone book down next to the phone however it lands and go back to my bedroom.

I'm not going to be able to sleep tonight, so I huddle up under my sheets and wait for morning. Every time the wind calls out, I think it's some crazy bloodthirsty Ethiopian so, even though it's boiling hot in my room, I shut my window and sweat, and sweat, and sweat.

***

I show up early for work, hoping to catch Barbara before we open. When I come into the restaurant, I don't see Barbara, but Alan and

Mandy-Mandy are busy cleaning up the dining room. In three years of working at A Panini for Your Thoughts, I have never seen Mandy-Mandy being productive before work, or after work, or really at any point in the day when tips aren't up for grabs. Today is different, because she's scrubbing at the front counter like there is an awful piece of grime refusing to come off. She's got an enormous smile spread on her face and, when she sees me, she says brightly, "Good morning, Thor! It's great to see you this morning."

Meanwhile, Alan is mopping our red tile floor. I don't think it has been mopped in days, and it shines clearer than I would have expected. I guess, under all that filth, there's a pretty decent floor. Alan's wearing a black suit with a bright gold handkerchief poking out of the breast pocket. He's slicked his thin, black hair back, just like a stage magician might do. He winks at me, which I guess is supposed to make me feel free and easy, but it only makes me uncomfortable.

I want to pretend this is ordinary reality—that the invasion plan, along with Mandy-Mandy's snarly-ness, is a gross and twisted dream I've been having and that, really, we're all pleasant folks itching to do some good, honest work.

"You haven't even got the decency to return my goddamn salutations, you dopesy drundlehead?" Mandy-Mandy says to me, still all smiles. She turns to Alan. "You hear that? Nobody ever taught this kid his social graces."

"I'm sorry," I say, sharing a halfhearted smile with Alan. "I'm just surprised and you know. What with the lack of fight."

Mandy-Mandy succeeds in scrubbing off whatever spill she was working on and tosses her dishrag over her shoulder in triumph. "Today is the Orechiette Offensive. Today is the day we prove our worth to the world. Today is the day we get wrote up into the annals of history. Today is the day we bust some damn Ethiopians and make them weep and scream over the ruin we brung them unto. Today is a day of sunshine and violets, my dearest Thor-Thor."

Alan groans and starts mopping faster. "For the love of Jesus Christ, the holy Son of God, who lies bleeding and desperate against the cold, hard wood of the sacrificial cross, please do not go doubling up the names of my friends and esteemed colleagues."

Mandy-Mandy takes a stick of gum out of her pocket, unwraps it, and begins to munch on it. A slow, warm smile glows all over her face as she softens the gum with her jaws. "Today is a day of vengeance and carnage," she says, "and even *you*, Alan-Alan, cannot make me a single kilowatt less radiant and sunshiny." She grins, and I see the mushy pink mass of her gum oozing between her perfectly white teeth.

"Thor," Alan says, "why don't you go wake the twins and then see if any of our salad dressings need to be refilled?"

I nod and head into the back. I touch the badge that Bruce and Ronald gave me and think to myself, "Remember, Thor—no matter how bad it gets, you are the Moral Authority here."

Remus and Romulus are curled up snug in their sleeping bags. A bunch of knives, corkscrews, and meat tenderizers are scattered around them; they must have been playing last night. I clap my hands, loud, right in Romulus's ear. He doesn't wake up, but he twitches and grabs the handle of a nearby knife. I gently try to pry his fingers off the knife, but every time I touch him, he twitches again and holds on even tighter. Finally, I shake him by his shoulders and jump back. He whips up, slashing the air up and down with his knife, and then sees where he is and settles down. He sees me and smiles, big and loving. He playfully stabs at the air in front of me.

"Today," he grunts.

"Yeah—today's the day. Why don't you wake up your brother?"

Romulus's lips split open to show his grinning, yellowy teeth. With a high-pitched scream, he plunges his knife into the floor, a couple inches from Remus's head. When Remus hears the knife whoosh by his ear, he jerks his head up, looks at his brother with rage and hate, grabs Romulus's wrist, and tries to pull his brother down to the floor. Romulus grabs Remus's hair and starts twisting. The two brothers start flinging their fists at one another and wrestling around on the floor. Finally, they stop, panting and out of breath. They look at each other and start laughing, silent and creepy, and I know they're awake and happy and I can go check up on the salad dressings.

The Extra-Virgil Olive Oil and Vinaigrette needs to be refilled, so I'm about to go into the walk-in freezer and fetch a tray, when Barbara comes into the kitchen. Her face is so pale I can hardly even see her freckles. She is hunched up like she has some kind of pain in her stomach. She hasn't combed her hair at all, so it's not lying down straight and flat like usual.

"Man, oh man," I say. "What's wrong?"

Barbara shakes her head and stashes her purse behind our microwave. "I'm just ill," she says. "Don't worry about it."

"Is it your uterus?"

"Not today." She checks her reflection on the stainless steel surface of our industrial dishwasher and I can tell she is not happy about what she sees. "The doctor says I have an exacerbated aorta."

"What does that mean?"

"It means everything just sucks, that's what it means," Barbara says. She sounds mad at me, and I know she's in plenty of pain. "It means the last thing I need is this fucking invasion and to get all stressed out and imperiled."

"You should call in sick," I say, even though I know that Alan would never let that slide. The plan is in place, and it can't be changed. That's part of Fascism, too—sticking to the plan, no matter what ailments you've got or haven't got.

"Ha," Barbara says. She tries to smooth down her hair, but it isn't working, which makes her even angrier. "Today, of all days, I need the money." Alan is paying us time-and-a-half today.

"Man, oh man," I say to myself. "If I had two million dollars, I bet we could get you cured up in a snap."

"Yeah," Barbara says, "and if Ethiopians were peaceful and affectionate, then maybe we wouldn't have to smash up their restaurant—but you're no millionaire, and Ethiopians ain't good-hearted folk. Life is life, Thor. Things just suck, and you've got to deal with 'em." Barbara stops messing with her hair and heads to the walk-in freezer. "I need to cool off."

As the freezer door slams shut behind Barbara, my belly goes cold. Of all days, I need her to be my friend today. Today is the invasion. Today, we are going to be hitting out at the Ethiopians with amazing cruelty, and they will maybe hit back. Without Barbara, I will be all alone. So, swallowing hard and trying to slow down my heartbeat a little, I follow her into the freezer.

Our walk-in is jam-packed with all sorts of packaged foods. We've got noodles in big boxes, enormous jars of sauces and sandwich spreads, and bags of dressings and soups. Barbara is leaning on one of the shelves, breathing hard. She frowns when I walk in, but I've got to be bold. I walk right up next to her, lean on the same shelf, and start to talk.

"You know, I tried to call you last night," I say. I can see my breath curling up in front of me. "I was feeling so sad and I thought maybe you would be, too."

"Well, that makes you the only nice guy in the world, I guess."

"I tried both women's shelters, but they wouldn't tell me if you were there."

Barbara hugs herself and shivers. "Honestly, Thor—I'm waiting and waiting for you to get it, but you're just this hopeless idiot."

I cough so Barbara doesn't see how much hurt is flooding my face.

"I mean," she says, going on no softer, "people like Parker and Alan and Mandy-Mandy are cruel and I know you see that, but you just go on pretending you're going to stay this delusional goody two-shoes forever."

The cold air in the freezer burns my lungs as I breathe it in. I wish I were back in bed. I wish I hadn't gotten up today. I wish I'd run off with Mr. Hans. I wish I'd never worked at A Panini for Your Thoughts. I don't know what I wish.

"Let me tell you something," Barbara continues. I want to tell her to stop, but I don't think I can say anything without my voice going sobby. "People ain't good, and things ain't always going to work out just how you want them. Sure, my aorta's all exacerbated and my humerus is all maladjusted, and I hate the idea of fighting and invading, but am I gonna go in there and bust Mister Bogale Gojjam's Rasta-Raunt tonight? Sure, I am—not because I think it's good or right or all that, but because I need the money. And if I don't keep this job, or some job, then I gotta walk all the way back across this big, huge country and move back in with Parker, which fellow is not a subject of conversation that is even appropriate to get into at present. Sometimes life just bites, and I'm sorry to be the one to break it to you, but my guts hurt and I hate this invasion and I'm crabby."

Barbara.

Barbara, who I love, who I thought understood everything about kindness and honesty and hard work.

I feel some tears leak out from my eyes, but they freeze on my face before they get very far down my cheeks. This is not Barbara talking—Barbara, who is so nice and strong and peaceful.

"You don't mean that," I say, feeling a sudden rush of blood up into my head.

"I do mean that," Barbara says, but sounding more sad than mad. She is shivering out of control now.

"Barbara," I say. I don't know what is taking hold of me, but I grab tight onto her shoulders. She is tense, but she doesn't try to shake my hands off. We've got this invasion, and Alan is being warlike and driven, and I've been keeping secrets from Mom and Dad, and—if I don't keep Barbara on my side with me, then I guess I don't even have anything else at all. "You *don't* mean that."

I've got to say something, anything, to keep Barbara from totally giving up hope, so I blurt out: "What if I *did* have two million dollars, and we could get you checked out by a real doctor, and we could both quit this job and never have to invade another restaurant-nation as long as we lived?"

Barbara looks at me. Her cheeks and nose are red, and the rest of her is white and cold, and she is listening to me.

"There's this German," I say, not wanting to let any dangerous silence creep in. "He's a gay gentleman with a plan about these paintings he's got, or hasn't got. I'm not too sure. But he said if I help him, then I can get two million dollars. Now, it sounds like maybe he is some con artist, but he isn't, because he cares about helping me and he knows how bad the economy is, and he's super-rich, so two million dollars is like two pennies to him. He drives a red car that probably costs more than Alan's made in his whole lifetime. If we had two million dollars from this German, then we could get you cured up, and that would just be the beginning of all the great things we could do with that kind of money."

I can feel my metal badge through my work T-shirt, growing ice cold, and I know we ought to get out to where it's warm, but I don't want to leave until I know if Barbara's going to give me any reason to keep hoping. She shivers hard underneath my hands, and I bite my lip, cross my fingers, and hope, hope, hope, hope that I got Barbara to stick with me.

She doesn't say anything right away, and I start to worry that maybe she was just too cold to even really understand what I was talking about. Finally, she looks at me, her eyes moist and maybe even a little happy, but maybe just confused, and says, "Thor, two million dollars is so much money."

"Yeah, but that's okay."

"Just …" Barbara says, and pulls herself into my arms for warmth, "… I will just caution you that trusting it when men make you promises is something that is pretty dumb."

Barbara is in my arms, and she needs me to keep her warm in this big, cold freezer and, likewise, I need her to keep me warm. I guess this is one of those little moments of happiness I was thinking about last night and, right now, right here, I know it's worth all the bad things life throws at me to have this one little moment where I am all comfortable and safe.

"I mean," she goes on, "Parker made me lots of promises, and …" She doesn't finish talking, because her teeth are chattering so hard she can't even speak words so I can understand—so I squeeze her tighter, and she squeezes onto me, and everything is going to be okay as long as we need each other this way.

"Well," I say, suddenly the protector, "maybe we should get out of this cold, don't you think?"

"Y-yeah," she says, and then even smiles. "It's c-c-c- …" And I know she's trying to say "cold," but can't, so I smile right back at her and, best of friends, and maybe even more, we head back out into the Day of Invasion.

***

Everybody tries their best to make the lunch shift go on like usual, and it's almost like everybody being so chipper and normal makes things *un*usual. Remus and Romulus work a little too fast, Mandy-Mandy works a little too cute, Alan talks a little too smooth, and Barbara and I just try to do what we can do, working like usual, and knowing we have each other.

Not too many people come in to eat today. Little Greta comes right at noon and tells me about how she's thinking of maybe taking a trip to the moon, but how she's heard it's humid up in space. I get a couple of Beach People to keep me busy with getting them water refills every five minutes but, by the end of the lunch shift, my pockets are pretty empty. From time to time, Alan peeks out the front door and looks at the parking lot of the Rasta-Raunt. "They're doing a big business today," he says to me at one point. He's working hard not to let that bother him, but I know he's just as scared of the Ethiopians as the rest of us are. Lunch shift turns into dinner shift, and my hands are shaking so badly that Alan has Barbara and Mandy-Mandy carry all my food and drinks for me. Ronald and Bruce don't come in for their usual coffee. Alan tells me he saw their squad car parked out by the Rasta-Raunt. "They've defected," he says, straightening out the sleeves of his suit coat, like he could care less where Ronald and Bruce decide to get their coffee.

Every time I look at the clock, it's later than I think it is, and nine o'clock jumps out at me suddenly, even though I feel like I've been checking the time every minute or so. We lock up the restaurant, Alan counts up our sales—"Two thousand less than usual," he says with scowls flying every which way—and still nobody says anything about the thing we're all thinking about. I keep busy, taking the soup pans off their heaters, wrapping up all the leftover salads, and doing a deep scrubbing of every surface I can find. I'm busy trying to get a reddish stain off a cutting board at the deli station when Barbara puts her hand on my shoulder so suddenly that I fling my Brillo pad across the kitchen. It hits the wall and drops into a tub of Tuscan Tuna Salad. Barbara laughs at this, but it doesn't sound like laughter with any joy behind it.

"Are you ready for this thing?" Barbara asks. She's breathing loud and raspy and I know her aorta must be awfully messed up.

"I'm just ready to be all done with it, so we can go back to being a happy and normal restaurant-nation," I say. I wash my hands and reach into the tuna salad to get my sponge back. It's covered with mayonnaise, so I chuck it into the nearest trash bin.

"I've been thinking about that German," Barbara says. "Do you know what he's about?"

Before I can say anything, Mr. Tony Rigatoni strides into the kitchen, dressed up like he's running for president: his black pants are neatly pressed, and I can see myself in his shiny shoes. He's spinning a silver cigarette lighter in his hands.

"*Bella*," he exclaims, and kisses Barbara twice on both cheeks, leaving behind patches of gooey spit. Mr. Tony then turns to me and grabs me up in the tightest, most awful hug I've ever had. His arms are so strong he could crush metal to dust. Just as I think I'm going to die, owing to not being able to breathe, he lets go of me. I fall back against the counter, coughing hard for breath.

"Today," Mr. Tony says, with his teeth as clean as a dentist's office, "is the glorious day of *la nostra guerra*. Are you *preperati, miei bambini*?"

Barbara and I nod shakily.

"*Bene, bene*," says Mr. Tony. He flicks on his lighter and looks at me through the flame. "Tonight, you will pass through the *inferno* of war and come out the other side—*forte*!" He shuts off his lighter, puts it into his breast pocket, and grasps me by the shoulder. His fingers dig in below my collarbone and I am washed over with fear. He takes hold of Barbara with his other hand and starts leading us to the break room.

"The eleventh hour is come, *miei bambini*," he says. "It is time for our long-awaited war council."

***

Mandy-Mandy, the twins, and Alan have already set up the break room according to our plans—nine chairs around a small, square table. Alan's map of the Roman Empire hangs on the back wall. Mandy-Mandy is filing away at her fingernails, trying to make them pointy at the ends. Remus and Romulus both have metal spatulas, and each twin squirms in his chair, occasionally swatting his brother with his weapon.

"How do you like my death-claws?" Mandy-Mandy says to me, waggling her fingers near my face. "They're for clawing and shredding— and also for gouging." Barbara grips my elbow. Remus swipes his spatula across Romulus's face; red welts pop up where Romulus was hit. Barbara's grip gets tighter and tighter.

"Let's get some peace in the war room, my young hoplites," Alan says, taking a thin wooden pointer from the corner and thwacking it across the map. His forehead is sweating, but otherwise he's in his element, bossing around and strategizing. "The moment we've all been working toward quivers just inches away from our militant fingertips. Remus, Romulus, holster your spatulas for the time being, please."

The twins obediently put their utensils on the floor by their feet and look to Alan with shiny, hungry eyes. Barbara and I take our seats, and Mr. Tony slides up next to Alan. The two men look like brothers, almost. They've got their black hair slicked back the same way, and they're both wearing expensive suits, pressed to look even more expensive than they really are. The biggest difference is that Mr. Tony's smile is satisfied, but Alan's is small and stomach-achy.

"It's ten o'clock," Alan says to Mr. Tony. "Where are Numero Uno and Numero Due?"

"Correction, *mi fratello*," says Mr. Tony. "It is nine fifty-nine. My dear *squadristi* would never bear to be late for an appointment."

I hear the click-clack of wing-tip shoes walking in perfect synch across the tiles of the dining room floor. A moment later, Mr. Uno and Mr. Due are in the break room, each holding a bright red gasoline canister. They are both wearing black from top to toe and, standing stern with the gasoline heavy in their hands, they look like thugs in a gang movie. I look to Barbara, but she's turned her eyes down to the tabletop and won't return my gaze.

"Ha!" Alan says. "Mussolini could make the trains run on schedule, but you, sir," he says, turning to Mr. Tony, "have reined even the *delinquente* into the reliability of an unwavering timetable—Fascism at its finest." Alan's teeth are chattering some underneath his enthusiasm. He's staring at the gas cans, and seeing him stare makes me want to stare. Mr. Uno and Mr. Due set down the gas, and Alan clears his throat. "Well," he says, "but this was not really part of the plan."

Mr. Tony shakes Alan's hand. "It is not a point worth mentioning, *mi fratello*. Now, shall we call this *consiglio di guerra* to order?"

"I have no intention," Alan says, "of using incendiary tactics."

A little fly wobbles by me. I hold out my finger, hoping the fly will land on it, but my insect friend keeps looping crazily in the air until it slams into Alan's map and falls twitching onto the ground.

"Alan," says Mr. Tony, and the corners of his smile edge up toward his ears. He takes a step towards Alan, and I'm afraid he's going to accidentally step on the fly. I should get out of my seat and move the fly, so it doesn't get crushed.

"Alan," Mr. Tony says again, "you relinquished this operation to me, *o fratello mio*. This is not the time to—"

"It's absolutely unconscionable!" Alan says, and he points at the gasoline like it's a fearsome enemy.

"Oh, dry out your damn panties," Mandy-Mandy says to Alan. She jams a paper napkin into her mouth, chews it up with her spit, then pulls it out of her mouth and flings it at Alan's head. Barbara puts her head down on the table like she's going to sleep. I scoot to the edge of my seat. I could probably snatch the fly and be back in my seat before Alan had time to yell at me.

"Alan, *amico mio*," says Mr. Tony. He pinches Alan's cheek between his fingers and squeezes until all the color goes out of Alan's face. "Such tantrums are unnecessary on the day of battle." Mr. Tony snares Alan's wooden pointer and pokes it at Alan's belly button. Alan sighs and takes a step back, right onto the fly that I was going to try and save. If the situation had been the opposite, and it was up to the fly to save me, I wonder if the fly would have done it.

Alan makes a spinning gesture with his wrist. He opens his mouth to say something, but his eyes are shiny, and he shuts his mouth and makes his gesture again. Mr. Tony rubs his hands together.

"Well," says Mr. Tony, "let us begin, shall we?"

Mr. Uno and Mr. Due slide into their spots at the table and Mr. Tony starts handing out black shirts, black pants, black hats, and black gloves. This is it. I'm really, honest to goodness, about to pull off some sort of illicit heist, just like I was a criminal.

"Are there any questions about the evening's logistics?" Mr. Tony asks, as we all start putting on our sneaky black outfits. Alan looks up like he wants to say something, but it turns out he only needs to sneeze.

"I got something," Mandy-Mandy says. "It's no question, though. It's me just saying I'm going to bring a shredding knife, so if I see that Mister Bogale Gojjam, I can open his belly and feast up on his malnourished guts."

Alan grabs his wooden pointer and brings it down on the conference table with a whack so hard it makes his papers fly in every direction.

"Merciful Mother Mary of my holiest prayers and supplications," Alan says, his eyes looking toward heaven or gracious or whatever it is he sees up in the sky, "this simply will not do. No violence. Let's just—"

"You heard your boss," Mr. Tony interrupts, "and we must honor our bosses in everything. No violence or you're excommunicated."

"Exco-what-the-fuck-icated?" Mandy-Mandy does not look happy about this whole exco-whosits.

"Honestly," Alan mutters. I don't know if anybody but me hears him. Barbara's still got her head down on the table. I wonder if she's doing okay.

Mr. Tony nods to his *squadristi*. "Numero Uno, Numero Due, would you care to explain the concept behind excommunication to our lovely *sciattona* here?"

"Excommunication, put simply," says Mr. Uno, cracking his knuckles with such force I think I see sparks fly off them, "is the process by which we make it so you can't communicate no more."

Mr. Due stares hard at Mandy-Mandy. "The tongue being an important agent of communication and such, I regret to inform you that, in the event of excommunication, you would must needs part with it."

"Numero Due and I," says Mr. Uno, "are also under the impression that appropriate use of hand signals and facial expressions no less fall under the category of communication than does proper speech and suchlike verbal utterances."

"Therefore," says Mr. Due, picking some lint off of his lapel, "the most thorough of our excommunicative techniques is a process known as liquefaction, the which, unless you are aching to hear yourself referred to as a human smoothie, I urge you from the very cockles of my peace-loving heart to make every best effort to avoid."

Mandy-Mandy smiles sweetly at Mr. Uno and Mr. Due and mimes zipping up her lips. She pulls on her black shirt, bundles up her blonde hair, and yanks a black woolen cap onto her head. She holds up her index finger, which is filed extremely sharp, and ducks into the kitchen.

Barbara sits up and starts putting on the black clothes Mr. Tony gave her. I should do the same. I pull my black shirt over my head, and the cloth is itchy. I scratch at my chest, then my belly, then under my arm, then my side, and then my back.

"Thor," Alan says, "cut that out."

I frown and sit on my hands. It feels like ants are tracking up and down my body. I bounce up and down in my seat and try not to think about how much I want to scratch. I look to Barbara to see if she's having the same problem, but she's sitting perfectly still in her black shirt, staring straight ahead at the wall, steeling herself up for something awful. I hum under my breath. The gasoline fumes from Mr. Uno and Mr. Due's gasoline canisters float up into my nostrils. I'm dizzy.

Mandy-Mandy comes back into the break room with tapenade smeared under her eyes like war paint. Little greasy flecks of olive have dropped all over her cheeks. She yanks on her black gloves. "Let's go to war," she says.

Humming isn't working at getting my mind off my itchiness, so I try counting. It doesn't work either, because every time I say a number, I think about why I'm counting, and that makes me itch even more.

Mr. Tony grins and puts his hands on the twins' shoulders. Remus is busy playing this game he's just come up with, where he puts one of his gloves on his spatula and flips the glove over and over like a pancake while Romulus tries to grab at it. Every so often, Remus takes the glove himself, whacks Romulus first with the glove, then with the spatula, and then goes back to flipping.

"Why don't we get ourselves *preperati*?" Mr. Tony asks the twins, giving their shoulders a squeeze. Remus flips his glove into Romulus's face, sets down his spatula, and clambers into his black clothes in a flash. Romulus slithers under the break room table to his chair, retrieves his prowling outfit, and by the time he's slithered back under the table, he's already completely decked out in black. Those gas fumes are strong, and I feel them filling my head and making my eyes swim around.

The tag on my shirt burns the back of my neck. I whip my hands out from underneath me and set to scratching furiously.

"Thor," Alan says again, rapping one of his cufflinks on the tabletop.

"Sorry, Alan, but it itches." I can hear my heart in my ears. It sounds slow and thundery. There's a blurry layer of fuzz over my eyes. I rub them, trying to get the fuzz off, but … it doesn't work. I look over at Barbara and see two of her. I wave, but neither Barbara sees me.

"Thor," Alan says. I look at him and see two Alans. "How are you doing?" Both Alans move their lips exactly the same way. This makes me laugh. I pull my four gloves onto my four hands, which is an utter riot. I can hear myself laughing, but it sounds like I'm listening to myself on tape. Is everyone staring at me? I look around. Eyes, eyes, eyes, eyes, and more eyes.

I hiccup and my stomach might leap out of my mouth. I slam my hands onto my lips. The gasoline fumes are coating my insides. I hiccup again. Am I floating? I look at my four feet to make sure they're still on the ground.

"He can't do it," I hear Alan say, but he sounds miles away. "This was the worst idea. This is your fault." Is he talking to me? I check to see if Alan's looking at me, but his face is a blur of pink.

"Now is not the time for this," says another voice—Mr. Tony's?—loud, but murky.

"Why did you ..." says another voice, and then something else. My ears buzz, like two million little voices are whispering in them all at once. I look at my smudgy feet again, and they're definitely not touching the ground this time. I laugh and laugh. Where's Barbara? I look all over the room: pink smears, dark smears, but nothing that looks like her.

"Thor! Thor!" A female voice. I try to stand up, but I'm already standing up. Oh no.

"Thor! Thor!"

I try to respond that I'm right here, in the break room, ready as I'll ever be to do this invasion thing, but I open my mouth and some noise comes out, but not really words. I try again, but I'm laughing too hard to say anything. Everything is way too bright and I'm scared, and happy, and everything all at once. I try to say, "Help," but my tongue is made of vermicelli. Someone is talking to me. I turn toward the nearest pink blur, and I realize ...

I am flying! I am soaring through the air, into the sun! I can see the mountains, and Francesca, and Mr. Uno and Mr. Due's gasoline canisters look like bright red cherries, and Barbara is right here with me, and we're going to be fine.

***

I'm looking at a field of white squares. I hear water dripping somewhere far away. I feel something wet and warm and heavy on my forehead. Pressure on my ears. I pull my hands up in front of my face. I've only got two hands—that's a good sign.

"Thor?" Barbara says. I take a deep breath, close my eyes, and open them again. The white squares are ceiling tiles. The dripping water is the dishwasher. "You're okay?"

I try to see where Barbara is, but I can't move my head.

"It's okay," Barbara says. "I've got your head." The pressure on my ears releases and I can move again. I sit up slowly and the wet thing on my forehead falls into my lap, so I pick it up. It's a dishrag, which Barbara must have soaked in hot water. "You had a fall. Can you talk?"

I clear up my vocal cords and say, "Okay." I'm embarrassed at how raspy my voice sounds. "Okay," I say again, but it doesn't come out any better this time around.

"Can you stand?" Barbara asks. I turn my head to look at her. She's standing over me with Mr. Tony's pocket watch dangling by her side. I hold up a finger and then put my hands on the floor to make sure it's solid. The floor feels okay, so I push myself up on to my knees. My head's spinning, so I put my forehead on the ground and take a deep breath.

"Come on, Thor," Barbara says. I hear her opening the pocket watch. The sound makes the spinning move from my head into my stomach. "Stand up."

I look at the clock on the wall and take a minute for its hands to get steady in my vision. Five after eleven. I'm supposed to be inside the Rasta-Raunt right now, being the lookout. Remus and Romulus must already be inside, smashing things up. I feel for my badge, and it's still pinned over my heart, like always.

"The invasion," I say. My voice still grinds and creaks. "What's going on?"

"Thor," Barbara says, "please stand up. For me." I fight to get one foot flat on the ground. I push up with all my weight and Barbara steps in to take my arm, so I'm suddenly upright. I lean into Barbara, and I can smell her strong, citrusy perfume. I want to know what's going on, but I'm also tired and comfy, and maybe I should just curl up in Barbara's arms and go back to sleep and then, when I wake up, the invasion will be over and we'll be together.

"Thor," Barbara says, and gives me a good shake. My head whips back on my neck, and my vision starts to spin all over again. I hold Barbara's shoulder tight. "Thor, we need to get out of here."

"Is it the invasion?" I say, just to say something. I can't feel my feet under my body. I hear a man screaming outside, and Barbara looks out the window.

"Oh!" Barbara says. Another huge scream. I look out the window but just see a bunch of black shapes moving around. "Thor, move."

"The invasion," I say again, as I move one foot in front of the other. I let Barbara lead me out of the break room and into the kitchen. Everything is a mess. Dishes are broken up all over the floor and they shine like white shards of ceramic ice. The dishwasher door is open and suds are flowing out onto the tile floor. The smears on the wall make it look like a mob of kids just got done with a huge snowball fight, only they were using gobs of marinara sauce and olive oil instead of snow. Some of the overhead lights are shattered and jagged, and a couple of the stainless steel countertops have been bashed up.

"Whoa," I say. I grab onto a countertop to steady myself, but my hand comes down on a sharp piece of glass and a pain shoots down my arm.

"Thor," Barbara says, "I want you to listen to me." We're not walking anymore. I'm looking at Barbara's chocolaty eyes. Her breath is light and hot on my face, and something about the way she's talking to me stands the hairs on the back of my neck to attention.

"Why's everything smashed up in here?" I say.

"You need to find that German and go with him." I hear some crashing from outside the restaurant, like an entire Dumpster has been turned upside down. "I do not want to hear you say even one singular word more about this invasion. Alan should have listened to you," Barbara says, her eyes leaving my face and going off toward the window. "Alan should have listened to you, but he didn't, and now we need to get out of here."

My heart's beating so fast it buzzes in my ears. As Barbara and I walk through the kitchen and into the dining room, my eyes hum. The black leather on the stools in front of the takeout counter has been slashed through and yellow stuffing has fallen from the gashes onto the floor. The reflections of the fluorescent lights in the glass front windows are blinding suns. Barbara rushes me along, and I could count the copper-colored hairs on her arm. My hands are shaking as fast as my heart. I'm a rocket ship. I'm ready to blast off.

Barbara pushes me from behind, and I'm out the front door and into the foyer. The main door has been smashed from the outside, and glass bits are strewn over the foyer floor like dewdrops. Another push from Barbara, and I'm out of the foyer and into the night. One more push, this time on the back of my head, and I'm doubled over.

"Keep low," Barbara hisses behind me. "Don't let anybody see you. Get out of here."

I hear another scream and it sounds like words. Near the Rasta-Raunt, a bunch of black shadows are running around. I listen for the shouting again, and it comes from one of the shadows that's standing off toward the side. I can make out the words a little bit this time. It sounds like "Rocket," or maybe, "Stop it." Another big crash and one of the lights over at the Rasta-Raunt isn't shining anymore.

"*Move it*, Thor," Barbara hisses at me. "Now. *I mean it*." She shoves me again, and I fall onto the concrete curb. From the ground, I see the black sky and hundreds and hundreds of stars. Down here, the night is peaceful. I hear feet tromping around over by the Rasta-Raunt; they sound distant and almost calming. I listen to the quick, jagged sounds of Barbara's breath and feel the cool summer breeze on my face. It all seems so silly on the ground. It's a different world down here. Two million miles away, stars are burning with insane amounts of heat and chemical reactions and they don't care about A Panini for Your Thoughts or Ethiopians or anything else that seems so important when I'm standing up.

"Oh, come on," Barbara says. She curves her fingers underneath me and tries to pry me up off the asphalt, but I don't want to be moved right now. Barbara's being forceful, but her fingers feel like ticklish feathers. I smile up at one particularly cool blue star. It winks at me, and I wink back. I could fall asleep here and sleep the best sleep of my life. I'm yawning. I'm drinking the entire night.

"Fight it, Thor," Barbara says. "It's from your fall." Cool drops of water on my face. Rain? "Come on, Thor," Barbara says. "You need to find that German and get that money. Whatever it takes. Please. Please. Please." Barbara just keeps on saying, "Please," and every time she says it, she tries to pull my shoulder off the ground. I want to help her, and I don't want to. Raindrops roll down my cheeks and into the corners of my mouth, and they taste salty. Oh. Not raindrops. Tears. Barbara is crying.

"Thor, Thor, *Thor, Thor*," she's hissing in my right ear, but my left ear is still listening to silence. Barbara is shaking me, and my head is bouncing off the concrete curb over and over and over, but I just can't feel it. I can't feel anything.

"Oh, Lord," Barbara says, and she stops shaking me. "This is all just going to hell. I'm not usually what one would call a crier …" Barbara's voice is caught at the back of her throat by her tears, and I feel bad for her.

"It's okay," I say. "The stars are beautiful." I point up at the night sky and hope Barbara will come lie here with me and see how little our invasions seem when you look at the universe, huge and calm.

"Oh God, oh God," Barbara says, but not to me. I prop myself up on my elbows. Barbara blazes past me, running like gracious. She turns back to me as she runs, and screams, "Go, go, go, go, go, go, go, go, go!"

My skin goes tingly, and I think I ought to snap to it and follow Barbara to wherever she is running, but it's too late.

I hear a roar that isn't a human roar, or an animal roar, or any kind of roar I've heard before. It's an airy roar, like an enormous giant exhaling after a long day's work. It's a roar like a tiger coughing with enough force to send his phlegm flying for miles and miles. It's a roar like somebody would make if he had every drop of air crushed out of his lungs.

I hear a phenomenal roar, and then it isn't night anymore.

It isn't night because the sky is shining, bright and smoky. I look at the Rasta-Raunt, but there isn't a Rasta-Raunt.

There isn't a Rasta-Raunt because instead there's a tower of flames. At the top of the tower, the flames are vomiting sparks into the sky. My heart pounds at my ribcage, and I need to find Barbara — but there's no Barbara.

There's no Barbara, because she just hightailed it somewhere and she tried to warn me about something, but I didn't listen, and there's a big fire across the street where Rasta-Raunt used to be, but maybe something even worse is coming. I'm on my feet and running, but where am I going? The smoke is pouring into my lungs and now I'm doubled over, coughing, coughing, coughing. There's screaming far away somewhere, awful screaming, and it's a human doing the screaming, but it somehow sounds like an injured animal, an injured and despairing animal, so I keep running, but I can't tell if I'm heading toward the fire, or away from it, and I think I'm not the only one running, but I can't tell. I look for faces but I only see darkness, and I look at the sky, but there's too much smoke for me to see the stars, and I remember about the Big, Big Anvil, always pointing toward the Pacific Ocean, and I look for it on the horizon, but owing to the smoke, and the darkness, and the blindness, it's not there, so I can't figure out what way is west and what way is east and what way is safety and what way is danger, but now I've got two bright eyes glaring at me, waist-level, and they're headlights, and the car's already pulled up next to me, and the door's popped open, and Mr. Hans is there in the driver's seat, making his beckon at me, his face tight and unhappy, saying, "Get in, get in, get in," so I get in, and I click my seatbelt, and then we're soaring, soaring, soaring into the night and leaving behind A Panini for Your Thoughts, and we keep soaring and soaring, and we're leaving behind Gruff Valley, and we keep soaring and soaring, and all I see is blackness, mile markers, and a median strip.

"What is it that happened back there, mein herr?" Mr. Hans asks.

"It … it …" I try to talk, but I can't. I'm laughing too hard. I know there's nothing funny, but the muscles in my belly keep convulsing and convulsing. I laugh, and laugh, and laugh. I laugh until tears come rolling down my face, and I'm not sure if I'm laughing or crying, but I guess I'm doing both. Mr. Hans drives, and I laugh, and we keep on soaring down the highway toward whatever place it is we're going.

***

Our hotel room is small, but I've got a double bed all to myself. As soon as we crossed over the state line, Mr. Hans said I needed some rest, and he was right. I've got too many thoughts running around in my head to sleep, but I like lying down on the soft mattress and looking out the window at the parking lot.

The shower hisses on the other side of the thin bathroom wall. Mr. Hans is singing an old German song in a deep voice. I should find out what's going on, but part of me feels like if I just go to bed tonight, I'll wake up tomorrow morning and everything will make sense.

I roll onto my stomach and drop my hand over the edge of the bed and onto the carpet, which is old and crusty. I think about my blue carpet back home, and I know Mom and Dad are going to be worried about where I am. Maybe Alan called them to let them know what happened — but, then again, even Alan doesn't know where I am. There's a slick black phone on the night table between my bed and Mr. Hans's, but I don't know how these things work in hotels. If I call home, will I cost Mr. Hans money? Of course, if I call home, I don't even know what I'd say.

The stream of water in the bathroom stops running, and I hear Mr. Hans walking around as he dries off and runs the sink for a while. I flip back over onto my back. The ceiling is exposed wood, and I can see the rafters running across it in stripes. A long yellow pipe runs over my bed, with a bunch of smaller pipes branching out from it near the bathroom wall. I see a big red dial on the pipe and wonder what would happen if I twisted it.

The bathroom door opens, and Mr. Hans comes out into the bedroom with his blonde hair wet and slicked down. He's wearing an old white undershirt and red flannel pajama pants, and he's keeping his feet warm with white-and-black slippers made to look like penguins. He walks to the window and looks out it for a while, his hands holding on to each other behind his back. After a minute, he lets out a low, long whistle that doesn't have much tune to it.

"Well," he says, I guess to me, "what a day it has been." He raps on the glass with his knuckle, and it suddenly hits me how quiet it's been up until right now, with neither of us talking.

"Yeah," I say back. My voice sounds too loud. In fact, I sound like somebody else. I sound like a guy who has been involved in invasions and running away with Germans, and not like Thor. I sound tired, like I've been traveling all over the world. I want to say something else, just so I can test out that weird, tired voice again, but I don't have anything in particular I want to say.

"Can you explain to me what it is that has happened tonight, mein herr?" Mr. Hans asks. He turns from the window and sits on his bed. I've only ever seen him in the parking lot before, so he seems like a total stranger, sitting on the thick, zigzagged hotel comforter in his pajamas and slippers. I guess he *is* a stranger, come to think of it.

"I'm not sure," I say.

"It was big explosion at new Rasta-Raunt," says Mr. Hans, as if I don't remember there was a big explosion at the new Rasta-Raunt.

I eye that big, red dial on the ceiling pipe again. Maybe it controls all the water to the entire hotel, or the electricity. Maybe if I turn it, I'll turn on all the sprinklers. I point at it and ask Mr. Hans, "What's that red thing do on the ceiling?"

Mr. Hans looks up and says, "It looks like it would be for gas main, for heating in wintertimes."

Gas. Those red gasoline canisters that Mr. Uno and Mr. Due had.

I'm feeling chilly, so I climb under the sheets to warm myself up. Mr. Hans is watching me shiver. He raises his eyebrows at me.

"Well, back at the restaurant," I say, "we had these two guys that were pretty fierce, and they had red containers with gas."

"Hm," says Mr. Hans, frowning. "What is happened after these gentlemens had cans of gas?"

"I don't know. I was too shivery to keep focus, and there was two of everything, and then I was flying. Then it was just me and Barbara in the restaurant, and everything had been smashed. I guess that sounds pretty stupid, huh?"

I wait for Mr. Hans to respond, but he doesn't.

"Well, Barbara said to go, and I did, but then we got outside and it was dark and beautiful, but then burning, and not so beautiful. And that's pretty much what I know."

"Hm," says Mr. Hans again. "It sounds like maybe you has had panic attack, mein herr. Has crazy flying sensations happened before, yes?"

"Panic attack," I say with a frown. "That sounds bad. I don't know. I hope not."

Mr. Hans slides out of his bed and stands between my bed and his. Since I'm lying down, Mr. Hans seems extra tall, and this makes a little lump of spit get caught in my throat. He's big and still a stranger and nobody knows where I am. Why didn't I think about this before? Mr. Hans takes a step closer. He smells like white hotel soap, and I notice how neatly his fingernails are trimmed. Could some guy bash up my face with hands that clean and tidy?

Mr. Hans throws his arms over his head and arches his back the way a cat does. His biceps look huge. How did I get here? My mind can't help going back a few years to before the invasion, to before Mr. Hans, to before The Money Situation. One night, I brought a cup of pesto home from work, boiled up some pasta, and made dinner for Mom and Dad. Dad was drinking a dark kind of beer, and I watched the bubbles float up to the surface and make a cloudy foam at the top of the glass. Mom ate carefully, twisting up her pasta with her fork into a neat little bundle, and sliding it onto a spoon. I asked her how she did that, and she tried to teach me, but I ended up splattering flecks of pesto all over the table. Dad thought that was the funniest thing he'd ever seen, and he pounded me on the back and said my dinner was even better than his mom used to make. Later, I heard Mom humming to herself as she did the dishes, like she used to do when she was happy. If I had a time machine, I'd pull it out right now and zap back to that night. I'd tell myself, "Well, Thor, enjoy all these good times you're having right now, because your life is going to keep on moving along and you need to be ready for when times get harder."

Mr. Hans yawns, and his mouth looks like an enormous tunnel leading to blackness. "Well," he says, "do you mind if maybe I turn on television? Maybe we will perhaps be able to see primetime news report on Rasta-Raunt fire." I nod.

Mr. Hans flicks off the lamp, turns on the television on the opposite wall, kicks off his penguin slippers, and climbs into his bed with the remote control still in his hand. The reception on the television isn't so good, and I hear static behind the newscasters' voices like a whooshing ocean. Their faces are blurry on the screen, but I can tell there's one man talking, and one woman. They're saying something about a fundraising drive for people affected by the economy. I can feel my breath getting steady. What's done is done; maybe it'll take a few days or weeks, but all this will get sorted out, and I'll be back at A Panini for Your Thoughts with Barbara and Alan, and I'm going to be happy.

The newscasters say something about wanting to raise a million dollars, and the thought of Mr. Hans's two million dollars floats into my head like a happy dream. Maybe Mr. Hans will make The Money Situation go away. I just don't know.

The next thing I know, Mr. Hans is saying my name. I hear something crackling, and my eyes focus up to see a lot of red on the television screen. "They talk about your fire, mein herr," Mr. Hans says all excited, turning up the volume. My heart starts pounding. The fire on the television looks worse than the fire in real life did. I can see little charred bits of Rasta-Raunt poking out of the flames like twigs in a bonfire. Smoke is covering the top half of the television screen, and it flickers red and blue as it reflects the lights of the fire engines. Little guys in yellow are standing at the bottom of the screen, firing off high-power hoses into the blaze. The fire is huge compared to the firefighters' tiny streams of water.

The picture on the television switches to show the face of some cop who hasn't shaved in a while. "We don't generally see arson on this level in Gruff Valley," says the cop. He scratches his chin with his fingernail. "This was a large-scale enterprise which required definite premeditation."

"Do you have any hope of tracking down the Victual Vandals?" asks a male voice from somewhere off screen.

"Well," says the cop, and he looks under his fingernail to see if he scratched off anything interesting from his face. "We always have hope." He smiles, and the skin around his eyes bunches up into a wrinkly mess. "But you never can tell. We suspect the culprits are responsible for some vandalism at another restaurant across the way, and we'll certainly conduct a full investigation, but arsonists are notoriously good at covering their tracks."

The screen shows the fire again, and it looks smaller. The little yellow firefighters have moved in closer, and it looks like one main firefighter is showing the others where they ought to go. The woman newscaster's voice starts up again.

"That was Officer Louie Justice of the Gruff Valley Police Department, who is heading up the investigation of this incident. Later this evening, I spoke with Mister Alan Forsythe, who manages the neighboring business, A Panini for Your Thoughts."

Alan's face pops up on the television, and I want to rush up to the screen and let Alan know I'm safe, but of course the Alan on the screen wouldn't actually be able to hear me. Alan rubs his eyes with his fists and it seems like he's looking straight at me.

"You can see the vandalism for yourself," says Alan, waving his hand at the dining room behind him. The camera moves over the dining room of A Panini for Your Thoughts, and I see tables turned over, ketchup bottles smashed all over the floor, and the windows cracked and banged up. "But I thank the Almighty Lord, author of all things seen and unseen, that the thugs responsible for this did not visit absolute destruction upon my humble enterprise, as they did upon that of my friend and esteemed colleague, Mister Gojjam."

Now it's Barbara on the television screen. Barbara! Her hair is flung out in multiple directions, and the skin under her eyes is sagging, but she's safe. She coughs before she starts talking, and her eyes move around fearfully. I wish I was with her and could hold her hand and tell her it's all okay.

"This was just absolutely not what we needed right now, what with the economy," says Barbara. Some little words appear under her face on the screen, saying, "Barbara Hackbush, A Panini for Your Thoughts employee." She sniffles and rubs her nose with the back of her wrist. "I don't think it's even necessary for me to get into all the emotions and horror that are completely devastating me right now. I would say that whoever rampaged all through our restaurant and our neighbor's is just a total brute what deserves to be executed, and maybe more."

I want the television to keep showing Barbara, but now her face is replaced by the face of some dark-skinned fellow whose mouth is open and quivering. He's got thick lips that seem to shake and shake, and he's got his eyes scrunched up tight, with enormous tears flowing down over his cheeks.

"When I spoke with Mister Gojjam," says the woman's voice, "he was devastated by his loss and could speak only about his daughter, who remains in Ethiopia."

A strange, awful howl shrieks out of the television and runs straight into my heart. Mr. Gojjam flings open his eyes, which are glistening with torture and sadness. "My daughter," he says, his voice thick with some kind of accent, "she will not be come to this country. I had wanted to bring my daughter here, but now … now it is …" And Mr. Gojjam doesn't finish, but instead he closes his eyes again and wails.

The fire shook me, but Mr. Gojjam's scream drills into me and makes every bone in my entire body shiver with sadness. Mr. Gojjam's nostrils flare out wide and dribble filmy strings of snot onto his lips, but he does not stop to wipe off his face, because he is too grieved over what we did to his restaurant.

I think again about that time machine I wish I had. I wouldn't go back three years. I would go back to a week ago, when Mr. Tony started talking about this invasion business, and I would bring a picture of this man screaming and crying over his losses, to show Mr. Tony how it would end up. I would make Alan stop the invasion, and if Alan wouldn't or couldn't, then I would go to Bruce and Ronald and tell them all about what plans Mr. Tony had cooked up. I can see clearly now it would have been the right thing to do, but I can't go back and change how it happened. I reach into my pocket, even though I know that there's nothing in it, hoping that maybe, somehow, some miracle happened and a time machine will be in there after all. Of course, all I can feel on my fingertips is the lint on the lining of my empty pocket. I want to cry the way that Mr. Gojjam is crying, but I don't deserve to feel that kind of sadness. He is innocent, and that means I'm guilty, and guilty people should not be allowed to feel bad for themselves.

Mr. Gojjam flashes off the screen, and now the broadcast is back to the man newscaster and the woman newscaster, sitting in their studio.

"A real tragedy," says the woman without really making it sound like she thinks it's such a tragedy at all.

"Of course we'll keep you posted on any developments in the Case of the Victual Vandals," says the man, "as they arise." They lean back in their chairs like they've just said the final word on the whole deal.

"When we come back," says the woman, "find out why one Chipper Creek grandmother is fighting City Hall … and how City Hall is fighting back."

The picture on the television screen turns into a big hamburger being roasted on enormous flames, and a lady with a soft voice starts talking about how hungry she is. Mr. Hans turns off the television and the room goes dark and quiet. I hope Mr. Gojjam has a wife here with him so that he's got someone to talk to tonight. I roll over onto my stomach and clutch my pillow tight to me.

"Mister Hans," I say, "what do you think about that poor Ethiopian fellow?"

Mr. Hans doesn't say anything for a while, and I think maybe he fell asleep, but just as I'm about to give up waiting for an answer, he says, "I think he will make lots of money from insurance company."

I stick my hand inside my pillowcase and squeeze a puffy handful of pillow. It bothers me that Mr. Hans doesn't seem bothered by Mr. Gojjam's loss. Maybe Mr. Hans sees something I don't see. "Well," I say, "but his daughter and all."

"He will get such press and sympathy from disaster at restaurant that when he rebuilds, money will come quick and easy."

Another set of headlights washes over the room, and I can see Mr. Hans is stretched out in his bed with his eyes closed. He must be tired, and I don't want to harass him, but I don't understand why he isn't shook up about this Rasta-Raunt. "Well," I say, "at least it was really low of whoever burned down that place of his."

"Don't you think it was probably these gentlemens you said about that had these cans of gas?"

"Yeah," I say, "but we weren't supposed to burn it down. We were just going to bang up some dishwashers." Why keep secrets? Mom always told me honesty is a big part of being good and, even if I'm not as good as maybe I wanted to be, it's time to start making up for all the wrong I've done.

"So you knew about plans for set fire to Rasta-Raunt?" Mr. Hans says. He doesn't sound surprised; in fact, his voice is thick and heavy like he would rather go to sleep.

"Well, like I said, the fire was not part of the plan," I say, "but Alan brought in his friend, Mister Tony, and we've been talking about this Orechiette Offensive for a week."

Mr. Hans laughs. "Orechiette Offensive is much better name for it than Case of Victual Vandals."

Why is Mr. Hans taking this so casually? I want him to yell at me and tell me I'm an awful guy for ever going along with all this. I want him to turn me in to the police and make me feel as bad as I made Mr. Gojjam feel. "They told me we had to do it, or else we'd be in real danger," I say, "but I don't think that's true."

"Oh, it is true, mein herr," says Mr. Hans. "It is business. One must look out for oneself. Your boss did what he must do, and you should not feel like this is bad thing. If Ethiopian man is smart, he will know what to do to recover from loss of Rasta-Raunt."

My head sinks into my pillow. Maybe Mr. Hans is right but, if he is, I don't know why I feel so bad about Mr. Gojjam. The hotel pillow is soft on my cheek, soothing, and no matter what, there's always tomorrow. So, without even really knowing I'm about to do it, I slip into sleep.

***

The next morning, Mr. Hans and I head down into the parking lot. Now that it's daylight, I can see a little better where we are. I don't recognize the landscape, but it's more desert. The sand stretches out as far as I can see, but it's not rocky, dirty sand like we have in Gruff Valley. The sand here is small-grained and white and looks like a fresh, clean sheet covering the earth. The rising sun is painting the sheet all kinds of soft reds and pinks and purples, and the sky is as clean as the ground, blue and cloudless. Little dark mesas sit out in the far distance, but they must be miles and miles away because I can cover them up with my pinkie. When I breathe in, I feel the desert air running into my lungs, pure and clean, and I feel happy and energetic, like I could run for miles and not even break a sweat.

"You look like you are in high spirits, mein herr," says Mr. Hans, as we load into his flashy red car. "You are ready for help me to adventure?"

I roll down the window as Mr. Hans turns on the engine, lean my head out the window, and sniff. It's early enough in the morning that the air is still cool from nighttime, and the coolness tickles my nostrils. "Yeah," I say. Sooner or later I will need to figure out about Barbara and Alan and our invasion, but I got a good sleep last night and looking out at the white sand makes me feel like I'm in some sort of fairy tale. All my problems will still be around when I come back from wherever we're going, but for right now I want to stop worrying and let Mr. Hans make the decisions. "Where are we going?"

"We must see mein American friend, Renegade Cowboy," says Mr. Hans. "He owns mystery shack and pyrotechnic shop across State Line. We will recover stolen Tintoretto paintings from Renegade Cowboy, and you will be tiny step away from collecting two million of dollars."

I nod like I understand, and stick my hand out the window. As we breeze along, my hand floats up and down on the air, and the air feels cool between my fingers. I watch the little green cactuses blip by on the side of the road. Mostly, they're short and stumpy, but every so often I see a big cactus towering above all the others like a king, with its arms raised up to gracious. "Can I brush my teeth somewhere?" I ask. I don't have anything with me other than the work uniform and the black clothes I'm wearing, and my teeth feel a little gummy.

"Sure," says Mr. Hans. "We will stop at next service station and buy you toiletries for hygiene."

"Thanks," I say, and watch out the window. A breeze is making one of the cacti's arms wave, so I wave back. I see a flock of small brown birds scatter into the blue sky and turn into dark shadows against the sun. I'm two million miles away from the rest of the world, and this feels good. It hits me that every single day in my entire life, I've always been around people. Every day, there have been cars and houses and lights and noise. If somebody had told me a few months ago that some day I'd find myself in the middle of the desert with only a German for company, I probably would have worried I'd feel lonely—but I don't feel lonely at all. I feel big and free, like I stretch on for miles and miles, just like the desert itself.

"Hurrah!" I yell into the air as we whip along. The sun, which I've always thought of as too big and too mean, is glimmering at me and making my face feel warm. "Hurrah!" I yell at the sun. "Hurrah!" I yell at the cacti and the scrubby sagebrushes. I see an armadillo sunning itself by the side of the road, and I yell, "Hurrah!" at that, too.

"Hurrah!" Mr. Hans screams, loud and German.

I laugh and laugh, because his voice is so huge.

"Hurrah!" I yell at Mr. Hans.

"Hurrah!" he yells back at me.

Mr. Hans pushes a button on the ceiling and a glass sunroof slides open, sending even more air streaming into the car. The air blows into my eyes and makes me flinch, but in a good way. My hair is flying all over the place, and Mr. Hans grins at me.

"Hurrah!" we yell together. We pass a faded green sign that says, "State Line, 160 miles." I point at it, but Mr. Hans has already seen it. We look at each other and laugh like maniacs. "Hurrah!"

Mr. Hans pushes down on the accelerator and, *vroom*, away we fly through the desert like a couple of eagles gliding away and away toward gracious knows what.

***

"Who is Mister Cowboy?" I say. We've stopped at a little diner at an outpost about fifty miles from the State Line. Mr. Hans said I could get anything I wanted, so I have a plate of spaghetti and the biggest glass of milk they've got. I feel guilty drinking milk when Mom and Dad are stuck at home, not drinking milk, and probably worried about me, but Mr. Hans said we'll have money enough for twenty gallons of milk, and more, by the time we go back to Gruff Valley.

"Mister Cowboy," says Mr. Hans. He takes a big bite of his sausage sandwich, and I see the muscles in his neck at work as he chews at it. "Is American hero," he finishes saying, covering his mouth with his hand as he speaks.

Our waitress, a sort of hefty woman with globs of lipstick on her mouth, comes up to the table and asks if I want a refill on my milk. I want to say yes, but I don't want to be greedy, so I say, "No, thanks." She winks at me, and I notice her eyelashes are covered with black clumps of goop. Mandy-Mandy would not think this waitress lived up to her maximum cuteness potential.

"Just let me know," she says, and goes off to a pair of trucker men in another booth.

"Why is Mister Cowboy an American hero?" I say. I try to loop my spaghetti around my fork the way Mom showed me to, but I just end up flopping noodles onto the grimy tabletop and splashing tomato sauce onto my face. So, I lower my head into my plate and scoop pasta into my mouth.

"He is American hero," says Mr. Hans, "because he help mein family."

"Okay," I say, and wipe my mouth off, leaving a little orange "o" on the back of my wrist.

Mr. Hans takes another bite of his sandwich and yellow mustard dribbles down his chin. He takes the paper napkin from out of his lap and dabs at his mouth. "You know, correct, that at one point, your country was in much fighting with mein country?"

"Sure, I guess." I take another bite of pasta. The noodles are gummy and the spaghetti sauce is watery. Remus and Romulus make better spaghetti, but I'm hungry and, of course, it's never good to let food go to waste, so I keep on eating.

"Well," says Mr. Hans, "in times of wartime, much things gets stolen, and was stolen from mein family two very expensive paintings of Italian master Tintoretto."

"That's too bad." I try to sop up some of the thin spaghetti sauce at the bottom of my plate with a piece of garlic bread, but the bread just goes soggy and starts to shred in my fingers.

Mr. Hans picks up a French fry and jabs it at me. "Ya, it is very bad indeed, mein herr." Mr. Hans tosses the fry into his mouth and closes his jaws around it. "Paintings are today of worth of ten millions of dollars. Mr. Cowboy is rescuer of treasure of mein family, and for him I give two millions of dollars for holding on to fortune of mine. And for you I give two millions of dollars, too, as well."

I push around the strands of spaghetti that are left on my plate, reddish and wet, like tiny earthworms.

"Mister Hans," I say, "I don't want to be rude, but I'm wondering why you're being so kind to me, offering me two million dollars. You know?"

"Well, mein herr," says Mr. Hans, "your role is most important of all. I say paintings are worth ten millions of dollars, correct?"

"Sure," I say.

Mr. Hans grins at me, and his gold tooth shines dully in the greeny fluorescent lighting of the diner. "It will be job of you, most trusted herr, to transform invaluable paintings into valuable moneys."

The diner has big glass windows along the walls, and the desert sun is streaming through them, beating in on me. My good feelings about the sun are starting to fade away. I look out the window, spotted with smushed-up bugs, and the white sand is pulsing out so much brightness I have to scrunch up my eyes in order to look at it. I'm the wrong man for Mr. Hans's job.

"I'm really sorry to say this, mister," I say. A huge, black bird with a wingspan as wide as a car or so glides around and around in a dizzy circle high up in the sky. "But I don't even know if I'm the fellow you want. It sounds like a big feat, which is maybe more than I can do."

Mr. Hans tosses down the crust of his black bread onto his plate and pushes his plate away from him, like he's done eating. I eye his bread crusts. I'm not hungry now, but I could probably save the crusts for a snack later.

"No, mein herr," he says, looking down at his pink shirt to make sure he didn't spill anything on it during lunch, "it must be you. There is no other herr that will be of similar excellence. Mein 'feat,' as you call it, will be most easy to perform, and you will be surprised how quick you will be in ownership of most coveted sum of money."

"I guess I just wonder," I say, wiping my hands on my pants. "Don't you think you might maybe be better at selling your paintings than I might be?"

Mr. Hans smiles at me but is looking at my pants like he doesn't like how I smeared my hands on them. He hands me a napkin, which I take, but I don't know what to do with it now that I've already wiped off my hands. I try folding it into a little paper crane, but I'm not sure what folds to make.

"Do you know what means 'a grudge'?" Mr. Hans asks me.

"Sure."

"Do you remember how I said mein country was once in state of warfare with your country?"

"Sure," I say.

"Do you know what it is to be German individual in this country?"

"No," I say. My crane is a hexagon.

"Art community is full with scum, mein herr. For you to sell these most precious paintings, they have worth of ten millions of dollars. For me, this German fellow that is not loved by governments and art communities, worth is far less, and perhaps not worth even so much as five hundreds of dollars."

"Wow," I say. Our waitress with the lips plops over to the table, crumples my napkin, and drops it onto my plate. No more hexagon. She whisks away our plates. No more bread crust snacks for later. She drops a slip of paper between me and Mr. Hans.

"Whenever you're ready, guys," she says, tapping the slip with a long, red fingernail.

"Ah," says Mr. Hans, "we will make bill settlement now, please." He shifts on his chair so that he can pull his slim leather wallet from out of his back pocket. He flips open the wallet and picks out two crisp, new twenty-dollar bills. It looks like he's got plenty more bills there in his wallet. "You may keep this change," he says to the waitress, handing over the money, and putting his wallet back in his pocket.

The waitress rocks her head back like she just saw a car wreck. "You sure?" she says, holding the money by its edges like she doesn't want to get too attached to it.

"Ya," says Mr. Hans, waving his hand like the waitress is holding some worthless piece of blank paper, and not forty whole dollars. "Money is created with purpose in mind of spending it."

"Well, thanks," she says, and holds the money up to her heart. "Let me know if there's anything else you need," she says, and scurries back to the kitchen as if afraid Mr. Hans might change his mind.

"That was nice," I say, and it hits me that Mr. Hans must be for real. Not once in three years at A Panini for Your Thoughts did a table of two ever leave me a tip like Mr. Hans just left for the waitress with the lips. There just isn't that kind of money running around out there. If Mr. Hans is willing to give out fifteen or twenty bucks to a waitress he never even knew before today, then maybe he would be able to give two million dollars to a real friend who helped him to sell some paintings, which paintings he couldn't sell for himself on account of the art community not liking him. Holy mostaccioli.

"Are you ready to get back to the road, mein herr?" Mr. Hans says, making a steeple out of his fingers. I nod. Does two million dollars come in one-dollar bills? Could I hold two million bills in my hand at the same time? I bet not. I wonder if two million bills would even fit in my house.

"Let us go, then," says Mr. Hans. If I counted to two million, how long would it take me? Counting to ten takes no time at all, but how many times would I have to count to ten to get to two million?

I feel a hand on my wrist. Mr. Hans is standing over me, pulling gently on my hand. "Let us go, mein herr," he says again. I smile and follow Mr. Hans out of the restaurant and, as we get in his car and start back onto the highway, I'm counting in my head.

***

I'm up to 1,264 when we stop at a gas station to fill up, and I watch the numbers on the gas pump tick up and up. I'm up to 1,315 when I go inside with Mr. Hans to buy a toothbrush and some toothpaste. I'm up to 1,402 when I step out of the bathroom, my teeth clean and shined up. At 2,000, we're somewhere way into the desert flats, and I can't see the distant mesas anymore. At 3,000, I haven't even seen a road sign since before 2,000. By 4,000, the little scrubby sagebrushes are greener and taller, and I'm up to 4,621 when I actually see a tiny pine tree, which I point out to Mr. Hans. The next thousand numbers go by, and the sand gets more and more like dirt, while the plants get more and more like tall grasses and shrubs. At 7,897, Mr. Hans points hurriedly at some green sign off in the distance, and by 7,904, we're close enough that I can read it: "State Line."

I let out a holler, because why not? And when I go back to counting I realize I've lost track of what number I was on.

"I hope you are ready to meet most excellent herr," says Mr. Hans. "It is twenty minutes and we will be at mystery shack of Renegade Cowboy."

I don't care that I lost count of my numbers. I didn't even get close to two million, which makes me think two million must be enormous. I pull down the sun visor and look at myself in its mirror. My hair is blown around and my face is red from too much desert sun, but at least my teeth are brushed. I grin so I can look at my teeth and they're nice and white. I put the sun visor back in place and lean back, because millionaires, I guess, are casual about everything.

"Sure," I say. "That sounds great."

***

We pull off the highway onto a lonely exit that's got nothing but weeds and meadow grass and a gray-blue clapboard service station that looks like it's been slapped together in a hurry. Mr. Hans drives into the gravel parking lot of this service station, and I see a plywood sign painted with red lettering and nailed up next to the screen front door:

"X-pereince the mistery! Rennegade Cowboys Mistery Shack!"

On the other side of the door, there's another plywood board, painted with blue lettering:

"Fire Work's! Cherry Bom's! Rennegade Cowboys Pyrotexnix Super-Store!"

We park on a patch of blacktop that's got ragweed and moss popping up through it. I get out of the car, trying not to step on any of the broken glass that's strewed out all over the parking lot. My stomach gurgles from the bad spaghetti earlier. I don't like this place. I don't know where I expected American heroes to live, but probably in big glass mansions or maybe ranches stretching over acres and acres of fresh grazing land.

"Ah, we arrive." Mr. Hans rubs his hands together like he's trying to light a fire and does his catlike back-arching stretch. "We arrive at last," he says to me, like I've been waiting all my life to get here, to this broken-down shack surrounded by rusty chain-link fencing, brown grass, and old car parts.

Mr. Hans heads up to the screen door, and I don't have much else to do but follow him. All the paint is peeling off the shack's wood siding. I yank off a nice, long strip of paint as I step inside, and tie it into a paint knot.

Inside, the mystery shack is all jumbled up. Cardboard boxes sit all over the floor. Most of the boxes look like they've been damaged on account of water leaking onto them. A bunch of cheap metal shelves, all leaning shakily to one side or the other, are overstocked with firecrackers and sparklers and other sorts of bomb-looking things that have wicks and wires all over them. If a smoker came in here and lit up a match, this shack would burn into cinders way faster than that Rasta-Raunt did, for sure. Thinking about the Rasta-Raunt makes me think about Mr. Gojjam and his sorrows, and the spaghetti in my guts starts bubbling. I should not throw up here in the middle of Renegade Cowboy's store.

Thankfully, a wide-faced fellow in a ten-gallon hat comes on by to Mr. Hans and me, and I've got something else to think about other than wanting to puke. This fellow's wearing a button-down red flannel shirt and tight blue jeans. He's shorter than me and just a little pudgy. He smiles broadly as he walks up to us, his cheeks shining.

"Dudes, dudes," says the stranger, rather loud, and with a funny accent I can't place. "You want firework? Or you want see mystery?"

"We will be most happy for your mysteries, Renegade Cowboy," says Mr. Hans, and he bends down from his waist, bowing low to this fellow who I guess is Mr. Cowboy. Mr. Hans straightens up again and grasps on to Mr. Cowboy's shoulder. "It is good to see you once more, mein herr."

Mr. Cowboy's eyes and mouth pop into three circles of total surprise. He takes off his cowboy hat, and his hair is black and slick underneath. He bows to Mr. Hans the same way Mr. Hans just bowed to him, and then the two men hug each other. I pick up a bottle rocket from one of the shelves and turn it over in my hands. It's red, white, and blue with silver stars glittering all over. I've never lit off fireworks before, but Mom and Dad always take me to the shows on the Fourth of July, where the sky gets lit up with spider-web-like blasts of purple, orange, red, and green. If this place exploded, I wonder if the blow-up would be breathtaking and great, or terrible like at the Rasta-Raunt.

"You disappear for long time," says Mr. Cowboy to Mr. Hans. "I think maybe you never come back."

"Well," says Mr. Hans, "you have been hero for take care of mein 'mystery fortune' such long spans of years." Mr. Hans turns to me and lifts the bottle rocket out of my hands. "This is mein business partner, ein Crafthor Gunderson."

I wave and step in to shake Mr. Cowboy's hand, but Mr. Cowboy doesn't stick out his hand. Instead, he bows at me like he bowed at Mr. Hans, and like Mr. Hans bowed at him. I put my hand back at my side and bend myself at the waist, bowing back to Mr. Cowboy.

"How do you do, Mr. Cowboy," I ask, straightening myself again.

"Nice to meet you, Mister Gunderson," says Mr. Cowboy.

"Oh," I say, "you can just call me 'Thor.' Mister Gunderson is my dad." I pick at my black pants, which have started to stick to my legs from sweat. I wish I had different clothes to change into. My black prowling clothes still smell like smoke, and even though they don't itch so much as they did back in the break room, they're getting bunchy from me wearing them all last night and into today.

"Thor will be mein most trusted salesman for purpose of sell Tintoretto masterpiece," says Hans, putting the bottle rocket back on an overcrowded shelf next to a few cases of bullets.

"This is a nice shop, Mister Cowboy," I say, figuring it's okay to make a smallish lie, owing to politeness's sake. "Did you grow up hereabouts?"

Mr. Cowboy guffaws from his belly, blowing out his chubby cheeks. He slaps me on the back, like I just made a joke he loves. "No, dude," he says. "I grow up in Japan, and come to America when in my thirties. This land of opportunity. Man can own mystery shack and everybody let him be."

"Japan," I say. I can't even figure what question I want to ask first. There's a lot I don't know about Japan. "Do they do a lot of fireworks there?"

"In Japan," says Mr. Cowboy, "firework is called *hana-bi*, meaning 'flower-fire.' We have many festival for display of firework."

"Oh," I say. "That's very pretty about flower-fire." I will have to remember to tell Barbara about all these facts I'm learning. "How come you came here to sell fireworks? Don't you like Japan?"

Mr. Hans claps his hands and says, "Renegade Cowboy came to America because he know that he will be American hero, ya?"

Mr. Cowboy laughs and nods. "It is true, Mister Thor," he says. "American hero is my destiny. I help Mister Gunderson with protection of mystery fortune, and future is most lucrative."

One of the linoleum tiles on the floor is starting to come off, and I work my toe underneath it and start prying it up. "Don't you miss your mom and dad?" I ask. "I mean, it must be sad to be all far away." I bet Mom and Dad have gone to the cops. Bruce and Ronald are probably looking for me and interviewing Alan and Mandy-Mandy about whereabouts they last saw me. I might as well be in Japan. I do not want to cry, so I keep focusing on prying up the curling linoleum tile. I press up hard with my foot, and the tile crunches in half. "Sorry I broke your floor, Mister Cowboy," I say. I try to breathe in deep, so I can stop thinking about home, but the breath only goes as deep as my throat.

"Dude," says Mr. Cowboy, as he touches my elbow lightly, "it is no problem. And my parents live very close. We very happy." My breath comes a little bit easier. "Now, Mister Thor," says Mr. Cowboy, "maybe we look now at mystery?"

"Ya," says Mr. Hans, picking up the piece of tile I broke and sliding it onto a shelf full of cherry bombs. "We will pick up mystery-fortune, and so we can continue our adventure-quest. Maybe tomorrow, Crafthor, you will want to go back to your home, ya?"

Home! I am so happy I accidentally knock a green cylinder canister off a shelf. It bounces once and then rolls against my foot. "Sure," I say. "I mean, I don't want Mom and Dad to be worried, you know?"

"Ya," says Mr. Hans, looking at Mr. Cowboy, "I think it is best if we will not linger. We have much work to do if we will get Crafthor to his home in timely fashion."

"Yes, dudes," says Mr. Cowboy, "follow, please." He makes a beckon at us and starts picking his way through his maze of explosives and flower-fire. Even though he's a little pudgy, Mr. Cowboy can move quickly. Mr. Hans and I follow him between shelves packed full with cardboard boxes and tin cases and loose ammo. Mr. Cowboy takes us to a brick wall at the back of the store and moves aside a couple of wheeled plastic bins to reveal a busted wooden door about half my height. Red paint letters on the door say, "Want to see mistery? Twenty five cent!"

"Today," says Mr. Cowboy, "I will not make old friend pay quarter to see mystery!" He laughs like he made a joke, and Mr. Hans laughs too, so I laugh along. Mr. Cowboy digs into the hip pocket of his blue jeans and pulls out a key-ring stuffed completely full. He selects a golden key, uses it to open the padlock on the tiny door, and throws the door open.

Inside is a dank little crawlspace with two old paintings leaned up against the rotting wood walls. One painting has some lady in a blue robe. Her head is surrounded by sparkly gold stars. Her eyes are rolled up to gracious, and she's jutting out her hips to one side so her body is made into a narrow "S" shape. She's surrounded by little angels that have birds' wings sprouting from their backs. One of the angels has short blonde hair and rosy cheeks, and he reminds me of how Mr. Hans might look if he were just a kid and had wings for some reason. I have a sudden image in my head of a feathery Mr. Hans flying across the sky, which makes me laugh.

The other painting is scary and I don't like to look at it. It's got an old man with a dirty gray beard hanging down to his knees. He's holding on to the neck of an hourglass that's wrapped around with snakes and bones. The man's face is pulled down thin and narrow and I can see his cheekbones poking out over his hollow cheeks. He's barefoot, and a little lizard is racing between his toes. Worst of all is the painting's background. It's mostly just solid black, but there's a little bit of reddish orange at the edges, which is painted to look like flames. The flames give off a bit of light, and I see faint outlines of boulders and shipwrecks behind the old man. This poor old man is all alone in this terrifying dark world, and the flames make me think about Mr. Gojjam and how his restaurant is ashes, and how his daughter is so far away. I hiccup and taste spaghetti in the back of my mouth.

Mr. Hans is looking at each of the paintings like they're his long, lost kids, and he can't decide which one he wants to hug first. He takes hold of my wrist and squeezes and squeezes as he looks at the paintings. I try to wiggle my wrist out of his hands, but the more I wiggle, the harder he squeezes.

"This," Mr. Hans says. "This is … This is …"

"I have done good job?" Mr. Cowboy says.

"This is *fantastic*," Mr. Hans says. "*Thor*." He squeezes my wrist so hard I'm afraid he's going to snap my hand off. "We are now looking at ten millions of dollars."

I look again at the painting of the woman and the winged Mr. Hans, which I like better than the fearsome painting. The woman radiates light and warmth, and she's surrounded by puffy white clouds and strips of silk. It's a pretty painting, but I do not think I would pay ten million dollars for it.

"It is masterful execution of light and shadow interplay," says Mr. Cowboy, pointing here and there at the paintings. "Most elegant."

"Mister Cowboy," says Mr. Hans, "today is most miraculous and … and … wonderful day." He lets go of my wrist and carefully takes the fearsome painting out of the crawlspace. "Today is day when we add to our millions," he says, turning to me.

"I help you load paintings," says Mr. Cowboy, picking up the one of the woman. "And then we talk payment?"

Mr. Hans cringes and frowns. "You are good friend, Mister Cowboy, but this is most inelegant way to do business. When we are surrounded by such beautiful things as Tintoretto masterworks to talk such ugly and transient things as money."

"You are right, dude," says Mr. Cowboy. "I am apology."

I follow my two friends out to the parking lot and watch as they place the paintings carefully into Mr. Hans's backseat. The sun's starting to go down, and the whole sky is burning yellow-orange. I think about that awful painting with the lonely man, and about the fire last night, and miss Mom and Dad terribly. Somewhere off in the distance a coyote howls, probably looking for supper. My mind gets around to Barbara and her ailments. She seemed fine last night, but what if all the stress from the invasion has got to her, and she's lying sick and alone somewhere? Do they have doctors at women's shelters? The coyote howls again, and I want to howl back. That free feeling I felt in the car this afternoon as I sped along with Mr. Hans is totally gone. Now that I know I'm going to have to face another night not knowing where I am, or where I'm going, I feel like I'm trapped in a cage, even though all I can see is wide open prairie. I rip a long shred of dry paint off the doorframe of the store as I watch Mr. Hans and Mr. Cowboy. I tie a paint knot, like I did earlier, but my hands are still restless, so I tear the paint chunk, knot and all, into little pieces and scatter them on the porch.

"Are you ready to get on the road, mein herr?" Mr. Hans asks me.

I think about sitting in that car, which smells like Mr. Hans's pine tree cologne. I think about ripping down the highway as the sky gets darker and darker. I think about not passing another car for hours, and not even seeing billboards. I think about spending another night in a bed that isn't my bed, in a room that isn't my room, with some friend who might not be my friend, and I just can't do it.

The back of my throat starts fluttering, and I know I'm going to burst out bawling. I don't want to, but there's nothing I can do about it—I can already feel the fluttering moving to my top lip. I sink down to the ground and cover my face with my arms. I try to think happy thoughts, but everything that makes me happy is far away. I feel like I'm not the same Thor who used to go in to A Panini for Your Thoughts, happy and excited to work; even worse, I feel like I'm never going to be that Thor again. There's no point in trying to stop my crying anymore.

I feel hands rubbing my back and I hear voices trying to be comforting to me, but I don't know what's being said. All I can focus on is the sad hotness at the front of my face and the tears running through my fingers. Where do all the tears come from? Do I have some lake somewhere in my head, where billions and billions of tears are stored up, waiting until just the right minute to rush out of my eyes? Maybe if I cry long enough, there won't be any water left in the lake, and I'll never cry again the whole rest of my life.

"Mein herr, mein herr," I hear.

"Dude, dude," I hear.

"I don't want to get in the car," I say, embarrassed by how choked up and sobby my voice sounds. "I want to go home."

"Well," says Mr. Hans, "you must get in car in order to go home."

"No," I say. "I want to go home *now*."

Mr. Hans doesn't say anything more, and I feel the hands keeping on rubbing my back. When I finally stop crying, the sun's gone all the way underneath the horizon. Mr. Cowboy and Mr. Hans are kneeling down by me, concerned.

"You feel better, dude?" says Mr. Cowboy.

I nod, still feeling awful.

"Do you want to get in car and drive to hotel?" Mr. Hans asks.

I shake my head *no*.

"Do you want to stay here?" Mr. Hans says.

I shake my head again.

Mr. Hans pauses for a moment, and then says, "Do you want me to sing a song?"

I shrug and shiver. Even though there's still a little bit of light left in the sky, all the warmness is gone from the air. Mr. Cowboy puts his chubby arm on one of my shoulders, and Mr. Hans puts his arm on my other shoulder. As we all sit on the porch of Mr. Cowboy's shop, watching the oranges and yellows in the sky turn into purples and dark blues, Mr. Hans starts singing something slow and quiet and beautiful in a deep voice. I don't know what the German words mean, but I can tell from the music of the song that whoever wrote it was feeling a lot like I'm feeling right now. That makes me feel less lonely. Somewhere, way across the oceans, and maybe years and years ago, there was some fellow that understood me—and, even though we've never met, we're friends through this song he wrote. I close my eyes and feel the coolness of the night on my skin. The world seems bigger and smaller than I ever thought before.

***

The hotel room tonight is small and dark, and the red wool blanket on my bed is itching me. The air smells like year-old cigarettes and wet dog. Mr. Hans opened a window to air out the stink, but it hasn't done much good so far. I'm holding the hotel phone in my lap. Mr. Hans offered to let me call home, without me even asking him if I could, and so I've just got to figure out what to say.

"If you had a son that ran off," I say to Mr. Hans, "and you were hearing from him, what would you want him to say?" I poke around at the phone buttons and realize maybe Mr. Hans *does* have a son. Who knows?

"I would want to know that my son come home with two millions of dollars, first of all," says Mr. Hans. He's lying in his bed with thin-framed glasses on and an enormous book spread out over his lap. I asked him what book it was, and he told me it was German philosophy, all about the moon and the earth and what they mean. I asked him what they mean, but he told me that was a dangerous question.

"How would you explain about running off?" I ask. "If you were me, I mean."

"I would ask them to consider," says Mr. Hans, pulling off his glasses and wiping them on his undershirt, "that I am adult person, and can make decision to do what I will." Mr. Hans puts his glasses back on firmly, like he's done talking about all this speculation.

I unpin my cop badge from over my heart and trace around its surface with my finger. Something about the badge gives me courage.

Bruce and Ronald keep their cool most always, so I should try to do the same.

"Crafthor," says Mr. Hans, sounding a little cross, "what is it that makes you scared to call your home?"

It hits me why I'm nervous. Even though Mom and Dad are going to be happy to hear from me, they're going to be sad that I ran off. For some reason, it's easier for me to be happy when I'm far away from their sadness—but if I call, I'm going to hear their sadness and know I'm the one that caused it. I felt awful last night to hear Mr. Gojjam holler and wail over his misfortunes, and I know I'm going to feel that same terrible guilt when I talk to my parents.

"Hey, Mister Hans," I say. The brown tile ceiling is full of cracks and water spots, and a pair of moths is doing a circle-dance around the room's single light bulb. The room is grungy, and the smell is rotten, and this is exactly what I deserve for my lowness. "If I give you something, will you take good care of it?"

Mr. Hans closes his book but puts his thumb between the pages to hold his place. "What is this about?"

I hold out my cop badge to him. "Some cops gave me this," I say, "but it's all about justice and good morals, which justice and good morals I don't think I've been good about lately."

"Thor," says Mr. Hans, "you must not feel guilty for restaurant-burn. It was not your idea."

"I still want you to have it." One of the moths bumps into the light bulb and spins around, crazy, as it tries not to fall to the floor. Mr. Hans shrugs and leans across the space separating our beds to take the badge out of my hand.

"I will take care of most sentimental artifact," he says to me, and puts the badge on the nightstand.

"Thanks," I say. I feel a little better. Maybe I can never take back my part in the Rasta-Raunt fire, or in running off from home and the folks that care about me, but at least I can keep on trying to do small things that will maybe eventually add up to enough good to balance out the wrong.

As I dial my phone number, I feel like my heart has moved up into my head. Every time my heart beats, blood runs through the veins behind my eyes and through my ear canals. I hold on to the phone receiver with one hand and use my other hand to press on my eyes to stop them from pulsing.

There's one staticky, metal-sounding ring, and then it's Mom on the phone. "Yes?" she says, frantic and out of breath, like she ran to get the phone.

I look over to Mr. Hans, panicked, but he's sitting on his bed, reading about his philosophies, calm and unconcerned. I feel my eyebrows creeping together like earthworms.

"Yes?" Mom says again, her voice high-pitched and scared. "Yes, is this Officer Justice?"

"No, Mom … It's me, Thor."

I hear heavy breathing on the other end of the line, and a sort of shapeless sob. Some tears come into my eyes, but I fight them. I look at Mr. Hans, who's still cool and calm, reading his book. It seems weird that something so important to me and Mom is going on right now, and there's a guy in the same room as me, who is going on his normal life, like always.

"Baby, baby, baby," says Mom. The words are hard for me to understand around our bad connection and her crying. "Where are you? Are you safe? Thorrie, where did you go? Come home. Are you safe? What happened?" And then, before I can answer even one of her questions, I hear her yelling, "It's Thor! Thor's called!"

I swallow hard and look at the moths. The one that flew into the light bulb seems to have recovered. I wonder if maybe moth families go through the same sorts of things as human families. I hope they don't have to.

"Baby, where are you?"

There's a shuffle and a click on the phone, and Dad's voice pipes up. "Thor. Where are you?"

"Hi, Dad," I say. I hear Mom and Dad breathing over the phone lines. Mom's breaths are shallow and jerky, but Dad's are low and deep. My folks sound close enough to be in the next room. "I miss you guys pretty bad," I say. Mr. Hans raises his eyebrows, quietly closes his book and slips it onto the nightstand. He gets out of bed, points at himself, and points at the door before stepping out of the room.

"Baby, baby, baby," says Mom, "come home. Just tell us wh—"

"Thor," Dad cuts her off forcefully. "Where are you?"

"I don't know. But I'll be home soon."

"You don't *know*?" says Dad, and I know he's yelling. A little earthquake starts shaking in my stomach. I deserve all the guilt, because I ran off. "Thor," Dad goes on, "do you have any idea wha—"

"Dear," Mom says to Dad. "Stop it. Thor, hon—"

"*Gracie*," Dad snaps at Mom.

"Hey guys," I say. I've got an egg or something stuck down my throat. "I miss you pretty bad." A door opens and shuts in the room next door, and a whole army full of feet tromps around. Somebody is laughing on the other side of the wall. "But I'm coming home, maybe tomorrow, or the day after, and I'm on an adventure. But I'll have two million dollars, and The Money Situation will be over, and we can be all happy." Applause from next door.

"Thor," says Dad, fighting to get his breath steadied out. "Boys do not wander off and then come home with two million dollars." I can hear him trying to keep the yelling out of his voice, but it's only working halfway.

"Money isn't important," says Mom. "We just want you back."

"Oh," I say. I thought they'd be through the roof happy when they heard about Mr. Hans's two million, but they don't sound like they care at all. Maybe they didn't quite understand? "But money *is* important, but that's okay, because I'm going to come home with two million dollars, and we'll drink all the milk we want, and you can have chocolate, Mom, and Dad, you can have beer, and it'll be just like the old times."

"Thorrie, are you safe?" says Mom, still frantic. "Is somebody hurting you? If somebody's hurting you, just say, 'Yes.'"

"No, Mom, I'm fine, I swear."

"Oh, thank gracious," she says, and I can hear her sobbing and sobbing.

The people in the next room are shouting and laughing. I hear glasses clinking against each other, and people slamming down on tables.

"Thor," says Dad, "I don't know what this is about, but please just come home and we'll sort it all out. We've had the police looking everywhere for you."

"Oh," I say. The folks next door are chanting something loud and rhythmic.

"And if somebody is promising you money, Thor," says Dad. "I want you to listen carefully to me, okay? Are you listening?"

"Yes."

"If somebody is promising you money, I *do not* want you to go with him, okay?" he says.

"But," I say. I wonder how many people there are next door. It sounds like at least five or six. "Well, I just want everything to be right again."

"It will be, Thor," says Dad. "It will be. But you need to come home to us."

Mom stops crying long enough to gasp out, "You heard your father, Thorrie. Come home to us."

"And for things to be right," Dad says, "and listen carefully, Thor—*do not* go with anybody who offers you money. Do you understand?"

"Why not?"

"Don't you do it, Thorrie!" screams Mom, and the sound of her voice sends my heart racing around my ribcage like a terrified rabbit scrambling for its home.

"Okay, Mom," I say. Some glass shatters next door, and my neighbors roar like it's the funniest thing that ever happened.

"Do you understand?" Dad asks again.

"Yeah," I say. "I'm sorry I ran off. I've been so shook up lately."

"It's okay, sweetie," says Mom. "Just come home safe. That's the only thing … the only …" Her voice just breaks off into tears.

"Thor," says Dad, "tell us where you are, and I'll come get you."

There's a knock on the door. "Are you still on phone?" Mr. Hans asks from outside.

"One second," I say to Dad. I cover the mouthpiece with my hand and yell out to Mr. Hans, "Yeah, Mister Hans. I'll be off in half a second."

"Do not hurry," Mr. Hans says.

"Thor," says Mom, "who were you talking to? Who's there with you?"

"I'm really sorry, guys," I say into the phone, "but I have to go now."

"*Thor?*" says Dad.

"Please—I have to go. I'll be home soon."

"Stay on the line! Stay on the line!" Dad screams at me, but I lower the earpiece back onto the cradle and move the phone back to its home on the nightstand. I guess this is the guilt I wanted, but now that I have it, I want it out of me. I thought maybe guilt would feel like a rock in my stomach, or some kind of tangle in my head, but it's worse than that. Guilt is a liquid running through my veins instead of blood, touching each and every part of me, and making me poison. Someone next door is pounding on the wall, and he might as well be pounding directly onto the middle of my eardrums.

I feel like I'm sleepwalking as I slide out of bed to let Mr. Hans back into the room. I hoped that maybe when I went home, I could just be the same Thor as always, but I guess, no matter what, my folks are always going to know I let them down. I must look bad, because Mr. Hans grabs my shoulder as he comes into the room. When Mr. Tony grabs my shoulder, I feel like my arm might crumple like an aluminum can in his grip, but when Mr. Hans grabs my shoulder he squeezes just enough to make me feel a little warmer and safer.

"You has heard of perseverance, mein herr?"

I nod and sleepwalk back to my bed. I wrap myself in the itchy hotel blanket, even though it's not cold in the room. I pull the blanket over my eyes, but I can still peek through it. I want to hide—but I don't really know who from.

Some big hoot gets yelled out next door, and then the same hoot from a different voice, and then a bunch of voices all hooting at the same time.

"Perseverance," Mr. Hans says, "is most remarkable demonstration of fortitude in young man." He picks up his big philosophy book and bounces it around in his hands like he's trying to guess how much it weighs. "It means to face hardest things of world, to destroy illusion of perfect order, to gaze over edge of very brink of life, and to come through all of moral skirmishes with armor that is dented but not shattered." Mr. Hans whacks one of the moths with his philosophies, and the poor little critter leaves a dusty brown smudge on the wall.

"Why did you smush that moth?" I say from under my blanket. I bury my eyes in the crook of my elbow and hunch over, making myself into a little ball. It's hot and sweaty underneath the blanket, but I feel like a bug in its cocoon—safe, like nothing outside my Thor-ball even matters.

"I am sorry, mein herr," Mr. Hans says. I can hear him easing on into his bed, making the springs moan and groan. "Sometimes I do not understand meinself."

Even with my eyes shut up and covered, I can tell the room gets darker. Mr. Hans must have turned off the lamp. Even though it's bedtime, I don't want to sleep, so I don't. I stay balled up under my blanket and listen until Mr. Hans starts snoring. I listen to the cars whooshing by out somewhere beyond the hotel parking lot. I listen to the boys next door that have settled down and turned on some late-night comedy show on the television. I listen and listen, and as I listen, I think. I think about Barbara and Mom and Dad and pesto and Francesca and carpets and little bugs and big deserts, but there's no sense or order in any of my thoughts. I just go on flickering through them like I'm looking at a slide show that got shuffled out of order. I listen and flicker and sweat in my little cocoon for as long as I can keep myself awake.

***

The next morning, Mr. Hans tells me we're going to see Mr. Pierre Baguette, an art dealer from Switzerland.

"How far will we have to drive?" I ask, as I climb into Mr. Hans's hotrod. I'm still wearing my work clothes from two days ago and they're starting to smell. Would it be rude for me to ask for something else to wear?

"It is back in direction we have come from," says Mr. Hans, revving up the engine and sliding thin sunglasses onto his nose. "Perhaps if we get this important business taken care with today, you will be able to return to home this evening. And you will have your money in your hand."

As we pull out of the parking lot, I look at the prairies around us. I always hear about the prairies being lush and full of grasses taller than a fellow's head, but this prairie is as plain as the desert I came from. The grasses aren't green, but brown and crispy-looking, like they haven't had a good drink of water in a long time. Little white and gold cornflowers poke out of the grasses, stretching towards the sun. Wispy clouds float around in the sky, soft and gentle like gigantic dandelion spores. As far as I can see, this greenish-brown prairie stretches out far off in all directions, doing the same old thing.

Mr. Hans puts on a CD of crazy electric German music, which I guess means he doesn't want to talk. That's fine. I might be going home today. Yesterday, I wanted nothing more than to go home, but today I can't feel anything but guilt when I think about how I talked to Mom and Dad last night. Home is where Mom and Dad will not ever be able to trust me again. Home is where Mr. Gojjam is wailing and sad. Home is where Alan gets ruthless. What do I have at home? Barbara, I guess.

I pull down the sun visor and look at myself in its mirror. I don't grow much of a beard, but I see a few black hairs poking out of my face on account of my not shaving. My hair is messed around, the white parts of my eyes are pink with tiny red veins, and I've got fuzz from last night's blanket caught up in my eyebrows and clinging to my cheeks and nose. The fearsome Tintoretto painting glares behind me in the backseat. The old man in the painting is staring at me, thinking what a bad guy I am.

"Mister Hans?" I say, but he doesn't hear me over his music, which sounds like lasers shooting and a big, staticky heart beating. "Mister Hans?"

"What is it, mein herr?" he yells over his music. A drum beat starts going, cymbals crashing all over the place.

"Who is that old man in the painting?"

"Ah … herr is Chronos—Greek god of time."

"Oh." I look at the man in the painting again, hoping maybe he'll seem less scary now that I know his name. He still looks back at me, miserable and stern, though. "Why is he lonely? Where's his family?"

I can't see Mr. Hans's eyes on account of his sunglasses, but he blows out through his lips like he wants me to not be asking questions. There's a quick crashing noise on Mr. Hans's music, like somebody just smashed through a window, and then the laser gun noises continue.

"Chronos sees misery that is wrought by time and growth, and sees common mistakes of mankind repeated over and over and over." Mr. Hans sounds bored, like this is all stuff I should already know. "So of course man in such situation would be lonely and most unhappy."

"Oh." I turn around to look at the painting. I wave at *Chronos*, but of course *Chronos* doesn't wave back because he's just a painting. "But doesn't he also get to see all the *good* things people do?"

Mr. Hans turns his music up louder and rolls down his window. Wind whips into the car, smelling like cow manure, fresh and grassy. "Perhaps," he says, "you would like to take opportunity to sleep? You did not fall to sleep until very late last night, mein herr."

When Mr. Hans closes his lips, he shuts them so hard that I know he's not going to open them again for a while. He doesn't want to talk about *Chronos*, and I guess I don't want to talk about *Chronos* either. I shut up my sun visor so I don't have to look at the painting, and recline the seat.

"Is Mister Baguette pretty nice?" I say, forgetting that Mr. Hans doesn't want to talk. Mr. Hans exhales loudly through his nose and doesn't answer, so I shut my eyes and feel the warm prairie breeze blowing around in my hair.

***

Around noontime, the highway crowds up with other cars. I'm happy that this gives me something to watch, other than the prairies turning gradually back into desert. As we whip by cars, and as cars whip by us, I look at the other drivers. I see a young cheery-faced girl singing along to something on her car radio as she keeps rhythm by drumming her hands on her leopard-print steering wheel cover. I see an older dark-haired woman turning her head over and over to talk forcefully to some infant in the backseat, then to look back at the road, then to go back to scolding. I see a bare-chested fellow who's all bald, except for a long, wild string of gray hair that's sprouting from the side of his head and getting blown around by the wind. I see grumpy people, pretty people, laughing people, and bored people. I feel like I'm at the zoo, looking on as the animals go on with their regular lives without even knowing that I'm watching. I wonder what people would think if they looked in at me. They'd probably never guess what I've been through recently. I smile, feeling like I've got a special secret.

Out on the horizon, I see the faint gray outlines of huge buildings sticking together in a giant clump that pokes out of the ground like a tree made out of rectangles. Dark, ugly clouds are spread out in layers above the clump of buildings. I want to ask Mr. Hans if those buildings are near where we're going, but he hasn't said anything since he told me about Chronos, and I don't want to be the one that starts up conversation again.

A humongous truck cuts into our lane, just inches in front of our car's nose, and Mr. Hans presses on the horn. "People here do not know first thing about how to drive motor-vehicle," he says, red in the face.

I wait for Mr. Hans's face to go back to its normal color, and then I decide maybe this is a good time to get him talking.

"Where are we?"

Mr. Hans raises his eyebrows and cuts in front of a little station wagon, just like the truck cut in front of us. "You have not been looking at road signs, mein herr?"

"Oh," I say. I see a green sign coming up on my right, and I read it as we whiz by: "Center City: 15."

"We're going to the city?" I ask. Gruff Valley is a city, but not a big city. The city we're approaching looks to be a big city. Before The Money Situation, Mom and Dad once took me down to Pacific City. I don't remember the overall of it, owing to I was young, but I remember there were lots of dogs, and the dogs all seemed happy because there were lots of things around to sniff. I also remember we bought pretzels and used them to feed the seagulls that walked around everywhere with their chests puffed out, like they were governors. The buildings stretched up extremely tall, and I wanted to grow up to be as tall as the buildings; I was too young then to know there are certain heights which a human being cannot grow up to be.

"Center City!" yells Mr. Hans, and he honks his horn four times, victorious for coming this far. "Center City!" he yells again and, without looking at me, whacks one of his hands down onto my knee. This doesn't hurt, but it jangles me. I look out at the skyscrapers. As we get closer, they look less like a blob of shapes and more like individual buildings and, as the numbers on the green signs go down from fifteen to thirteen to nine, I can make out rows of windows and stone carvings on the faces of the buildings. Soon, the tree of rectangles has turned into a forest of rectangles, and then we're in the middle of the forest, with brick-and-glass buildings towering all up around us, and all sorts of people running here and there like forest creatures. Mr. Hans slams on his brakes so he doesn't hit a woman who's pushing a shopping cart right in front of his car. The woman glares at Mr. Hans, says something to herself, and goes on crossing the street.

"Welcome," says Mr. Hans, "to Center City."

Our car is surrounded by other cars, and so we crawl along slowly. This means I've got time to look around at all the different people and buildings. We pass by three Italian restaurants, all crushed together on one block, and I wonder if one of them ever invaded the others. Some shops have signs in Chinese characters, and others have handless plastic people in their windows. I see a couple of fruit shops that don't even have walls, so crates of oranges and grapefruits sprawl out into the sidewalk, with people crowding around them like hungry ants crowd around breadcrumbs. A fellow on the corner is vomiting into a trashcan, while a woman with a pocket-sized dog walks by him without stopping to find out if he's okay.

"We should check on that guy," I say to Mr. Hans, but we've already driven past him. "Do you think he'll be okay?"

"Mein herr," says Mr. Hans, "we must all look out for ourselves in this world."

I turn around in my seat but can't see back to where the man was. Mr. Chronos is looking at me from the backseat, so I face front again. "But he looked sort of sick," I say.

Instead of answering me, Mr. Hans points up ahead to a glittery glass building with enormous gold numbers above the front entry. Men and women in business clothes pile in and out of the revolving front door. These folks dress snazzier than Alan. They must be rich. I bet they've each got millions and millions of dollars, closets full of suits, and refrigerators full of meat and milk and juice. I wonder what it would be like to be one of those rich fellows, walking around like I had important places to be. I straighten up in the seat and try to make my face serious by pulling my mouth down into a frown.

"What kind of building is that?" I ask, sounding bored.

"You will see soon enough, because this is the moment when you will earn your millions."

My frown now is completely and totally real. I don't know what I will have to do, but if it means going in that building with all those rich people and trying to work out financial mumbo-jumbo, then I hope Mr. Hans knows I do not usually deal with more than thirty dollars at a time.

"So what am I going to do in there?" I say, trying to keep my voice from getting quivery. Mr. Hans finds a free spot along the curb and slides his car forward and back, forward and back, trying to wedge it between two other cars.

"First, mein herr," he says, pulling the car forward about an inch, and then backing it up another inch, "we will get you into clothing that is more suitable for future millionaire."

Nobody has ever called me a future millionaire before, and hearing this makes me uncomfortable. I move around in my seat like I'm sitting on sand and can't find a spot I like. It doesn't seem like Mr. Hans is too interested in answering my questions, so I look back at the rich people's building. It stretches up high into the sky, and I can see lights on in all the windows, even though it's the middle of the day and their electric bill must be through the roof. Some of the people coming out of the door look happy, like they just ate a terrific meal, and some look pretty unhappy, like they just had a demanding day at work but didn't get any tip money to show for it.

Mr. Hans turns off the ignition and looks over at me with a smile. There's not much sunlight to reflect off his gold tooth, and his grin makes me chilly. He claps and then sticks out one of his hands like he wants me to shake it. I grab Mr. Hans's hand with my own, and he squeezes as he pumps my arm up and down.

"Congratulations," Mr. Hans says, sounding more cheerful than he has all day. "This is moment when we both become rich men. Your job is easy and will not take so long."

"That's good," I say. I think back to my old cop badge and wish I hadn't given it away. I wonder if it would be rude to ask Mr. Hans to give it back to me just long enough for it to give me some courage.

"In trunk of my car, you will find small suitcase. It contains suit for you to wear, basic items of toiletry, and extra set of keys to mein hotrod." He points out at a building with a big red awning and steep marble steps. "You may change clothes in restroom of lobby of that hotel. When you have made yourself into presentable herr, you must enter bank, and ask for Pierre Baguette." Mr. Hans gestures back at the building that has all the rich people going through the revolving door.

"Okay," I say. As we sit in the car, lots of people are trotting past us. It was neat to see so many people at first, but now I'm starting to get a headache, what with watching them all. The crowded sidewalks remind me of how full and busy the lunch shifts would get at A Panini for Your Thoughts, and thinking about that kind of stress is making my blood push frantically through my veins. A dirty guy with a big scowl and not many teeth bangs on the rear window of Mr. Hans's car, and electricity goes through my skeleton. Mr. Hans honks his horn, and this scares off the dirty gentleman, who goes hobbling off lopsided, like one of his legs is longer than the other. I feel my chest, right over my heart, but then remember for the second time that I gave up my badge to Mr. Hans last night. If I'm going to be doing dangerous work, I need to have it back. "Mister Hans?" I say. "Remember that cop badge I gave you last night?"

"Mein herr, we must not waste time if you would like to get back to your family tonight with two millions of dollars." He licks his lips, making it look like millions of dollars is something tasty. "Mister Baguette will help you to move most precious artwork from hotrod and then have you fill out all necessary paperwork to make sure all is most legal. He will give to you payment in form of cash, and when this has happened, you must load money into hotrod and then blast car horn two times quick. I will be waiting for you in hotel lobby, and when I hear your signal, I will come to drive us away, two most rich gentlemen."

"Do you have my badge, Mister Hans?" I ask. Mr. Hans scrunches up his face, and I know I'm being rude to ask for it back, but I need it.

"You need to be listening, mein herr," Mr. Hans says, and raps my knuckles. I feel a sting of pain, and tears pool up in my eyes. I take my hand off my chest and put it onto my knee. Suddenly I undo my seatbelt, grab the door handle, pull open the door and fling my legs out onto the curb. I'm almost onto the sidewalk when I feel Mr. Hans's hand on my shoulder, his fingers digging in tight under my collarbone and pinching on my nerves. I scream out of surprise and hurt, and Mr. Hans yanks me back into the car, smashing my head against his shoulder.

"Help! Help!" I scream, not really knowing why. "Call the cops!" I struggle to get out of the car door, but the more I fight, the harder Mr.

Hans pulls back on my shoulder. I scream and scream, hoping that any of those people passing on the sidewalk will stop and get Mr. Hans to stop roughhousing, but nobody sees me, or at least they all act like they don't see me.

"You must stop disgusting outrage," Mr. Hans snarls in my ear.

I open my mouth and try to scream again, or tell Mr. Hans to let go of my shoulder, but the only thing that comes out is a soft whimper. I twist up my face, trying to bear up with the pain, but Mr. Hans is going to rip my arm off.

"Stop," I say, my voice choking out through my throat.

"Get back in car, all the way, and close door," says Mr. Hans, pushing down even tighter on my collarbone. My eyes are vibrating; I can't keep focus on any one thing.

"Let go," I say, trying to squirm free.

Something hard slaps across my face, and bubbles of pain float through the air. There's an awful, hot throbbing on my cheek and under my eye. My eyes snap focused, and I can see Mr. Hans raising his hand, ready to hit me again.

"Don't," I say. It's hard to talk. My lip is eight sizes too big. "Please." I slide my legs back into the car and shut the door. A woman walks by, pushing a stroller. She stares at me as she goes, and I wish I were in that stroller, being taken away somewhere safe by someone that cares about me.

"Why?" says Mr. Hans, his face red. "Why you wanted to run away?" He lets go of my shoulder, but my arm keeps on hurting just as much as if he were still holding on to it. I should try to make another break for it, but I know that Mr. Hans is faster than me, and stronger than me, and whatever he wants from me, he's going to get it, whether I fight back or don't fight back. I look up into Mr. Hans's eyes. He's glaring at me like I'm some weak little wretch, and my throat fills up with this sad sense of just how unfair life can get to be.

"You hit me," I say, my voice going sobby. Mr. Hans's forehead wrinkles, and I think he's about to yell, but instead he just drills through me with staring eyes. "I'm sorry," I say, hoping that Mr. Hans will look away. I feel hot in the car, and I just want to get out so I can breathe fresh air.

"I have put all mein trust in you," says Mr. Hans, not moving his eyes off me. "I have offered to you two millions of dollars and treated you like honorable business-partner, and when it comes to you to play your exceeding small part in mein plans, you wish to run off and not fulfill responsibility." He shakes his head a millionth of an inch, and my heart falls into my feet. I let down Mr. Gojjam, I let down Mom and Dad, and now I guess I'm letting down Mr. Hans, too.

"You shouldn't hit folks that have been good to you," I say softly. I put a hand up to my face, but it hurts to touch.

"You are right," says Mr. Hans. He puts his hand on my knee, and his forehead smoothes out. If my cheek didn't still feel like it was ready to bust open, I'd think I just imagined the whole thing. "I was most wrong to hit you," he says, "but, mein herr, I do not want for you to make enormous mistake." He gives my knee a squeeze, and somehow that lightens up the pain in my shoulder just a bit.

Mr. Hans points out his window to the traffic crawling along. A little group of yellow cabs are honking back and forth at each other, and a kid on a bicycle pedals by between the lanes of traffic. "Life, mein herr," Mr. Hans says. "Life." He smiles at me, and I feel fuzziness in my head. Mr. Hans squeezes my leg again, like "life" is this hardship we're going through, but it'll be okay because we're going through it together. "Do you know that sometimes our life is directed for us?" I hear sirens off somewhere in the distance.

"We are all put on course by some power of fate," says Mr. Hans, "and must do what is our duty."

I start to crank down my window, but Mr. Hans squeezes a pressure point on my knee, and so I stop. "Sorry," I say, and Mr. Hans lets go of my knee.

"At the end of times, Thor, we will all be judged based on how we bore up against difficulties of our lives. Think of your family, mein herr."

I run my hands along the leather surface of Mr. Hans's dashboard. My family.

"They are quite poor, yes?" Mr. Hans says, and I nod. "Then, it is fate of yours to do what you can do to make lives of others less full of suffering. And so if you have opportunity to take two millions of dollars, and, at last minute, you flee away like criminal dog, and so your mother and father must scrape along day to day when they could be living in riches and not worrying about financial problem, then would you say that you are herr who understands concept of duty?"

"I guess not," I say, and suddenly I'm wrapped up in Mr. Hans's arms. He squeezes me tight, and I can feel his alcohol-smelling cologne floating up into my nose and stinging behind my eyes. My skin starts sweating underneath his, but that doesn't stop him from holding on to me. I put my arms around Mr. Hans's broad back and try to squeeze him back the way that he's squeezing me.

"It is not always easy," says Mr. Hans, "to do what is right." I don't know why, but I feel tears stinging my eyes and getting tangled into my eyelashes. "But we must do our duty."

"Yeah," I say. I swallow hard, and Mr. Hans lets go of me. He puts his hands on my shoulders and looks me up and down.

"It will be over soon. You will change into suit, you will go into bank and find Pierre Baguette, and you will come into car. You will give me signal, and we will drive away. I will take you home, you will see your parents, you will return to your restaurant, and all will once more become well. Do you feel like you can do this?"

I nod.

"Mein herr," says Mr. Hans, a smile splitting his face open, "this is most wonderful." He rubs me on the head, like Mom always used to do, and I know he's sorry for hitting me. "And I only have one more instruction, and you must listen carefully, yes?"

I nod again. Mr. Hans's smile has flown across the car and landed smack on my face.

"You must not, mein herr," he says, "under any of circumstance, mention that you know me, that these are mein artworks, that this is mein hotrod, or that you do anything other than come to sell artworks that you happen upon at art auction in Gruff Valley. I must not be involved, mein herr. This is most important."

"Sure," I say. "Is this because of how all those art dealers think badly about Germans?"

Mr. Hans pushes a button on his side of the car, and my door unlocks. He gives my head one last pat, and nods. "Yes, mein herr," he says, "you are most exactly right. Excellent young herr."

I feel for my cop badge, but, again, it isn't pinned on my chest. No problem. I know I can do whatever mission without it.

"Here, mein herr," Mr. Hans says, unlocking his own door, and stepping out into the street. I get out of the car as well, taking a deep breath of fresh air. "I will unlock trunk for you," says Mr. Hans, with a big wink, "and then I will leave you—for it is time for you to do what is your duty."

Mr. Hans pops open the trunk, and I see a small black duffel bag inside. I lift it out, thinking how nice it will be to at least change out of my black invasion outfit, but when I turn to ask Mr. Hans if I should shut the trunk, he's already shuffled into the crowd of people going by on the sidewalk and disappeared.

***

I look at myself in the bathroom mirror and somebody who isn't Thor looks back at me. What is looking back at me is some deluxe gentleman. I move my hand, and the deluxe gentleman moves his hand. I stick out my tongue, and the deluxe gentleman sticks out his tongue, too. I know I am him and he is me, but this deluxe gentleman is somebody that decks himself out to the nines and tens in Mr. Hans's suit and combs down his hair.

The suit Mr. Hans gave me looks nice on me, even though it would probably look nicer on him or on Alan or Mr. Tony. It's got a dark blue coat and a fine, clean white button-down shirt with a gold handkerchief folded up in the breast pocket. My pants are the same dark blue as my coat, and I'm even wearing a stripy gold tie that clips on to the front of my collar. I grab my tie by its knot, and feeling it in my hand gives me the same feeling that holding on to my badge used to give me.

A fellow in a suit that's even nicer than mine—purple silk and teardrop stitches—breezes on into the restroom and gives me a hurried nod. I raise my eyebrows up at him, like we're both in on the secret of how nice it is to be rich, and he starts laughing and shaking his head. I start laughing and shaking my head, too, copying him a little, and he brushes past me. The gentleman, who a week ago might have sat in A Panini for Your Thoughts, just another Business Person with demands and timeframes, is now my friend and we're sharing a joke about something.

I blow a little fog onto the bathroom mirror, which is framed in gold curlicues that must cost a fortune, and write "Rich Man Crafthor" with my pinkie finger. I take one last look around the shiny, black bathroom, and grab Mr. Hans's duffel bag, where I've stuffed my old work clothes and black invasion clothes. I wanted to throw out the invasion outfit in order to forget about the guilt and the itchiness, but I should have it in case Alan asks for it back. As for my brown uniform shirt, there's no way I could get rid of it. On the one hand, it's got all kinds of sentiments for me and, on the other hand, I've got to have it for when I go back to work at the restaurant. Even after I'm a millionaire, I can't see myself leaving the restaurant—at least not until Barbara is healthy and ready to start up our own panini restaurant somewhere.

I walk out of the bathroom, stepping heavily so that I can hear my shiny brown shoes clicking on the black tile, through the hotel lobby, and out into the street. The sunlight on the street blasts me, making me wince slightly. Even so, I smile at the sun because I'm a deluxe gentleman now, and even though the sun might still be bigger than me, I am rich.

Pierre Baguette's bank towers up in the sunshine like a gigantic sword. There are more windows than I can count, and each window reflects the sun and other buildings nearby. When I move my head up and down, the sunlight bounces around the bank's gold-and-glass surface, tracing glittering designs in the air. I feel for Mr. Hans's car keys in my pants pocket and I unlock his hotrod. I toss the duffel bag in the trunk, take a look at myself in the side-view mirror, and, straightening up my lapels, lock the car back up.

As I stand at the street corner, waiting for the light to change, I make my back very straight. A scruffy guy with a red tattoo on his neck looks me up and down as he walks by, and I pretend I don't see him. I stuff my hands into my pockets, and then take them out again, not really sure if rich people put their hands in their pockets.

The light changes, and I cross the street to the bank. As I walk up the marble steps to the front entrance, I smile and nod at the other well-dressed people. Nobody smiles back, but when I step into the bank lobby, I'm too stunned to even care. The lobby ceiling must be four or five stories high, painted dark red with clouds and angels around the edges. Enormous stone columns as thick around as trees shoot up into the air. The slick white floor is so polished I can see my reflection in it. I wave at myself and then try to figure out where I should go.

I see a large desk in the middle of the lobby, with a curly-haired woman sitting behind it on a tall stool. She's busy typing at her computer, but I don't see anybody else that looks like they might be able to help me, so I step up to the desk and smile my best smile.

"Hello," I say. "My name is Crafthor Gunderson."

The woman tears her eyes away from her computer screen. "Can I help you?"

"I am supposed to see Mister Pierre Baguette on account of some artworks."

"Do you have an appointment?" she asks, drumming her fingers on her keyboard.

"I don't think so."

"Hold on," she says, and rolls her eyes. She pulls a phone receiver off her desk, pushes a button, and says, "Mister Baguette? A walk-in for you, concerning the art trade." The woman reads something off her computer screen as she listens to Mr. Baguette's answer.

"Were you sent by a Mister Hans Hess?" the woman asks me.

I start to nod, but then remember that Mr. Hans told me not to let anybody know he sent me here, so I turn my nod into a head-shake.

The woman snorts out a mean little laugh and says into the phone, "That's ambiguous, but I'd say yes. Should I send him up?"

"Oh," I say, "I wasn't sent by Mister Hans, or even by anybody else. My name is Crafthor Gunderson, and I'm just trying to sell some valuable artworks …"

I stop talking, because the desk woman is not looking at me. She is watching her computer and listening to Mr. Baguette. I reach into my pocket and make sure that Mr. Hans's car keys are still there. I jingle the keys as I wait for the desk woman to finish up on the telephone.

Finally, she hangs up, and, without looking at me, says, "Mister Baguette will see you." Her fingers type so hard she rattles her keyboard. "Take the elevator to the fifteenth floor. When you step into the hall, turn right, and Mister Baguette's office will be the third on your left."

"Thank you."

I walk around the front desk to the set of glass-fronted elevators. I push the button that has an up arrow, and the doors of one of the elevators slide open. I step inside and hit the button marked "15." The doors slide shut with a ding and, the next thing I know, my stomach is in my feet and my feet are pushing against the ground. I hold my breath and close my eyes. A few seconds later, I hear another ding and my stomach is back where it ought to be. I open my eyes in time to see the doors slide open again, showing me a wood-paneled hallway that must be the fifteenth floor.

I turn right and, counting three doors down on my left, I see a huge oak door with a gold nameplate: "Pierre Baguette, Appraisal and Valuation." I dust off my shoes until they shine, take a couple deep breaths, and knock.

Almost immediately, the door opens up, and I'm looking at a blonde fellow with sharp blue eyes and a chin so smooth I'd think he was fifteen years old if he wasn't so tall and important. His hair is spiked up carefully, and even though he's not wearing a suit coat, I feel like he's dressed fancier than me. I put a hand on my chin and feel how stubbly it is.

"You were sent by Mister Hans Hess?" asks Mr. Baguette, smiling at me with perfect teeth, and making a beckon that I should step into the office.

"No," I say. "My name is Crafthor Gunderson, and I am not sent by anybody."

"Of course," says Mr. Baguette. "Have a seat." He closes the office door and then settles into a leather swivel chair behind his desk. I sit down in a similar chair on the other side of the desk, and it feels like I'm sitting in a forest of pillows.

"I would just like to remind you," says Mr. Baguette, "of a saying that we have in Switzerland. 'I don't know, and I don't want to know.' Whether you were sent by Mister Hess or whether you are, as you say, acting as an independent agent, I have no interest in prying into your motivations." Mr. Baguette presses his fingers together into a little house and rests his chin on it.

"I just know," I say, "that I have two paintings in my hotrod, and they're worth ten million dollars."

"In whose estimation?" says Mr. Baguette, but before I can say anything, he shakes his head and laughs. "Never mind. I don't know, and I don't want to know. Well," he says, undoing his finger-house, "why don't we have a look at these paintings?"

"Sure," I say. Mr. Baguette stands up, so I stand up too. He leads me out into the hallway again, but when we get to the row of elevators, I say, "Are there stairs we can use instead? The elevator makes my stomach feel awful."

Mr. Baguette nods and leads me to a small silver door marked "Fire Exit." We head into the stairwell, and as we clatter down the steep metal staircase, Mr. Baguette says, "So, how did you come into possession of these paintings?"

I stop walking so I can think what to say, but Mr. Baguette keeps clattering on ahead of me. The concrete walls in the stairwell are less fancy than all the gold and marble in the rest of the bank. Some sort of brown liquid has dribbled over the walls, leaving a crusty stain. Mr. Baguette realizes he is walking alone, and he stops to turn back up to me.

"I don't know!" I call down to him. "And I don't want to know!"

"I suppose that's a fair answer," he says. He waits on the stairs while I hurry to catch up with him. Once we're walking together again, I feel like I have to walk twice as fast as Mr. Baguette—he's so tall that he goes a lot further in one stride than I do.

"So," Mr. Baguette says, "what, if anything, *would* you like to speak about, Mister Gunderson? What do you do for employment?" We reach the bottom of the stairwell, and Mr. Baguette holds the door open for me. I cross out into the lobby and make toward the front door as fast as I can, wanting to get a lead on Mr. Baguette for whatever reason. After a couple of seconds he's already right up next to me anyway, not even breathing hard.

"Please, Mister Gunderson, don't answer that," Mr. Baguette says with a smile. "Prepare to have your mind blown." He holds the front door open for me, and I step out into the sunlight. I hurry down the marble stairs, but they're too crowded with people coming and going for me to get much ahead of Mr. Baguette. "I'll bet," he says, coming right up behind me, "you work at some kind of restaurant. Italian or French, maybe. Or Polish."

I stop walking, and Mr. Baguette bumps into me. I lose my balance and have to grab on to the wooden railing to keep from falling down the steps. I guess Mr. Baguette did sort of blow my mind. Continuing on down the stairs and along the sidewalk with Mr. Baguette alongside me, I say, "Why do you think that?"

"I just mean," says Mr. Baguette, "that Mister Hess has a very distinctive type, when it comes to business partners. Make no mistake, Mister Gunderson: I don't care a whit whether you were sent by Handsome Hans or not, but, between you and me, I would be very surprised if you weren't."

"Center City sure is busy," I say, as we wait for a chance to cross the street. The cars are packed so tight together there would barely be room for me to squeeze between them. When the traffic signal changes, I lead Mr. Baguette across the street and over to Mr. Hans's hotrod. I try to stare up into Mr. Baguette's face without him noticing, so I can tell if his expression changes when he sees how nice a car I have. It doesn't.

I unlock the back door and for some reason Mr. Baguette seems more impressed by the paintings than he does by the car. He pulls out the creepy picture of lonely old Chronos and gasps.

"This is unbelievable," he says, his voice going quaky. "The *masterful* interplay of light and shadow. I had no idea that Handsome Hans had works of such quality in his collection."

"Yeah, it's a pretty nice painting," I lie, ignoring the part about Mr. Hans. "Here's the other one," I say, and pull out the nicer painting with the heavenly woman. "I like this one better. I like the angels."

Mr. Baguette stares at the nice painting for a moment, with his tongue sticking out between his teeth. Finally, he nods, and says, "Yes, the beginnings of a great talent are certainly on display in that canvas." I'm glad Mr. Baguette likes the painting.

"Mister Gunderson," says Mr. Baguette, "let's bring these back to my office. I'll have you complete the necessary liability paperwork, and then I'll provide you with your payment in full."

"Oh," I say. I want to put my hands in my pockets to show that I don't care about money, but I'm still holding the painting, so I just roll my eyes.

"You are quite an accomplished appraiser, by the way," says Mr. Baguette, looking *Chronos* up and down. "Ten million dollars is precisely how I would have placed the worth of these two canvases, taken together. You must have quite a background."

Mr. Baguette smiles at me like he's making a joke, so I laugh. I shut the car door with my hip, and Mr. Baguette and I carry the paintings back to the bank. Even as we pass people on the street, nobody seems interested to stop and look at the artworks. If I carried an old painting of a scary-looking guy down the streets in Gruff Valley, I'd be getting a lot of questions. In Center City, though, women chase after their kids, elderly folk get pulled around by their pet dogs, everybody dodges the folks on bicycles, and nobody seems to pay any mind to anything that isn't right in front of their face. I let Mr. Baguette walk in front of me so I can follow him instead of trying to cut through the crowds myself while holding a clunky painting.

When we get to the bank, security guards rush to open the front doors for us. I smile at them, but they don't smile at me. Mr. Baguette heads straight for the stairwell, and the security guards come with us to open doors and, I guess, look out for bad guys.

The painting did not seem heavy on the street, but by the time I get up to the fifteenth story, my shoulders ache and I've got sweat on my forehead and under my arms. I check to see if Mr. Baguette's forehead is sweating, too, but he looks just as cool and smooth as ever. The security guards follow us into Mr. Baguette's office and when he props up his painting against the back wall, I let out a sigh that I hope nobody hears, and set my painting next to his.

Mr. Baguette slices his hand through the air at the chair where I was sitting earlier and says, "Have a seat, Mister Gunderson." He looks at the security guards and straightens his tie. "Thank you for your help," he says to them, "but my colleague and I are going to need a moment of privacy while we conduct our transaction. Would you kindly convey the Tintorettos to the vault?"

The security guards both nod and, as they hoist up the paintings, I wipe the sweat off my forehead with the cuff of my suit coat and sit in the comfy chair, just like Mr. Baguette asked me to. I take one last look at *Chronos* and wave goodbye as the guards carry the paintings out of the office.

Mr. Baguette shuts the door behind the security guards and then settles into his office chair across the desk from me.

"As I said, Mister Gunderson," he says, "I don't know who you're working for, and I don't want to know. However, bank protocol and international law require a certain degree of accountability. So, if you can see your way to completing these brief liability forms, I will have my associates prepare your compensation."

Mr. Baguette opens a metal file cabinet next to his desk. He pulls out a couple of forms and slides them across the desk to me, along with a thick silver pen. I check out my reflection in the pen, and my face is stretched out long. I smile, and it's the widest smile I've ever smiled.

I look through all the forms before filling anything out, to make sure they don't ask anything too tricky, but they all seem simple, so I write my name where they ask for it, I put my birthday where they want me to, and I sign where they ask for my signature. As I write, Mr. Baguette talks into his phone. I hear him say, "ten million dollars," and my heart sends an electrical jolt up to my brain. I look up to see what Mr. Baguette looks like when he's talking about such a big amount of money, but he just looks normal. When I look back down at the form I was filling out, I see the pen has drooled out a big black smudge, and so I ask Mr. Baguette for a fresh sheet.

When I've finished all the papers, I slide them back to Mr. Baguette. He looks through them and then gives a nod, like he thinks I did a good job on them.

"It's been a pleasure to meet you, Mister Gunderson," Mr. Baguette says. We shake hands across the desk. If it is this easy to make two million dollars, I do not understand why there are people in the world who don't do it.

"You will find," Mr. Baguette continues, as he leans back in his chair and rubs at his temples with his knuckles, "that Mariel, at reception, will have your payment ready for you as you leave."

Mr. Baguette takes a pencil from a cup on his desk and nibbles on the eraser. I shift in my pillow-chair, not sure if I am supposed to leave or stay. Mr. Baguette is looking up at his ceiling, so I check to see what's up there, but it's just a ceiling.

I think we might sit here forever, staring up at the ceiling, so I stand up and say, "Thank you, Mister Baguette. It's been a real pleasure to sell off my paintings to you."

Mr. Baguette nods slowly, without looking at me, and I'm not too sure if he heard what I said. Half of the pencil eraser comes off in his teeth and he spits it into his hand with a "pthew." I turn around and head toward the door.

"Please wait, Mister Gunderson," says Mr. Baguette. I turn back to him, but he's still staring off into the sky. "Perhaps you would be so kind as to do me a small favor."

"Sure."

"I do not know, nor do I want to know, if you came here with Mister Hans Hess, but, if you did, I would ask you to please give him a message. Please tell him that it's professional, not personal, and that he's the only herr with whom I would ever … well … join forces. Just tell him that." Mr. Baguette's cheeks are flaming pink, and I feel my own face get warm just watching him. "Can you remember that message?"

"Sure," I say. I step over to the desk and put a hand on Mr. Baguette's shoulder. "But I wasn't sent by Mister Hans, or even by anyone else."

"Yes," says Mr. Baguette, nodding. He looks up at me, and I see more sadness than I would have thought such a tall, well-dressed gentleman could ever have in him. "Here," he says, and takes a thin golden ring off of his desk. He puts the ring in the palm of my hand and I close my fingers around it. "Give that back to him, if you would."

"Okay," I say, shifting from foot to foot. "But I never met Mister Hans."

Mr. Baguette nods again and clears his throat. He looks towards his door and says, "I understand that. Thank you for your business, Mister Gunderson."

Mr. Baguette starts scribbling around on some of his paperwork like he's forgotten I'm standing in the office with him. As I step out of the office, I turn back to look at him, but he's busy writing, so I exit into the hallway and head down the fire steps.

When I first get home, I will surprise Mom with a whole bouquet of flowers, and Dad with a twelve-pack of beer. I'll have to set aside the rest of the money at first for Barbara's doctor bills, and pay whatever it takes to get her right again. After that, Barbara and I can buy a house together, and a restaurant, and then, whatever's left I can spend on presents for Mom and Dad and Alan, and all the rest.

I come into the lobby and step up to the desk, where the woman was not that nice to me before. Now that I'm a millionaire, I wonder if maybe she'll be nicer.

"Hello again," I say to her. She types for a moment, and then finally turns her face toward me.

"Can I help you?"

"I am supposed to pick up ten million dollars," I say, spreading my feet apart and taking a stance I'd call pretty confident. "On account of Mister Baguette said so."

"That's right," she says with a little nod. "Alistair and Hernando will assist you. Please step into our accounting room." She waves her hand at a wooden door back near those awful elevators. I stand at the desk a bit longer to see if she'll say anything more to me, but she just turns her attention right back to the computer and types away.

I walk to the accounting room and put my hand on the doorknob. I shut my eyes, count to ten, and then open the door and step into the room.

The tiny accounting room is pretty ordinary, compared to all the expensive rooms all over the rest of the bank. The walls, the ceiling, and the floor are all hardwood, and the only furniture in the room is a short desk and a couple of scratched-up wooden chairs. The two security guards who helped Mr. Baguette and me with the paintings are standing next to a big black chest, looking like stern-faced statues.

"Hello again," I say. "Are you Mister Alistair and Mister Hernando?"

"Yeah," says one of the fellows, and he undoes a clasp on the front of the chest. He lifts off the lid. The chest is stuffed full of stacks and stacks of five-hundred-dollar bills. Suddenly I'm on my knees. I put out a hand and run my fingers over the bills at the top of the chest. Every bill is a month's worth of tip money. Twelve bills is a year's worth of tip money. This chest must be a lifetime's worth of tip money.

"Hello," I whisper down to the money. I climb back onto my feet, but I have to lean against the desk to keep myself propped up.

The security guards close the chest and latch it up again, like they see that kind of money every day. They probably do.

"We'll escort you to your car, Mister Gunderson," says one of the guards.

"Do you see a lot of folks that have this kind of money?" I ask.

Hernando and Alistair look at each other and shrug. One of them says, "It's not uncommon."

"I never thought I'd see ten million dollars all in one place."

The security guards shrug again and lift up the chest between them. I focus on putting one foot in front of the other as I walk to the door and open it for the guards. I follow Alistair and Hernando through the lobby and out into the street. When I breathe, I try to get the air down as deep into my lungs as I can, because that helps keep my legs from shaking too much. I show my guard friends where I've parked, and I unlock the backseat of the car so they can slide the chest inside.

"Well," I say, after I've shut the car door, "is that it?"

"That's it, Mister Gunderson," says either Alistair or Hernando, and each of them shakes my hand. "Best of luck."

Without another word, the guards are walking back to the bank, and I'm standing on the sidewalk in Center City next to a bright red hotrod with ten million dollars in the backseat. I jingle the car keys in my pocket and tell my heart it doesn't need to be beating so fast. What should I do next? I see myself sitting at the breakfast table with Mom, Dad, and Barbara, and we're all talking and laughing and eating bacon. I see myself in front of Barbara, on one knee, holding up a box with a beautiful diamond ring inside. I see a panini restaurant, done up in gold and marble like a bank, with fountains of pesto and the warmest down sleeping bags for Remus and Romulus.

A car blasts its horn, and I'm back in Center City, standing by Mr. Hans's hotrod. I need to signal for Mr. Hans to come drive us away. Fighting to keep my whole body from trembling, I climb into the passenger seat, lean over the console, and press on the horn two times. I keep my eyes on the door of the hotel where Mr. Hans is waiting so I can see him come out. With all the noise from the traffic and pedestrians, I wonder how Mr. Hans will be able to hear the signal.

Just as I'm about to signal again, Mr. Hans comes out of the hotel entrance, walking casually toward the car. I grin at him and stick a thumbs-up in the air, but he doesn't pay me any mind. As soon as Mr. Hans gets into the car, though, I yell out, "Hurrah!" and pat him on the back like he's some kind of champion. A half-smile crawls onto his face.

"Well," he says, "I assume that business-transaction has occurred in proper way?"

"Yeah!" I say, pointing into the backseat. "We have ten million dollars in that chest there!"

"And two million of dollars are yours," says Mr. Hans, "for job well done."

I want to sing or whoop or grab Mr. Hans up into an enormous hug, but he merely sticks out his hand for me to shake it.

"We must," he says, "now get you home to parents. You have been big help to me, but every adventure-quest must end in homebound journey."

Mr. Hans starts the car and, as we get stuck in the city traffic, I feel my excitement start to drain out through my feet. I turn back to look at the chest of money and try to guess how many bills must be inside. I want to talk to Mr. Hans and ask him all sorts of questions, like what he's going to do with all the money he just earned, but I know he doesn't want to talk, so I just sigh and sink back into the passenger seat.

It takes us an hour and a half to get out of Center City, and when I look back at the city skyline, I can see the sky starting to get gloomy and twilight-blue. In front of us, a bright pink strip of sky burns right on top of the horizon. I feel lonely.

"So long, Center City," I say, sort of to nobody. Mr. Hans keeps driving along in silence.

A few minutes later, Mr. Hans finally talks. "Well, did Pierre ask anything about me?"

I feel in my pocket for the ring that Mr. Baguette gave me. "I didn't even mention you at all," I say. Maybe I'll just leave the ring on the dashboard when I get home, so that Mr. Hans will find it later.

"It's okay. I would not be surprised if maybe Pierre said something about me?"

We drive along into the darkening night. I close my eyes and listen to the whap-whap of the tires as they roll over the uneven highway. Soon I'll be back with Mom and Dad. I want everything to be the same as it always has been, but I don't know. Maybe with two million dollars everything will be different.

"Well, Mister Hans, I guess he did mention you, a little." Mr. Hans raises his eyebrows but doesn't say anything. "He said to give you this ring," I say, putting the gold ring into the cup holder in the center console. "And he said that it's professional, not personal, and that you're the only herr that he'd ever want to join forces with."

I can't hear Mr. Hans breathing anymore. I think I see his top lip shaking a tiny bit, but the car's getting darker and darker, so I can't really tell.

"Are you okay?" I ask.

"We would have been," Mr. Hans says, and sniffs, "an excellent pair."

"Yeah, I sure bet so. Mister Baguette was pretty tall."

Mr. Hans doesn't say anything, so I close my eyes again and keep listening to the whap-whap of the tires as we drive back west, toward home.

***

"Hey," a voice says. I yawn and stretch my arms out over my head. "Hey," says the voice again, and someone's shaking my shoulder. I open my eyes and see Mr. Hans leaning over me. The windshield is covered in dewdrops and, through it, I can see the bright orange sky.

"Is it the morning?" I ask. I don't remember falling asleep. I look out the window, seeing if I can spot anything familiar. I see small hills of sand glowing in the rising sun and, in the distance, blue outlines of mesas. One mesa has a little rock horn jutting out on one side. "The Big, Big Anvil!" I say. "We're home!"

Mr. Hans nods. His eyes look dark and saggy from driving on through the night, but he's smiling. "Yes, mein herr, we are back inside town limits of Gruff Valley. I pulled into rest area to nap, but time has come, mein herr, to move on. We must divide up money, and return you home to family."

A huge smile slides onto my face, and I want to grab Mr. Hans and scream, or sing, or bounce up and down. I'm back where I belong.

I press my nose against my passenger window, and now that I know what I'm looking at, I can see a little better that of course we're in Gruff Valley. I see the smokestacks from the carton factory pushing up over Carleton Hill and, down in a valley nearby, the little houses of the Gruff Acres subdivision. The green sign posted at the rest area where Mr. Hans has parked the hotrod says, "Bluff View Scenic Overlook."

"We're home!" I say again.

"We must divide up money," says Mr. Hans. "Do you have duffel bag from when you went on bank-journey?"

"Oh—I put it in the trunk."

"Then, I will send you home with duffel bag full of cash. How does it sound to you?"

"It sounds good." The rising sun pokes up over the mesas, spilling golden light into the car. Mr. Hans's face shines.

"In that case, patience yourself and I will make necessary cash transfer."

Mr. Hans steps out of the car, and I do the same. I didn't realize how badly my legs needed a stretch, but now that I'm standing out in the breezy morning, I straighten them up as much as I can and feel my muscles shaking with pleasure. I take a deep breath … and the air slides into my lungs, pure and smooth.

"It sure is a nice morning," I say to Mr. Hans, swiping a finger through the dewdrops that have collected on the hood of his car. Mr. Hans doesn't say anything to reply. He's popped the trunk open and is suspiciously looking all over the parking lot of the viewpoint, even though we are the only people around.

"How fast is your counting, mein herr?" Mr. Hans asks, as he opens up the rear door and puts his hand on the chest full of money.

"I'm pretty good with counting and can count really fast."

"Our difficulty is that we do not want to be caught at scenic overlook with millions of dollars. We must transfer two million of dollars from chest to duffel bag, and do so in a manner of quickness."

"Makes sense to me," I say, and then frown. "Two million is a lot to count in a manner of quickness, though."

"This is why I propose to count money, while you act as lookout. I am expert," says Mr. Hans with a smooth smile, "of counting large money-sums."

"Okay," I say.

"I will be scrupulously fair."

"Okay." A cloud of smoke puffs out of the smokestack at the carton factory. They must be starting up work for the day. I bet Alan's getting the day started right now, too. I'm not there to wake up Remus and Romulus, so maybe Barbara's doing it. Alan's probably greeting the deliveryman and helping him unload all his boxes of tomatoes and dry pasta and sugar packets. I want to be back at the restaurant too—smelling the focaccia coming out of the oven, mopping the floor so clean I can see myself reflected in it, and watching the twins let loose with their knives, chopping onions and garlic into bits.

Mr. Hans starts loading money from the chest into the duffel bag, and I watch the road winding up to the viewpoint. A square patch of sunlight on the asphalt disappears and then reappears as a cloud passes across the sun, but no cars come along. I listen for motor noises, but I can only hear birds singing their morning songs, and little rustling sounds as Mr. Hans counts out the money. Mr. Hans can count really fast. I try to count silently along with Mr. Hans, but he's so much faster than I am that I give up and go back to watching for cars. I see a green Jeep rolling up the road.

"Hey, Mister Hans, we've got a Jeep coming."

"Pity," says Mr. Hans, zipping up the duffel bag. He puts the duffel bag in the chest of money, and closes the lid. "This will slow us down."

Mr. Hans shuts the car and locks it. I keep watching the Jeep as it crawls up the hill.

"Well," says Mr. Hans, putting his hand on my shoulder, "at least we can take advantage of distraction to enjoy breathtaking vista of Bluff View." We walk over to the edge of the overlook and peer out into Gruff Valley. Up here, the wind can run along quicker than it does down in the valley, and breezes whistle in my ears.

"I came here once with Mom," I say, "when I was little. I remember I was afraid of falling over the edge." A wooden fence stands between me and the drop-off, but its planks are rotted through, and I don't think it was built too sturdily in the first place. I kick at one of the fence posts, and the wood splits.

"See? This fence is old and broke-down, and I bet a kid could break right through it."

Mr. Hans pats my shoulder a couple of times and points off into the sky. "See the eagle," he says.

I squint into the rising sun to see what Mr. Hans is pointing at, and after a moment I can make out the black shadow of a bird with a huge wingspan gliding in the orange sky. I watch the bird float around. It doesn't flap its wings, but it lets itself get carried along wherever the wind chooses to take it. That must be such a strange feeling—to be blown around like a feather, high above the earth. If I jumped off the edge of the bluff, I'd fall straight down and get busted up on the rocks. This does not seem close to anywhere fair.

"I think we are safe to continue counting," Mr. Hans says softly. I look around at the road, and I don't see the Jeep. It must have turned off toward town.

"Okay," I say, and we go back to Mr. Hans's car.

It takes Mr. Hans about fifteen more minutes to finish counting out the money into the duffel bag, and I play lookout the whole time. Mr. Hans pushes the duffel bag full with my two million dollars into my arms and winks at me.

"You have been most helpful to me, and now you are rich man."

I unzip the bag and peek in. Bills, and bills, and bills. I open my mouth to say something, but I don't have anything to say. Instead, I zip the bag back up, drop it on the asphalt of the parking lot, and throw my arms around Mr. Hans's middle, squeezing him tight. I squeeze and squeeze with every bit of energy I can bring into my arms, and bury my face in his shoulder.

"Thank you, thank you, thank you, thank you," I find myself saying. The words get muffled on account of I'm talking into his shirt, but Mr. Hans pats me on the head and I know that he understands what I'm saying.

"Ssh," says Mr. Hans, patting me again. "You must not thank me, for it is simple business transaction." He grabs me by the shoulders and pushes me away. "You must not be careless with your salary," he says, poking the duffel bag with his toe.

I smile, knowing I'm blushing, and pick up the duffel bag. If I try to say anything, all that will come out will be "thank you" again, so I keep my mouth shut as I get into the passenger seat. Mr. Hans gets in the car and starts up the engine.

"Mein herr," he says, "we must say our goodbyes now, because I will drop you off by your house and then journey on. I do not wish to linger in sentiment."

"Well, you should come by the restaurant sometime. Maybe I can get Alan to comp you an appetizer."

Mr. Hans chuckles and holds out his hand for me to shake. I grab his hand and he squeezes.

"It has been my pleasure to engage in business-activity with you, mein herr. Perhaps it will be destiny for our paths to cross one another in a future day. Perhaps it is our fate to never again be drawn together." He drops my hand, and I hit my knuckles on the center console. "It will be how it will be."

"Yeah," I say, and I bounce the money up and down on my lap. "It's been nice to meet you, too."

Mr. Hans pulls out of the parking lot and starts driving down the road into Gruff Valley. I keep bouncing the money on my lap, and as we get closer and closer to home, I bounce the money faster and faster. I tell Mr. Hans which way to drive to get to my house, and he follows my directions without saying anything. We drive around the city park, past the dump, and then we turn at the old scrap metal yard, with its big sign that says "Redemption" in golden letters. We pass under the railroad tracks and make a big loop at the roundabout next to Pie and Hooch, coming out near the cemetery that has a big gargoyle that reminds me of Alan. I see the vacant lot where Mom says not to cut through at night, and then, beyond the locksmith and the rental car spot, I see home.

"*That's it,*" I say to Mr. Hans, pointing straight ahead at my house. After Center City and its skyscrapers, my house looks tiny and beat-up. Long strips of our siding are gone, and the paint job is splotchy. I never noticed how much our roof sagged in before.

"You will be okay if I drop you here?" asks Mr. Hans, pulling off to the curb a few houses before mine.

"Oh," I say, bouncing the money up and down. I wonder if Mr. Hans doesn't like my house. "That's my house up there. You can come in if you want. I bet Mom and Dad will want to meet you."

"Mein herr," says Mr. Hans, "I think that it is time for us to move on our separate paths. You have your money, and I have mine, and that is end of our business."

"But you could still meet my folks, at least."

Mr. Hans sighs through his nose. "I am quite shy," he says. He digs around in his pocket, pulls out something I can't quite see, and places it in my hand. "It is yours. I think you deserve it most excellently."

I look to see what Mr. Hans gave me, and my cop badge looks back up at me like an old friend. I move to pin it on my chest, but I'm still wearing Mr. Hans's nice suit, and I don't want to poke holes in it.

"Your suit!" I say. "You want it back, I bet." I run my hand along my stripy gold tie and look at myself in the rearview mirror. "Thanks for letting me borrow it, though. It made me feel like a deluxe gentleman."

"No, mein herr. It is your suit. It would not fit me. You must keep it, and be deluxe gentleman, and whenever you wear it, you will think of adventure-quest and your friend, Hans."

"Of course I will!"

"Look here," says Mr. Hans. He takes the badge out of my hands and pins it through the buttonhole at the top of my lapel. "This way you can pin on, but will not make holes in polyester fabric."

"Thanks," I say. Mr. Hans and I shake hands again. I should say something important and meaningful, because this is the end of our adventure-quest, but I don't know what.

"You must promise me you will be good herr," Mr. Hans says.

"Sure will, Mister Hans."

"Money can buy you objects, but cannot buy you good taste."

"Sure."

"You are author of your own destiny."

"Oh," I say, and want to add something smart, but only come up with another "Sure."

Mr. Hans drums his fingers on the steering wheel. "You must go now."

"Okay." I grab on tight to the bag with my two million dollars inside and get out of the car. "Thanks, Mr. Hans!"

"It has been my pleasure," he says with a little nod.

"You should come visit the restaurant soon!"

Mr. Hans nods again, and I close the passenger door behind me. Before I can think of what I want to say next, Mr. Hans is already driving down the street, waving at me. I have just enough time to raise up my hand in return before Mr. Hans's hotrod motors around the corner, and I'm left alone half a block away from my house, wearing a spiffy suit and holding two million dollars.

I take a deep breath in through my nose and smell the old grass-and-dirt scent of my neighborhood. Before I know what I'm doing, I'm grinning like a little kid and sprinting up to my house. I climb up our uneven porch steps and press my ear up against a crack in the front door. I hear somebody clomping around inside. It must be Mom, since Dad's probably already left for work. What will I say to her? I slam on the door with my fists and then put my ear back up against the crack.

The footsteps inside stop, and I pound on the door again. I hear the footsteps running to the front door, and so I take a step back and spread my arms open so I will be ready to give Mom the biggest hug I ever gave her as soon as she opens the door.

In a moment, the front door is open, and I'm looking at Mom and screaming, "Mom!"

Mom's eyes get huge, like she's looking at a ghost, and her chest goes up and down, jerky, like she's having trouble breathing. I step toward her and wrap my arms around her, but she's not hugging me back.

"Oh, Thorrie," she whimpers in my ear. I can feel her trying to get out of my hug.

"Mom, I'm home."

"Thorrie," she says again, and pushes at me a little. She wants me to let her go, but I can't. I want her to know that I'm never leaving again, ever.

"Thorrie, please," she says, and then she's not struggling with me anymore. Mom sighs, loud and tearful, and relaxes into my hug. I stagger a little under her weight. Catching my balance, I plant my feet firm, and hug Mom even tighter.

"It's okay, Mom. I'm back for good."

"I'm sorry," Mom says, choking out her words between her tears. "I haven't slept at—"

"It's okay," I say, and Mom's hugging me back, and we stand in front of my house, with the door hanging open, and two million dollars in a duffel bag hanging off my shoulders.

"Gracie!" booms Dad's voice from inside the house. "Is it him?"

"Dad's home?"

Mom doesn't answer me. She pulls her head off my shoulder and turns back to the house. "He's here!" she says, her mouth twisting into a smile that's sad and happy at once. "He's back!"

"Thor?" Dad says. I hear heavy footsteps thudding toward the front door.

"Hi, Dad!" I call into the house. "Dad, I'm back! I'm so happy!"

And now Dad's filling up the entire front hallway, breathing hard through his mouth. His face is red, his eyes are severe, and he's waving a sheet of paper around like it's on fire and he's trying to put it out.

"Thor," says Dad, and my heart thuds into my feet. "I don't have the words," he goes on, cold and firm.

"Dear," says Mom. She steps up to Dad and puts a hand on his chest, like she's trying to hold him back from coming at me. Dad doesn't even notice her hand; he keeps his eyes glued on my face as he shakes his head back and forth in disappointment.

"I'm sorry, Dad," I say, and try to put a smile on my face. "But wait till you see wha—"

"I do not have the words," Dad says again.

"He's back," Mom says. "That's the end of it." She turns to me. "Oh, Thorrie, come on in. Are you hungry?"

"Gracie," says Dad, finally taking his eyes off me so he can look at Mom. "I need you to leave us alone for a minute."

"I don't think you're in the right frame of mind," says Mom.

"Gracie," says Dad, his tone firm. "Go inside."

"We can talk it through as a family."

"Go inside," says Dad, louder.

Mom pulls back her hand, and she smacks Dad hard on the chest. She pulls her hand back again, but he seizes her wrist and yanks her back into the hallway. Blood rushes up into my face, and I charge into the hall.

"Let go of Mom!" I yell. I've got my hands up, ready to snare Dad's arms. Dad lets go of Mom and she falls against the wall, trying to hold onto her balance. A second later, Dad slams me against the opposite wall.

The drywall cracks under the force. Surprise buzzes in my bones like an electric charge.

"Don't hurt him," says Mom weakly.

"Nobody's hurting anybody," says Dad, his face close to mine. I try to wriggle away from him, but Dad's pinning me against the wall with his arm. Over his shoulder, I can see Mom straightening herself up.

"Nobody's hurting anybody," says Dad again, "but a father would like to have a word with his son, if that is alright. Gracie, why don't you call Officer Justice and let him know that the little delinquent has turned up?"

Mom twists up her face, trying to fight against her tears, and hesitates for a moment, before nodding and walking off to the kitchen.

"Dad, it's okay. I've got—"

"Where have you been?" Dad says, looking all over my face like maybe the answer's written there.

"Let me go."

Dad pulls me away from the wall and smacks me back into it. I hear myself screaming and feel flecks of drywall raining onto my new suit and over my shoes.

"Where have you been?" Dad asks again. He shoves a sheet of paper at my chest. "And what is this?" The paper falls to the floor, and I lean over to pick it up, but Dad stops me by thrusting his hand onto my chest. "How about you answer me?"

"Dad," I say, fighting to keep from yelling, "I think maybe you can just calm down, because I have been very busy on this adventure-quest to get money for this family, and I have two million dol—"

"And what's the story with these ridiculous clothes?" Dad says, poking at my cop badge. "Thor, I think that you'd just bet—"

"Stop it! How about you just stop it?"

Dad pokes at my badge again, harder this time and, out of some reflex, I swing out with the money bag. The heavy bag thumps into Dad's knees, and he roars out. He lets go of me, and I pick up the paper he was waving at me.

"Call the cops!" Dad screams back into the house, rubbing his knee with both hands. "Get this kid locked up!"

"Mom, help!" I scream, looking at the open front door, then down the hallway into the house. Blood buzzes in my ears. I mash the paper up in my hands, and then pull it open again. Dad looks up at me, angrier than I've ever seen him, and my head spins. I turn toward the front door, hold on to my bag of money, and yell, "I love you, Mom!" before sprinting out the door, into the yard, across the street, and then down the block, toward the next block, and then down the next block to the block after that, and on, and on, and on, my eyes watering and the bag of money growing heavier and heavier on my shoulder.

***

After about fifteen minutes of running, I stop by a rusty stretch of cyclone fence to catch my breath. My chest puffs out when I breathe in and collapses when I breathe out. My breath rips at my throat, and my legs are numb.

On the other side of the fence, some guys are carting around a load of lumber with an enormous forklift. I watch the men for a minute. The guy driving the forklift is tall and thin, and his bright orange hardhat sits up high on his head, making him look even taller. He's got huge teeth, which I notice because he opens his mouth wide every time he talks. His partner is short and heavyset, with black stubble thick on his face, and a dirty leather tool belt wrapped around his waist. The man with the tool belt is trying to guide the man on the forklift between two stacks of concrete blocks. The forklift edges forward, then backs up, then edges forward again, the ends of the lumber scraping against the concrete. The short man goes red in the face and starts yelling, but the man in the forklift just laughs and laughs. The forklift jerks forward, and lumber smacks against the concrete, sending the entire stack of wood clattering off the prongs of the forklift and into the mud. The tall man's face lights up with laughter, and I can't watch anymore.

I've socked my own dad, and yelled at him, and run off for the second time.

I'm still holding on to the sheet of paper that Dad threw at me, so I look down at it and feel sick to my stomach. My battle plan.

I remember about Mr. Gojjam and his screaming on the television, and how I caused that screaming. Dad knows what I did. Probably all of

Gruff Valley knows what I did—Ronald, Bruce, Little Greta. And Mom? I hope, I hope, I hope Dad did not tell Mom. I think about how hurt she'd get if she knew I hurt the Ethiopians, and that makes me hurt. I wish Alan had never had his stupid invasion idea.

I crease the battle plan down the center and rip it. Then, I rip it again. When I think about Alan, the muscles in my jaw get tight.

Rip.

Alan, who always said he was my buddy.

Rip.

Alan, who made me disappoint Dad and Mom and everyone.

Rip.

Alan, who ruined everything.

I toss my shredded battle plans into the air, and they drift around on the breeze like snowflakes before falling to the ground. I shift the strap of my duffel bag onto my other shoulder and take a deep breath. I cannot go to Mom, because of Dad. I cannot go to Alan, because. So I've got Barbara. And after that?

"Shut up," I whisper to myself.

I look back at the men in the lumberyard, and they're re-stacking the wood onto the forklift. The short man is chewing out the tall man, but the tall man is just smiling and shaking his head.

"Let's see some hustle," I whisper, just like Dad used to say to me. "Let's see some hustle," I say again, louder, as I hug the duffel bag against my chest. I've got to get to A Panini for Your Thoughts. I've got to get to Barbara.

***

"Oh my gracious," I say as soon as I round the corner to the restaurant. A Panini for Your Thoughts looks the same as ever but, across the street, where there used to be a Rasta-Raunt, there is some sort of metal skeleton, with shreds of burnt-up walls sagging off it. All the grass on Mr. Gojjam's property has gone black, and all the windows are busted up. Through the windows and the holes in the walls, I can see inside to what's left of the kitchen and dining room. The floors and tables and counters that used to be gleaming white and steel are covered over with grey ash. This restaurant can never be the same restaurant as it was before it got destroyed, and thinking that thought makes a sad lump collect in the back of my throat.

I walk up to the front door of A Panini for Your Thoughts, but even though I'm not looking at the Rasta-Raunt anymore, I can't get the image of the Rasta-Raunt out of my mind. When a bug gets smushed, it's the same bug as before, only tragic.

Our glass front doors are boarded over with plywood, and suddenly I remember the Rasta-Raunt wasn't the only restaurant that got smashed up that night. My heart feels the tiniest bit lighter. Maybe we aren't the bad guys after all. I was so woozy and terrified that night. Maybe something else happened altogether—maybe a terrible enemy came by and smashed up our restaurant and the Ethiopians' restaurant both. Then I could tell Dad it wasn't my fault, and I could be buddies with Alan again, and everything would work out right.

The minute I step into the dining room, I am grabbed.

Hands pat my back. Hands pat my legs. Hands reach under the lapels of my suit jacket and feel my chest and my ribs. Hands grab my duffel bag and other hands rap on my shoes.

"What's in the bag?" says one of the men who's patting me down.

"Hold everything!" says another man before I can answer. "It's Thor."

"Apologies, sir!" says one of the men, and the hands stop. There were three men patting over me, all of them wearing A Panini for Your Thoughts uniforms and dark sunglasses. I only recognize one of the men: Mr. Uno.

"Hey, Mister Uno," I say. "What's going on?" I look out over the dining room, and even though nothing's too different from how it used to be, I feel different from how I used to feel. The same kinds of customers are eating the same kinds of food, but they seem nervous or depressed to be here. Everything is shiny clean, but maybe too clean, like you'd get yelled at if you spilled a little marinara sauce. I catch a glimpse of a blonde ponytail—Mandy-Mandy's, I bet—as it swishes back into the kitchen.

"In these troubled times, *signore*," says Mr. Uno, "the security of our restaurant-nation has become our concern *principale*. There's the Albanian threat, and the British-Egyptian fusion *ristorante* has been particularly menacing. We do security searches now," he says, and thumps his chest, proud.

I see the blonde ponytail come back into the dining room, and I'm about to yell out a greeting to Mandy-Mandy when I realize that the woman with the ponytail is not Mandy-Mandy. This woman is a little plump and her face is round and rosy. A few more waiters and waitresses come out right on her heels, none of them folks I know. They're all blonde and healthy-looking, with blue eyes and firmness in the way they walk. All the men are clean-shaven, which makes me reach up and feel my own stubbly cheeks. I would not fit in with these employees; they all look clean and muscled, like Mr. Hans.

"Who are all these new people?" I ask, clutching tight to my money bag. "Where's Barbara?"

Mr. Uno grabs onto my shoulder and leans his face toward my head so his lips are almost touching my ear.

"It is good to see you, Thor," he whispers, "but I would not let Tony Rigatoni see you here, mein herr. You are lucky that he has a meeting this morning, but I would not linger."

"Who are all these Germans?" I ask, watching as one waiter carries out a Plautinus Pastrami to a couple of Beach People, makes a stiff little bow, turns on his heel, and walks quickly back to the kitchen.

"There are no Germans here," says Mr. Uno, and he clears his throat.

"You called me 'mein herr,'" I say.

"I did not call you 'mein herr,' *signore*," says Mr. Uno. "I called you '*signore*,' *signore*."

"Why did ..." I start saying, and then stop. The waiters and waitresses are marching out of the kitchen in a line, all stepping at the same time, and all twirling baguettes around in their hands. I turn to Mr. Uno to see if he will explain this to me, but he is watching the new blonde staff march around, proud, like he is the happy father of every last one of these waiters.

"Ah, the twenty-ninth," says Mr. Uno, rubbing his hands together. "There is artistry in order, *signore*."

"The twenty-ninth what?" I say. Some of the customers are watching the waiters march around and spin their bread, and other customers are trying to eat their meals without watching—but even the customers that are trying not to watch can't help glancing up from time to time to look at the dance routine, or whatever it is the waiters are doing. "Where's Barbara Hackbush? And why shouldn't I let Mister Tony see me here?"

"The Twenty-Ninth Waffen Grenadiers," says Mr. Uno. "Such a staff-army was never before seen in our Gruff Valley."

One of the waitresses stomps and thrusts her baguette in front of her, like she's pretending to stab a horrible enemy. She bares her teeth and looks up with her blue-green eyes, and immediately I recognize Mandy-Mandy. She must recognize me too, because her eyes open up wide and she breathes in a gasp of surprise. She looks away and keeps on going with her routine, but now she's a step or two behind the others. Mr. Uno makes a "tsk" noise and shakes his head.

"I'm not sure how much longer she'll be with us, *signore*," he mutters at me. "Her precision is not always what one might hope."

I wonder how Barbara's precision would stack up, and this makes me worried. I'm not so sure what Mr. Uno means, but if there's some sort of skill that is important for making money that Mandy-Mandy hasn't mastered, I can't imagine that Barbara, what with all her ailments, would be doing much better.

"Where's Barbara?" I ask again, but Mr. Uno puts his finger to his lips.

"The best part is coming up, *signore*."

The waiters spin their baguettes a little bit longer, and then the baguettes get slammed onto customers' tables. Next thing I know, the waiters have all pulled out long bread knives from their belts and are chopping up the baguettes into little slices with speed I've only seen before from Remus and Romulus. Some of the customers laugh and applaud, but most look terrified.

"*Ausführung!*" screams one of the waiters, and the entire staff stops cutting. Everybody bows to the customers and marches back to the beverage station. I catch Mandy-Mandy's eye, and she makes a beckon at me by jerking her head to the side before disappearing into the kitchen.

"Wonderful military exercises," says Mr. Uno, "would you not say so, *signore*?"

"Oh yeah. Very great, actually, but I am going to go say hello to

Mandy-Mandy and Remus and Romulus."

"Okay," says Mr. Uno, "but Tony Rigatoni will return in an hour or so, and if you are smart, you will be gone long before then."

I frown when I hear that, but I don't ask Mr. Uno any more questions. I pick my way through the dining room, trying not to whack plates off of anybody's table with my duffel bag, and remember all the times when I used to walk around the dining room with plates of food instead of with two million dollars.

I push through the swinging doors to the kitchen, and the place is swarming with clean-cut German-looking folks. I see skinny guys with muscles dressing salads and plump pigtailed women positioning parsley garnish on plates of Fettuccini de Medici. I scan over the crowd, looking for Mandy-Mandy, but with all the blonde, she doesn't stand out the way she used to. A tall fellow with clear eyes and a smooth face brushes by me on the way to the soups. I am about to ask him where Mandy-Mandy went, when I am almost pulled off my feet by something that whacks into my legs. I steady myself and look down. I start laughing. Remus is hugging onto my left leg, Romulus is hugging onto my right leg, and they're both looking up at me like I'm a hero.

"Thor!" says Remus, squeezing tighter on my leg.

"Thor!" says Romulus, squeezing tighter, too. The twins are hugging right on my knee joints and it hurts, but I'm so happy to see them that I just reach down and tousle up their hair. I dig my fingers under their arms and try to get them to loosen up their grips some.

"How've you been?" I ask them.

"Good," grunts Remus, and it's my turn to talk again.

"Behaving yourselves?"

"Yeah," says Romulus.

"Where's Alan?"

"Jail," says Remus.

"Jail?" I say, pulling on my tie. I try to frown, but I'm kind of happy, and I think my cheeks go red. Alan deserves to be in jail. He destroyed the Ethiopians. He made me hit Dad.

"Where's Barbara?" I ask, and a bell rings off by the panini station.

"An order!" says Romulus, and he lets go of my leg right away. He hits Remus, who lets go of me also.

"An order!" repeats Remus, and the twins scurry off to their sandwich station to start putting together whatever order the waiter rung in.

Jail. Iron bars. Rats running around everywhere. Stone walls with moss creeping around through the cracks and onto the floor. Some sort of awful cot that's only an inch thick and crawling with spiders.

"Psst, Thor," says a soft voice over my shoulder. I turn around and see Mandy-Mandy, but she whispers, "Don't look at me," so I turn back around and stare at the dishwasher churning out suds from its boxy metal body.

"I'm on break as soon as I buss off my tables. I'll meet you in the walk-in in two minutes."

I hear Mandy-Mandy walk back to the dining room, and I frown at the dishwasher. The dishwasher gurgles and clatters at me, so I stick out my tongue at it. We never used to get breaks, but I guess now, what with all the new wait-staff, it's possible to take a break. Mandy-Mandy must be furious—break-time cuts into tip-time.

I haul my duffel bag with me into the walk-in freezer and, while I wait for Mandy-Mandy, I look over the shelves of food. Everything looks just like it used to: stacks of beef patties, bags of chicken thighs, vacuum-packed cartons of spinach and mixed veggies, and clear plastic tubs of rainbow-colored gelato. I rub my hands together and blow on them, my breath drifting around my face like I'm a smoke-breathing creature. I try to make my breath into a smoke-ring, but I can't give it any sort of shape.

The freezer door opens; Mandy-Mandy walks in, looking more tired and run-down than I've seen her before. She's got worry wrinkles wriggling around on her forehead, and her eyes are underlined by dark crescents. Her hair doesn't shine like usual.

"Thor, what in the name of holy God do you think you're doing by showing yourself around here?" she asks, shutting the door behind her and wiping her hands on her apron. "Are you a verifiable lunatic?"

"I don't get what's the big deal," I say, casual, even though I can hear my heart thudding in my ears. "I work here."

"Thor," says Mandy-Mandy, putting her hands in her pockets and bouncing up and down a little for warmth, "the boss will not be happy to see you here."

"The boss is in jail."

"Thor," says Mandy-Mandy, and her eyes lock onto my face and start drilling into it, "do you really, honestly not see what is going on here? Alan is not the boss here."

"Tony Rigatoni is the boss?"

Mandy-Mandy bellows in laughter and bends over a little, like laughing is hurting her stomach. She laughs, but her laugh isn't a happy laugh—it's a hopeless and desperate laugh.

"Tony Rigatoni," she says, "is not Tony Rigatoni."

I raise my eyebrows, hoping that Mandy-Mandy will just come clean and tell me, with no muddle or mystery, what in gracious she is talking about.

"'Tony Rigatoni,'" she says, "is the silliest, most contrived pasta-themed alias I have ever encountered. The man you like to call 'Tony Rigatoni' is a scheming usurper and, yes, he's the boss here and, no, he will not be all sunshine and roses to see you, Thor."

I lick my lips, which are starting to tremble due to the cold. My legs are shaking too—though I'm not sure if it's owing to the cold or the confusion. I prop myself against a case of frozen ravioli and nod for Mandy-Mandy to go on talking.

"How to explain this to you?" Mandy-Mandy asks herself, rolling her eyes up to the greenish fluorescent tubes that light up the walk-in. "Alan is a businessman, but not a particularly smart one. Alan made choices that Alan no doubt regrets. Alan is rotting in prison, which probably he deserves, but I would say Alan is more so a bumbling moron than a villain."

I grip a little tighter to the ravioli.

"However, I guess jail time is just what you get for meddling with Germans," says Mandy-Mandy.

"With Germans!" I say.

"Tony Rigatoni is as Italian as tomato sauce, seeing as the tomato plant wasn't imported to Europe from the New World until fifteen nineteen and, even after that, was thought to be poisonous and so was used exclusively as decoration until well into the eighteenth century—in other words, marginally Italian at best."

"Jeez," I say. I think about Mr. Hans's blonde hair and crazy accent.

Mr. Rigatoni doesn't seem like him at all.

"Are you aware of the Sauerkraut Kitchen?" Mandy-Mandy says, glaring at me so strong I feel like I've done something I ought to be ashamed of. I nod, because I feel like she wants me to, but then realize I'm not aware of whatever Sauerkraut Kitchen it is she's talking about.

"No."

"*No,*" she says, and mutters some words at the ceiling like she's praying to gracious. "The Sauerkraut Kitchen? The fastest-growing Central European franchised eatery in the Continental U.S.? The most profitable hospitality corporation of this decade, whose powerhouse business model is fueled by its extreme efficiency, the unmatched loyalty of its staff, and its ruthless and voracious appetite for market share?"

"Oh yeah, sure," I say, nodding, as I rub my cheeks for warmth. "The Sauerkraut Kitchen. Yeah."

"Thor, your cognitive deficiency is an epic and catastrophic ..." but she breaks off her thought with a sigh. I have never once seen Mandy-Mandy stop herself in the middle of an insult, and I can feel the hairs on the back of my neck standing up like porcupine quills.

"That's not important right now," she says, glancing at her watch and frowning at it, "and I cannot afford to be back late from break." She looks down at the ground and chips at a hunk of ice with the heel of her shoe. "I'm up for review."

"*You*? Can't you just tell them you're going to punch their lights out or grind up some bread or something?"

"Shut up, Thor," she says, looking back at me, red in her cheeks. "These are tough times, and these Germans don't go easy on anybody. Sure, my scare-tactics worked on Alan, but it takes a lot more than focaccia in a food processer to make these Hessians flinch.

"Thor, Alan fell hook, line, and sinker for these dopes. Alan is a spinally-disinclined nincompoop. Alan thinks, 'If you can't beat 'em, join 'em,' which is the motto of somebody predisposed to failure. Mandy-Mandy says, 'If you can't beat 'em, you're a weak and pitiable waffle-head.'

"Alan thought that, rather than fighting tooth and nail against the unstoppable wave of progress that is the Sauerkraut Kitchen, he could trust Regional Manager Anton Richter—Tony Rigatoni, as you know him—far enough to enter into a tactical alliance with him. I guess Alan thought that, if he and the Germans could team up against some weaker enemies, then A Panini for Your Thoughts would be proof against German expansion. Alan, like you, Thor, is a slobbering fool who does not realize that trust is not a trait that results in success."

"Actually," I say softly, looking down at my hands, which are starting to go white from the cold, "I am not a slobbering fool at all."

"Shut up, Thor!" Mandy-Mandy screams, suddenly wet-eyed. "This is what happens when people make idiots of themselves! Hard-working go-getters that have their eyes on the prize go up for review." She clamps her lips shut, but I can see her face straining like she wants to say something. I start to shiver so bad my bottom teeth start clacking up against my top teeth.

Mandy-Mandy opens her mouth, but what comes out is not a sentence or even a word, but some kind of bone-shaking wail. Her face loosens up, and the wetness in her eyes starts running down onto her cheeks in thin streams. I pat her shoulder, but she flinches away like my fingers are charged with lightning.

"I'm fine," she snaps.

"So I guess the invasion didn't go so great?"

All of a sudden Mandy-Mandy is laughing again, but, again, not like she really thinks anything is too funny.

"Depends on who you ask," she says, wiping her eyes on the back of her wrist. "Sure didn't go so good for Alan. He got his restaurant smashed up and overthrown by Anton Richter's staff-army of Bavarian street thugs and then got locked up for an arson that he wasn't even in favor of in the first place. But if you ask the Germans? Sure. I'd say they'd tell you the invasion went precisely according to plan."

Mandy-Mandy looks at her watch and starts crying again. I have never seen Mandy-Mandy look so un-cute before, with her eyes running water, and her nose sniffling, and her makeup smudged around.

"And why am I even telling you all this?" she says, her voice husky with sadness. "I'm already late from my break, and I'm going to lose my goddamn job."

I reach out to touch her shoulder again but remember she doesn't like it, so I put my hand in my pocket and just look at her, not really knowing what would be the right thing to say. I want to ask her where Barbara is, but I don't think it's the right moment. Instead, I unzip my duffel bag and pull out a stack of bills. I don't know how much money I've grabbed, but there's so much money in the bag that I feel like I can spare some.

"Mandy-Mandy," I say. "I don't want you to lose your job, but here's some money in case maybe you do." I hold out the stack of bills to her, and she stares at the money, fascinated and afraid.

"Holy shit, Gunderson," she says, her eyes big and round and terrified. "Where did you get that?"

"It's from business."

"It's not from business," she says, taking the money out of my hands, carefully, like it might bite her. "I don't know what it's from, but I have my misgivings about whether or not it is likely to be from anything good."

"No, it's fine. I helped a German."

Mandy-Mandy ruffles through the stack of bills I gave her, and frowns at it. I have never seen Mandy-Mandy frown at money before, and suddenly I get an awful churning in my guts.

"You helped a German," Mandy-Mandy says to herself, her breath curling around her face in the cold air of the walk-in.

I hear somebody rattling at the door of the refrigerator and zip my duffel bag back up just before a slim blonde fellow with a red face and a feathery mustache walks in. He looks at Mandy-Mandy, who's stuffed the money into her back pocket, and looks at me, and frowns so hard his whole face crinkles up.

"This is not recreation-time," he says to Mandy-Mandy. "This is work-time."

"I understand," Mandy-Mandy says, not looking him in the eyes.

"Understanding," says the man, as he walks to the shelves along the wall and pulls out a carton of frozen meatballs, "is not evidenced in words, but rather in actions. If you understand that this is not recreation-time, but rather work-time, then your actions will fall in line with that understanding, and you will therefore cease recreating and commence working. Is that logical to you?"

"Yes," says Mandy-Mandy, through clenched teeth. "It is impeccably logical."

"Good," says the man, and his frown disappears. He even smiles a little, happy for being so logical. He hoists the box of meatballs onto his shoulder and starts out of the walk-in. Before he's fully out of the door, he turns to Mandy-Mandy and says, "Your continued employment at A Panini for Your Thoughts can be said to hinge intimately on your airtight understanding of such logical principles." He gives Mandy-Mandy a salute and heads back into the kitchen.

"God," says Mandy-Mandy, still looking down at the frosted-over floor of the walk-in. "Times are tough, Thor. Times are tough as holy hell. They let us keep our name and our menu, but we're through-and-through German. I'd give us another month or two, tops, until A Panini for Your Thoughts is just another Sauerkraut Kitchen."

I inhale, then exhale, trying to breathe the nausea out of my stomach. Home is not the same anymore. Work is not the same anymore. I have to find Barbara.

"I guess you've got to get back out there, then," I say to Mandy-Mandy.

"Yeah." She sighs, shudders a bit, either from the cold or just from emotions, and pulls the money back out of her pocket. "You'll have to take this back, Thor."

"Oh no," I say. Thinking about Mandy-Mandy passing up money makes me feel like earthworms are squirming all over my skin. "It's for you, you know, in case things don't go so good with the Germans."

"Thor," Mandy-Mandy says. She pushes the money up against my chest with one hand and latches onto my wrist, firm, with the other. She stares at my face so forcefully I have to look away to the stocks of chicken thighs, frozen spinach, and premade cobblers. Mandy-Mandy lets go of my wrist and grabs me by the chin, forcing me to look her in the eye. I squirm, but I bite my lip. I'm tough enough to listen to whatever she has to say to me.

"You are a good guy, Thor," she says. "You are an idiot, but you are a good guy. We're not all such good people."

"Oh, that's not true."

"Shut up, Thor. You may be a dunderhead, but you know as well as I do that I've been a snarling bitch, which snarling bitch is the persona necessary in order for me to achieve success in business matters."

"Oh, I wouldn't call you that."

"Thor," says Mandy-Mandy, and she squeezes my face with such strength I can feel her nails digging into my cheeks. Pain-tears sting at my eyes. "There are times when I look at you and wish I could be as honest-hearted as you are, and so you have to promise me that you will please, please, please take this money, whatever it is, and wherever it's from, and run far, far away from here to someplace where a guy of your character has half a shot of possibly succeeding."

The pain-tears are joined by some other kind of tears. I open my arms to hug Mandy-Mandy, but she pushes my chest so hard I stumble backwards.

"I do not want you to hug me," she says. "I want you to promise me."

"Sure, yeah," I say, but Mandy-Mandy shoving me reminded me of the way I shoved my own dad, and I know that no matter how far away I go, that's something that will always make me less honest-hearted than Mandy-Mandy thinks I am.

I hold out some money to Mandy-Mandy once again, but she just shakes her head at the offer.

"I can't take it, Thor. Please … just find somewhere to be happy."

She wipes her palms on her apron, sighs, and attempts a smile. Her eyes are dull and sad, not sharp and greedy like usual, and I feel gumminess at the back of my throat.

"Hey, Mandy-Mandy," I say. "Where's Barbara?"

Mandy-Mandy's eyebrows shoot up in surprise.

"Hackbush? Ha. Hackbush couldn't hack it," she says, and a clever, mean little smile shows up on her lips. "Hackbush is out on her cute little redhead ass."

"I need to find her. Where is she?"

"Bullshit, Thor. You don't need to find her; you need to take the money and run. This Hackbush is gone, but you can find another Hackbush wherever you go. I guarantee it."

"I love her. I love her and I'm going to run away with her."

"Oh, Lord. Thor, I am a woman at work, and I have already jeopardized my employment by standing here and yapping with you, and if you are too dense to understand that Barbara Hackbush is a weepy and unimpressive specimen, then I am not going to further put my job at risk by pandering to your moony-eyed illusions." Mandy-Mandy has blinked away whatever tears were in her eyes before and is now staring at me with all that cold cruelty I'm used to.

"Barbara Hackbush," says Mandy-Mandy, "has learned that Opportunity is just about as real as unicorns, and I would estimate that, if you were really such an unambiguous fool as to go hunting for her, you could find her hauling her patootie down the road, back to Kansas."

"Back to Parker who wronged her?" I say, my heart dropping into my feet like a ten-ton weight.

Mandy-Mandy sighs and frowns. "Just between you and me," she says, cracking open the door to the walk-in, "I would not hold your breath for Miss Barbara Hackbush." Mandy-Mandy slips back into the kitchen and shuts the refrigerator door behind her, leaving me alone in the frosty interior with my bag of money hanging heavy off my shoulders.

I drop my duffel bag to the floor and sit on top of it, covering my face in my hands. I want to disappear. I want to leave Gruff Valley and never have anybody think about me ever again. I punch at the duffel bag and wish it would disappear, too. Dad's gone cruel. The restaurant's gone German. Barbara's just gone.

And here I am, Thor, by myself with nothing left to feel good about.

Over the whirring of the refrigerator's cooling unit, I can hear the dishwasher clattering away out in the kitchen. I can hear plates clinking against one another and people calling out to each other, probably letting each other know that orders have come up or new tables have come in. Out there, people are working and having fun and being together, but I'm not. I'm stuck. I've got nowhere to go. I'm crying, and I don't know when I started, but I don't stop myself. I hunch myself over to try and warm myself up, and let myself cry and cry, because what else is there to do?

"Oh, Thor," says some woman's voice. "How about you do not cry but actually take steps to make your situation better, and all?"

I look around, but I don't see anybody. I cock my head to the side, hoping I'll hear the woman speak again, but it's so quiet and still in the walk-in that I think I must have imagined the voice.

"Hello?" I say quietly.

"Thor," says the voice, "you will not find me if you look for me. Maybe you recognize my crazy accent?"

"Francesca!" I say, a smile spreading onto my face. "What are you doing here?" I keep my voice low, out of habit.

"Thor, you silly young man, I'm not here. I'm in your head, of course. You know that, don't you?"

I smile and nod. "I'm glad you spoke up just now. I'm really in a sticky spot."

"No, you aren't," says Francesca. "You *think* you're in a sticky spot because you're a coward. But let's look at what we have here, shall we? You cannot go home right now, because you were aggressive with your father."

"That was bad," I say, chipping some ice off the floor.

"That *was* bad, but it is in the past and you cannot fix it right now. We must think about what you can do *right now*."

"Okay."

"You cannot go back to work, because Mister Tony, or Mister Anton, or whoever it is, is not somebody to trust."

"And plus Mister Uno says he's mad at me."

"And plus Mister Uno says he's mad at you, yes. But you have two million dollars, and you have Barbara."

"But Barbara's run off."

"So find her."

"But she's got a pretty big head start," I say. I look down at the ice I've been chipping away at and realize I've written Barbara's initials on the floor without even thinking about it.

"If you cannot catch up with her on foot, then you must find another way."

"But I can't drive."

Francesca is getting mad. "How about you stop saying 'but,' Thor? You either love this woman, or you do not. If you love her, you will be a man and find her—and if that means you have to learn to drive, then it means you have to learn to drive."

"Do you really think so?" I dry my eyes with my wrists.

"Only a scared little boy would think any other way."

I know she means me, so I slap my knees, stand up, and sling my duffel bag back onto my shoulder. "But I don't see any scared little boys in *this* refrigerator," says Francesca. "Do you?"

"*I sure don't,*" I whisper, and I grin. Every muscle in my body feels strong and full of energy. I can feel my blood whooshing around in my veins, and I feel like it's whispering a message to me: whatever you do, act now before you can think about it. There's a rental car place next to the locksmith near my house. If I show some hustle, I can be there in ten minutes. "I sure don't!" I yell out loud, and slam open the walk-in door. I race out into the kitchen, dodging clean-cut blonde men and women carrying trays of food. On my way out, I catch sight of Mandy-Mandy, so I grab her around the waist, smile at her, and give her a kiss on the cheek.

"Good luck, Mandy-Mandy," I say, louder than I intend. "Good luck, good luck, good luck."

I let her go and have just enough time to notice her mouth is hanging open in wonder before I sprint out of the restaurant without waiting for a reply.

***

"I need to see a driver's license," says the old woman behind the counter at the rental car place. Her name tag tells me her name is Stella, and her deep frown tells me she is not happy to see me, sweaty, out of breath, and still wearing the now-rumpled suit I got from Mr. Hans.

"I don't have mine with me, but I need to rent a car, owing to it's an emergency."

"If it's an emergency," says Stella, sucking her lips into her mouth like she wants to protect them from me, "then I advise you to call 9-1-1."

"It's a big emergency."

"You need to calm down, kid."

"Look," I say, leaning over the counter and pretending for a minute I'm as discreet as Ronald Harpoon. I shift my eyes to each side, lower my voice, and glower. "I got this situation going."

"I will call the police if you don't get out of here," says Stella. She also shifts her eyes to the side and glowers, matching me at my game. I don't move, but I don't say anything more. I lean heavier onto the counter and tell myself to think faster. I bounce the duffel bag on my shoulder and think about knocking Stella with it and running off with a set of keys.

"How much does it cost to rent a car?" I ask to buy myself time. "A cheap car?" I look at the pegboard full of keys behind Stella.

"I will count to five," says Stella, also leaning onto the counter. I can see big blue veins like worms on the back of her wrinkly hands. "And if you are still here, I will call the police and have you hauled off."

"Please."

"Five," says Stella, with a smirk starting to form. She likes being tough with me, so I guess I have to be tough with her.

"I don't want you to get hurt, but this is bad news for you if you keep counting."

"Four."

Could I really hit Stella with this heavy bag? She is old, and her bones are probably not too strong. I bet it would really hurt her. I bounce the bag on my shoulder again. If I swung at full force, she would snap in half like a breadstick. There would be blood and cracking and I don't know what else.

"Three," she says, picking up the telephone.

I'm staring at her, shaking, and I need to either hit her, or leave, or something, but I cannot remain standing here, leaning over the counter like some scared boy. I haul the bag up into my hands. I will swing it, who cares, nothing matters, I need to get to Barbara.

"I would not recommend you do what you are thinking about doing," says Stella.

"I don't want for us to get hurt," I say. I let go of the bag and grab one of Stella's hands with both of mine. "Please, let's think about what we can do for each other."

Stella starts laughing, cruel and false. "Oh?" she says, meanness making her old face ugly. "And what can you do for me?"

Not whack you. Not break you in half. Not push you over and take whatever car I want.

"I don't know," I say. My ears blaze. Stella's eyes shine. "I just need this so much."

One of Stella's fingers dances a little circle over the buttons on the telephone, teasing me. She stretches the corners of her mouth out to the side of her face in a flat smile. Every last one of my muscles tightens up.

"What's in the bag?" she asks, jabbing the "9" button and then letting her finger hover around the "1." "Anything good?"

"Just money," I say, keeping an eye on Stella's finger.

Stella's wrinkly brown lips form into a tiny "o," and I feel my lips do exactly the same thing. Money. Of course, money.

"I will pay you a thousand dollars."

Stella's eyes race to the front door before returning to my face. Her finger, no longer floating over the telephone, is now making a beckon at me to lean in further, so I do.

"Two thousand," she says, her old, meat-smelling breath making me draw back a little. "And I want to see it."

I haul the duffel bag up onto the counter and shield it with my body as I drag open the zipper just far enough to show Stella the money inside. Her smile gets wider but stays just as flat.

"In back," she whispers, and points at a little door marked "MANAGEMENT."

I move to the door behind the counter, while Stella shuffles quickly to the glass-paned front door, draws the deadbolt shut, and positions a small, black "CLOSED" sign in the window. While I wait for her, I rock all my weight to the front of my toes, and then back onto my heels. I keep rocking, forward and back, as she fishes around in a small pocket on the chest of her blouse and pulls out a big metal key. She unlocks the door and makes a beckon at me to go inside first.

Inside the office are a couple wooden crates set up like some kind of desk and covered with papers. Faded old posters of cats—some dressed up in ties and sunglasses, some batting at low-hanging Christmas ornaments, and some cuddled up in baby blankets—hang on the walls. All the staring cat eyes make me nervous, and I look back to Stella, but she does not notice the cats at all. She motions at my duffel bag, like she doesn't want to talk to me, so I unzip it and pull out two stacks of money.

I hand over the money, and Stella counts through it, silently and slowly. I keep up my rocking, wishing Stella would hurry up. I need to keep pushing on. I need to get to Barbara. The longer I delay, the more I worry I'm going to go chicken.

What will I do after I stop Barbara from going back to Parker? First, we will go to the best hospital around and get her checked out for every possible ailment, and pay whatever it takes to get her better. Then, I will write a letter to Mom and tell her how sorry I am for hitting Dad and how, if they will only just forgive me, they can move in with me and Barbara, and we will have all this money. Barbara and I will find a beautiful house looking out over the ocean, and when Mom and Dad move out to our mansion, I will get Remus and Romulus to come over and cook up the biggest feast ever, with bacon and pesto and milk and juice, and everything any of us want. We will sing and be happy, and I will take whatever money is left and open up a brand new panini restaurant with sparkling red floors and stainless steel kitchens.

"Fine," says Stella with a nod. She opens up a tiny metal safe in the corner of the room and crams the money inside.

"Please," I say, fighting to keep my fantasy clear and happy in my mind. "I need a car now."

Stella doesn't say anything, but walks out of the office, back to the counter. I follow her and watch as she pulls a key off the pegboard.

"Automatic transmission okay?" she says, dangling the key just beyond my reach.

"Sure—transmission is fine."

"Get out of here," says Stella, and she tosses the key over the counter and onto the ground. I have to bend down to pick it up. "It's the green sedan along the back wall. The rear window is cracked, but it runs fine. Have it back tonight or you're toast."

I bounce the key in my hand, about to say, "Thank you," but I stop myself from saying anything. I don't want to thank Stella, and I don't want to see Stella, so I turn around and head out silently to the parking lot.

Wandering around to the back of the building, I see a line of cars parked right up against the wall. I see a couple of little green cars, but only one has an ugly spider-web crack spread across the rear windshield. I run my hand along the metal surface of the trunk. I'm glad that the car is so small, because I don't know how I'd feel about running a big, monstrous truck around on the road. I feel like my little green car will keep me safe and low to the ground.

I unlock the trunk and drop my duffel bag inside. Then, after wiping my palms on my wrinkled suit pants, I let myself into the driver's side and slide behind the steering wheel. The car looks completely different from the driver's side. The console, usually trusty on my left side, is now trusty on my right side. If I want to look in the mirror, I have to look over my left shoulder instead of my right. Worse, I've got numbered dials staring up at me like I'm supposed to know what to do with them. I buckle myself in and reach out to pet the dials, like maybe this will make them friendly to me. I reach out my feet and find a couple of pedals down underneath the dashboard. I step on one and then on the other, but nothing happens. I'll just have to start up the car and trust my luck.

Thankfully, I remember watching Mr. Hans drive his flashy red car, so I try to do whatever it is he used to do. First, I put the key into the keyhole and twist. The car twitches a few times, then growls and makes a satisfying "on" roar. I twist the key again, just to be sure, and the car grinds and squeals in a way that Mr. Hans's car never ground and squealed, so I stop twisting. The car stays on, though, so I try out the pedals again. One makes the engine roar harder and the needle of one of the dials lift up; when I press on the other, the pedal presses back, so I suppose it's the brake.

I smile at myself in the rearview mirror. I'm getting the hang of this. Now, I look at the console. The big lever in the middle has been pulled into a position marked with a "P." Other letters mark other positions. I try to remember what letter Mr. Hans would pull the lever to when he wanted to go backwards. "D" is for "Drive" and "N" is for something else, so I tug the lever into the "R" position. "Rearwards"?

My mouth goes completely dry as I carefully, carefully, put my foot down on the speed pedal. Success! The car backs away from the wall, an inch at a time, and I am driving! I am driving a small green car, and I will rescue Barbara, and we will run away together in this small green car!

Backing up, I have to look behind me and in front of me at the same time, so I check out my cracked back windshield, then whip my head around to look out the front windshield, and then back up an inch and stomp on the brake pedal. Check behind, check in front, inch back, and stomp. Check behind, check in front, inch back, and stomp. I'm not making great time, but I'm staying safe and staying out of trouble, both of which are important when it comes to rescuing Barbara.

Finally, I'm all the way backed out of the parking spot, and I'm ready to make the car go forward. I move the lever on the console from the "R" position to the "D" position. The car makes another grinding whine and gives off another shudder and, suddenly, instead of inching backwards, I'm inching forwards. I try to keep my breathing steady as I pull out of the parking lot and into traffic.

Driving, I figure out, is not so hard. Even though I am in a hurry to get to Barbara, I know the most important thing is to stay safe and under the radar, so I keep in the right lane and jerk along pretty slowly, keeping the speed needle hovering between the mark for fifteen and the mark for twenty. The car does not go smoothly, the way that Mr. Hans's did, and every time I stomp on the brake pedal to slow myself down, the car squeals and shakes, and I can feel my ribcage flying forward, but I breathe steadily and continue onwards. Other cars honk and roar past me, but that is not important.

As I drive along, I pass familiar places—the blue cinderblock storage units, the trailer park with the friendly rainbow sign at the entrance, and the paint store where I used to go with Dad to watch Mr. Maher mix the colors together—but they look slightly different, owing to I'm driving past them instead of walking past them. It takes me about an hour, inching forward and then stopping, and inching forward and then stopping, to get out to the big eastern highway on the edge of town. The road widens out, and there aren't so many buildings and trees out this way, so I can see out for miles and miles along the road. I push down a little harder on the speed pedal, and the speed needle crawls up to thirty. My heart pounds with excitement. The open road, and me in charge.

I cruise along, keeping my speed where it is, and try to relax. The mesas and mountains all glow bright orange in the early afternoon sun. I wish I had Mr. Hans, or at least his crazy German music, to keep me company, so I start humming under my breath. After a while, humming isn't enough, so I start singing quietly. Eventually, even that isn't enough, so I get louder and louder, until I'm singing at the top of my lungs. I try to remember the nice German song that Mr. Hans sang to me at Renegade Cowboy's mystery shack, but I can't get the tune in my head, so I just sing the songs I know, about dragons, and moonlight, and tears. I start singing the song about the postman and remember how sad Mom was the last time we all sang it together, and I don't feel like singing anymore.

Sometimes, big trucks rumble by me and honk with tremendous force. I wonder where they are all going. What a life! To drive around the country in a big and powerful machine, honking at anybody you think is too slow! How would Barbara like it if I became a trucker?

As I drive, I keep my eyes trained on the shoulder of the road, looking for any sign of Barbara. Sometimes I see cacti and trashed-up trailers and smashed coyotes, but I don't see any people. The desert keeps rolling on and on as far as I can see, glowing yellow, but getting more and more orange as the afternoon drags on.

"Where are you, Barbara?" I say to myself, but of course I don't know the answer.

The shadows from the mesas grow long and purple as the sun starts to sink down low in the sky. The desert sands darken from orange into red. Where will Barbara sleep tonight? Is she going to curl up against a sand dune somewhere? Or will she keep walking through until morning?

"Oh, Barbara," I say out loud. I try to get the image of her cold and alone and hungry out of my head, but I still see her lying in the dark desert night, the only person for miles and miles, thinking about what a long walk she's got before her until she makes it back to Kansas.

I see a little red dot far up ahead on the shoulder. Barbara? Then again, maybe I'm only seeing what I want to see, but ... as I inch closer in my small green car I keep seeing this red dot. In fact, I begin to see that the small dot is a head of hair attached to a body. I get closer and can see that this person has got a green rucksack strapped on to her back and that she's speed-walking toward the east. I bite on to my lower lip, but I can't stop the smile that breaks onto my face. Barbara!

I honk the horn. I wait a second and then honk again, and the walker turns around. I see her face and, of course, it is Barbara, looking every bit as kindly and lovely as always. When she realizes the honk came from me, and that I am behind the steering wheel of a small green car, her mouth drops open with amazement. She lets her rucksack fall off her shoulders, and it sends up a cloud of dust into the air when it hits the ground. After this moment of shock, her face lights up with a wide smile, and she starts jumping up and down and waving both of her hands at once. I can't hear her, but I can tell from her mouth that she is yelling,

"Thor! Thor!"

I pull up onto the shoulder, giving Barbara plenty of space, and pull the lever on the console into the "P" position. I twist the key in the ignition, but I hear an awful grinding sound from the engine, so I twist the key the other direction, and the car shuts off. I throw open my door and rush out to Barbara. She is rushing toward me, and we meet together in a huge hug that makes me want to melt happily into the ground and spend the rest of my life with Barbara as some puddle by the side of the highway.

Barbara's breath is warm on my neck, and I give her shoulders a squeeze as we keep on hugging.

"I'm so glad I found you," I say. "You can't go back to Parker."

"Oh, Thor," says Barbara, her voice thick and sad but somehow happy, too, "I have to go back, because how could I not? You know what I mean?"

"No, I don't know." The sun slips down behind one of the mesas in the distance and gives it a halo of bright yellow light.

"Because, Thor, that restaurant you left is not the same kind of restaurant that's left now. It's all awful these days, and what's left back in Gruff Valley?"

"I know. I've been back there, and, yeah, it's awful, but that doesn't mean you have to go back to Parker."

"Well," says Barbara, finally pulling away from me. She glances down at the ground so I don't have to see her teary-eyed, and then gazes out at a point way off on the horizon. "I'm just dying to hear what all options you would say are exactly available at this current point in time, you know? Because I don't know about you, but personally, I am suffering from any number of acute ailments at present, and money does not grow on trees or under the ground or even, really, in planters on top of the unemployment counter. When times are tough, a woman has to go where she knows she can keep herself healthy, and if that 'where' just so happens to be the home of some certain individual whose name I will not spoil our current how-do-you-do by mentioning, then it seems to me that, without some kind of miracle or good fortune that does not actually happen to real people in reali—"

"It's a miracle!" I say, and pull Barbara back into a hug, though she doesn't hug me back this time. Barbara feels slack in my arms, so I let go. She's looking at me, confused, with her eyes squinting and her lips slightly apart.

"Are you making fun of me?" she says, her head cocked to one side.

"No." I feel my legs shaking under me. "You know that German I told you all about? And how there were these two million dollars?" I try to take a deep breath, but the breath doesn't get very far into my lungs before I hear myself already talking again. "I'm going to rescue you, Barbara, and together we'll get this restaurant! There'll be pesto, but maybe I'll be a trucker. Oh, and the ocean. We're going to live by the ocean! Rich, basically!"

Barbara takes a few steps back and almost looks scared of me. I try to fight the smile off my face. I try to look like some cool cucumber, suave and romantic, like sweeping women away into romantic situations is the sort of thing I've been doing since I was ten years old, but I can't stop myself from shaking.

"If you are making fun of me," says Barbara, "then I don't think this is the sort of humor that I am especially eager to respond to."

I do not trust myself to say anything.

"But if this is some real, genuine situation," she goes on, staring, "then I guess you'd better start by telling me what this is all about, and where you got that car, and, well, everything, really."

"Well," I say, fighting to get my words out clear and reasonable, "it is just so incredibly good to see you, you know?"

Barbara smiles, a little uncertain. I smile back at her, not sure what to say for now, and hoping my smile is saying everything for me. Neither of us says anything, and we stand out by the side of the road, as cars and trucks rumble by, and as the air gets cooler and cooler, smiling—her smile shaky but hopeful, and my smile huge and loving and squeezing tears out of my eyes. I take Barbara's hand in mine and hope she can't tell how much it's trembling.

Finally, a swarm of birds passes overhead, cawing and flapping, and something about this must strike Barbara as funny, because her timid smile bursts open and she presses my hand, hard, as she laughs and laughs. I laugh to see her laugh, and she leans against my chest and wraps her arms around the back of my neck.

"This is crazy, Thor," she struggles to say through her laughter. "Look at us! We are crazy people, in the middle of a crazy desert."

"Yeah."

"And if you are lying to me, Thor, I will never ever, ever, ever forgive you."

"Barbara, I would not lie to you. We are rich people."

Barbara sniffs and looks up at me, her eyes brown and beautiful. "If we are rich people, then I guess maybe we should get ourselves a place to sleep tonight, instead of making ourselves prey to wolves and coyotes and whatever else we might find out in a desert like this, huh?"

"Yeah," I say, and pat Barbara on the top of her head. She grins at this, so I grin back. "Yeah. Let's maybe find a motel. I'm getting good at driving this car."

"And on the way you can tell me all about your adventures and our happy future life and why we are rich people?"

"Yeah. And tomorrow we will take you to a real doctor and get rid of those ailments once and for all."

"Oh, Thor," sighs Barbara. She pushes her lips against mine and we are kissing. My whole face feels warm against Barbara's, and I realize I've closed my eyes without even thinking about it. I wrap my arms tight around Barbara, and she wraps her arms tight around me, and I know that, no matter what, we are together and in love. Even though we both want to find a place to stay for the night, I don't want to let go of Barbara, so I keep on hugging her and letting her kiss me, happier than I ever thought it was possible to be.

***

I lie on my soft hotel bed, staring up at the clean, white ceiling. I see me and Barbara sitting on a stone wall, looking out at the ocean. I try to think that story through to its end, but it's already changed: now me and Barbara are running through a green field full of bright purple flowers. Now we are kissing in front of a warm fireplace. Now Remus and Romulus are holding up a velvet cushion with a gold ring at our wedding. Now Barbara is meeting Mom and Dad, and her cheeks are rosy and radiant on account of modesty.

There's a knock on my door, and I'm back in my hotel room in the desert. I check the clock by the side of the bed, and it's nine-thirty at night. I walk to the door, the thick hotel carpet rubbing nicely on my bare feet, and open it to find Barbara.

"Couldn't sleep?" I say. I didn't want to make Barbara feel awkward, so I got us separate rooms when we checked in. She seemed happy about that, so I know I did the right thing; we have the whole rest of our lives to share a room, so I don't want to rush.

"I'm just so happy," she says, yawning big and looking more tired than happy. I step out of the doorway so Barbara can come into my room if she wants, but she stays standing in the doorframe, looking in at me.

"Well, I'm happy too," I say. "Really happy."

"Yeah," says Barbara. She looks at my feet, and I wiggle my toes, nervous. Usually Barbara's got more to say.

"You're the most beautiful person," I say, "and we're going to be so happy to be together."

Barbara smiles, but her eyes stay glued to my feet.

"I wish I was as good as you, Thor," says Barbara, and she sounds so lost and sad my heart up and empties.

"You're plenty good, Barbara," I say, touching her elbow. "You're the best woman, and the prettiest and most wonderful."

"Oh, Thor," she says, and I see thin, teary trails on her cheeks. "Oh, Thor."

And Barbara's shaking like a volcano ready to burst, and then she does burst, and she starts crying and crying. I wrap her up in the strongest hug I can give as she shakes and shudders and buries her face in my shoulder.

"It's okay," I say, brushing some of Barbara's hair off her forehead. "Don't cry. This is the start of some big, great thing that's romantic." I kiss her forehead, which feels hot and maybe a little feverish. Maybe it's making her self-conscious to have me watch her cry, so I look out the doorway of the room into the badly lit hallway. I look at the design on the carpet—little golden bunches of grapes—and up at the fluorescent tubes on the ceiling. I look back at my bed and its rumpled blankets, and then out the window into the dark night. Some headlights sweep over the room, making everything orange, and then they disappear.

"Oh, Barbara," I say, and kiss her forehead again. "Cheer up."

"Thor," she says, still with her face buried into my shoulder. "Do you realize you're the only guy what's ever been good to me?"

I don't know what answer she wants, so I give the honest answer: "I didn't realize, but I could have guessed."

"I'm sorry," she says, and peels her face off of me.

"Don't be sorry."

"Don't tell me how to be."

"I'm sorry."

"No, *I'm* sorry." She kisses me gently on my lips. "I mean, I'm really sorry."

"Hey, you can cry however long. That's not going to stop me from thinking you're the best woman."

Barbara looks over my shoulder to the clock next to my bed, and says, "Holy Jeez, it's only ten and I'm exhausted."

"Do you want to come in and we can make coffee, or have a glass of water?"

Barbara squeezes my shoulder and kisses me again, this time on the cheek. She rubs at her own cheeks with the back of her sleeve to dry up all the tears.

"I'd better get some sleep," she says. "Whenever you think about me, think good things, okay?"

"I can't think anything else but good things about you, Barbara. You know that."

"Oh, Thor," she says, and kisses me on the cheek again. "I hope you sleep real good."

"You too."

"Can I have the car keys?" Barbara asks. "I left my backpack in there, and I need my toothbrush."

I take the keys from my nightstand and hand them over. Barbara looks me in the eye for a second and seems like she's about to say something, but then she sniffles and looks down at my feet again. She hurries out the door and shuts it behind her so fast I don't even have time to give her a goodnight wave. I think about going after her, but I don't know if that's what she wants. This is all so difficult.

I go to my window and look out. The sky is black, but the stars make up sparkling patterns of light. I try to make designs out of the stars by connecting them together in my mind as I wait to hear Barbara go back into her room. I connect four stars to make a square. I attach a triangle to the square, and it's a house. The house shape-shifts into a squirrel. The squirrel is now a tiger.

I finally hear Barbara's door open and shut, and I check the clock. It's ten thirty already. I wonder why it took Barbara so long to get her backpack. Maybe she needs to be alone for a while to deal with her rough thoughts. I look back out at the stars and wonder what Mom and Dad are doing tonight. I need to get back to being their son. I don't know how long it will take the doctors to fix up Barbara's ailments, but as soon as that's done, I will go back home with so many apologies. I look at the slick phone on the nightstand and think maybe I should call Mom, but after how I left this morning, I need to be really sure what I want to say when I talk to Dad again, and I'm not ready yet. Tonight, I just need to be happy that Barbara's in the next room over, that we've got enough money for the best doctor in the state, and that nothing broken can't be patched up.

***

When I wake up, it's four in the morning and lights are flashing red, white, and blue right outside my window. I hear a knock on my door and the voice of a nervous woman.

"Mister Gunderson?"

"Barbara?" I say, even though the voice isn't Barbara's. My stomach is sinking into my mattress. I seize my blanket with both fists and squeeze my eyes shut.

"It's Lucky from reception," says the voice outside my door. "There are some people here to see you."

"Is it Mom?" It's not Mom. Whoever it is, my skin is telling me it's somebody I don't want to see.

"It's two gentlemen, Mister Gunderson. They're waiting for you in the lobby. I'm so sorry. I'm to see you down."

Even with my eyes shut, I can tell that the colored lights are still flashing outside my window. I'm not going downstairs. I wish Barbara and I had stayed in the same room after all.

"Mister Gunderson? Will you come with me?"

I open my eyes and rap on the wall that my room shares with Barbara's. Then, I realize she's probably still asleep and wish I hadn't knocked. I press my ear against the wall, but I don't hear her moving around. I guess I didn't wake her.

"Mister Gunderson, you really need to come with me."

I wish I hadn't said anything when I first heard the knock on my door; then I could pretend I wasn't in the room. Who comes for a visit at four in the morning? Two gentlemen? Remus and Romulus? Shouldn't they be asleep? Mr. Uno and Mr. Due? Maybe. Alan and Mr. Tony? But Alan is in prison.

"Mister Gunderson."

"Oh, I'm so sorry, ma'am, but I'm just not in the mood for company right now, it being the middle of the night and all."

I slide out of bed and look out the window at the parking lot below. The red, white, and blue lights are coming from a cop car parked a few spaces away from my rental car. Oh no. Where there are cops, there are bad guys.

"Mister Gunderson, your guests have made it very clear that if you won't come down to the lobby, there will be a great deal of trouble. They said that you'd be cooperative, though."

I look down at the concrete parking lot. If I get the window open, I could maybe jump down and get to the car without hurting myself too badly. But Barbara's got the car keys, and I couldn't leave her here. Whatever's going on, it's an emergency, so I rap on her wall again and hope the wall is thin enough that I can talk to her through it without Lucky hearing.

"Mister Gunderson." Lucky's voice is soft and kind. "I'm so, so sorry. Will you please come with me? If there's a fuss, everyone will be disturbed. Your guests are really very friendly. Please don't be nervous."

Barbara isn't answering my knocking, so I have to try another way.

"Barbara!" I yell as loud as I can, pounding on the wall. "Barbara, wake up! Wake up! It's an emergency!"

"Please keep your voice down. Your friend, Miss Hackbush, has already checked out."

I pause, my fist mid-air, ready to strike the wall. The air feels thick. I let my hand fall to my side, but it moves slow, like it's moving through water. My eyes swim to the door. Lucky's voice drags on, slow and dreary. Monstrous.

"I called a cab for her three hours ago. Didn't you know? She left you a note. Please come down to the lobby. I don't want to bring the police up here. It'll wake everybody up. They seem so nice. They just want to talk to you. They said they know you. They told me to tell you not to be scared."

I look at my hands, and they are somebody else's hands. I flex my fingers, but it takes too much energy to keep them straight, so I let them droop again. Barbara's hands are white and dotted with freckles. If she were here, I would take her hand and look for constellations in her freckles. I'd tell her about all the pictures I saw in her freckles, and maybe she'd be embarrassed and start blushing, and then I'd kiss her on the cheek, happy. Together, we'd break through the window and run out to the car like we were stars in a caper movie. We'd change our names and drive forever.

"I'm so sorry," says the door. "There's really no way out, you know. We've got the entrances guarded. I'm so sorry."

I take a deep breath. The air is cold in my lungs. Wherever Barbara is, I hope she at least took the money with her, because it's all over for me.

I shuffle to the door. Should I put my shoes on? Maybe if I stay barefoot, I won't have to go to the lobby.

"Can I see the note?" I ask, pressing my mouth up to the crack between the door and the doorframe.

"Can I give him the note?" says Lucky to somebody. I hear a few people moving around outside, and then Lucky says, "Here you go."

A little white envelope pokes its way through the crack under the door. "Thore" is written in big, black letters across the front. I bend and pick it up. I rub my thumb along the side of the envelope. I want to open it, but I also don't. The envelope is holding in something awful; once I open it, I will never be able to get that awful thing back inside. That awful thing will be out there in the world forever.

I bite down on my tongue until it hurts and rip open the envelope.

"Should I get the master key?" asks Lucky to somebody.

Inside the envelope there's a note written on a piece of hotel stationery. I have to squint to read in the dark room, but Barbara's handwriting is huge: "Dear Thore,"

"Mister Gunderson," says Lucky, "if you don't come out, I'm afraid we'll have to come in."

"Come on out, Thor," says a male voice from out in the hallway. "It'll be okay."

I keep reading:

"Your a guy whats been good to me and I remember it. Actually your are to good. You are not some slimeball like Parker, you are a real good guy."

I hear a key wiggle around in the lock on my door. The door opens, and light from the hallway spills onto the stationery in my hands. I glance up and see the small woman from the front desk massaging her hands together, nervous. Bruce Billington is standing next to her, wearing his sunglasses and, for once, not smiling.

"Hi, Bruce," I say, and keep reading:

"But I am not good like you and so Im so so so sorry because you deserve a good woman whats not going to run off on him. And I do not deserve a good guy like you, I deserve a slimeball like Parker so whenever you get sad think about me and how I'm way more sad because I am with a slimeball but would rather be with a good guy like you."

"Thor," says Bruce, and he touches my elbow, gentle but firm.

"I did not take all the money because I am not that bad but I took some of the money because I know thats what you want for me even though I don't deserve it."

The letter goes onto the backside of the stationery, but I've read all I want to. I look up at Bruce and see myself reflected back in his sunglasses.

"Will you come with me, Thor?"

"Okay," I say. I look down at my hands and discover I'm tearing the letter into little bits.

Bruce nods at Lucky, who smiles unhappily and backs away down the hall.

"We're going to go on a drive," says Bruce, "so I think you should get your shoes on."

I drop the bits of letter onto the carpet and they scatter over my feet as they fall.

"I don't need my shoes."

"We're not coming back here," says Bruce.

"I don't care."

"We can't go anywhere until you put your shoes on."

"It's okay. I can stay here."

"No, you can't stay here."

"Why not?"

"Because you're under arrest for grand theft auto. So we have to go to jail."

"Okay."

Bruce stares at me, and I stare at my feet. The carpet feels nice on them, but not as nice as my blue carpet at home. Will I ever see that carpet again? Will I ever see Mom and Dad again? I wonder what it must be like to be Bruce Billington, strong and good and always smiling.

"Are you going to put your shoes on for me?" asks Bruce.

"Okay."

I go to the bed, still drifting along like I'm floating in the ocean, and pull on my right shoe and then my left shoe. They feel heavy on my feet as I float back across the room. I glance at the mirror on my way to the door, and I can tell that the suit I've been wearing around for two days now is way too large. Bruce is holding out a pair of handcuffs, and the metal shines in the light of the hallway.

"I don't need these, do I?" he says. "You're going to come peacefully?"

"I guess so," I say, as I drift towards Bruce. I take his hand, and his grip is strong and certain. I don't return the grip, but I let my hand rest limp in his. We're walking down to the lobby, or Bruce is doing all the walking, and I'm floating along next to him, attached to him like I'm an extra leg. After we've passed through the lobby, we're out in the parking lot, and there's another cop—Ronald—holding my other hand.

"Hi, Ronald," I hear myself saying.

Ronald nods sharply.

We get close to the squad car, and the whole world becomes red, then white, then blue. Ronald opens the back door for me. The lights darken deep shadows on his face, and my ears buzz with fear.

"What's jail like?" I say.

Ronald just shakes his head.

"We all thought better of you," he says, and shuts the door.

Bruce and Ronald get into the front seats. Some kind of cage keeps the back seat separate from the front seats, and I want nothing more than to be up in front, in the driver's seat, or at least the passenger's seat. The back is where the bad guys—the miserable, sad, and wrong guys—sit, but up in front is where you sit if you don't get arrested, if you don't go on invasions, if you don't get violent with your own Dad, if you're somebody that is worthy of loving the most beautiful woman in the whole world and having her love you back. I lean my face up against the cage as Bruce starts up the car and drives us out of the parking lot and back to the highway.

"Can I sit up front?" I ask. "Please?"

Ronald turns around to face me, his sunglasses black and horrible.

"The front seat isn't for you."

"Just try to get comfortable back there," says Bruce. "It's a long ride back to the station. Maybe get some rest, because it'll be a long day. Ronald is going to tell you your rights."

Ronald starts speaking, and I try to pay attention to what he's saying, but he isn't talking like a friend; he's saying some kind of list that he seems bored by, like it's a list he says twenty times a day. I don't want him to tell me this list. I want him to tell me everything will be okay, that we'll be friends, that we'll find Barbara, that nothing broken can't be patched up.

But Ronald keeps on talking in his same monotone, and I want to cry, but I feel like there's not a drop of water in my whole body. I feel like there's nothing inside me but tired space. No heart, no bones, no muscles. And I shut my eyes.

***

When I wake up, the horizon is just starting to lighten up, and we're pulling up to a dull, boxy building surrounded by double-thick chain-link fencing with barbed wire coiled on top. A bunch of men in baggy orange clothes are walking around in a line on a big gravel field.

"This is jail?" I say.

"You'll be here for a while," says Ronald, as Bruce parks the car.

"Okay."

"You're going to have a talk with Officer Louie Justice, okay?" says Bruce.

"Okay."

The cops get out of the car and open up the back door. I slide out, and Bruce and Ronald get on either side of me and hold my arms as they walk me into the dirty brown jail building. I let myself go slack as the cops lead me into a concrete lobby with exposed light bulbs giving off glaring white light. I watch armies of brown spiders tumble over each other as they try to climb up the legs of an old wooden desk. Ronald lets go of my arm to write something down in a dusty book that's sitting on top of the desk, and then he and Bruce lead me through the lobby into a smaller room with a bent lamp in the corner. Ronald disappears while Bruce remains standing in the doorway.

"Ronald's getting you a change of clothes," says Bruce. "Do you like orange?"

"Sure," I say. There's a hard little bench jutting out from the wall, so I sit. I put my face in my hands and hope that Bruce won't keep talking to me.

"You didn't mean any harm, right?" says Bruce.

"I don't know."

"We've been looking for you ever since that invasion. You didn't know what you were getting into, right?" says Bruce.

"I don't know." A spider finds its way up to the bench with me, and I swat at it.

"Why did you take that car?"

"Barbara."

"Who's Barbara?" asks Bruce.

I swat again at the spider, and I guess I kill it.

"I'd rather just not talk right now."

"Okay."

Ronald comes back with a neatly folded bundle of orange clothes. He hands the clothes to me, and I look at them and set them next to me on the bench.

"Thanks," I say.

"You're going to have to put those on now," says Ronald.

"Oh, okay."

The cops step out of the room for a minute, and I take off the suit Mr. Hans gave me and put on the orange clothes. The new clothes are baggy and comfortable, but I don't like the way the fabric rubs on my skin. I try to fold my old suit up neatly, but I wrinkle the pants, so I unfold the suit and try again. Still, the buttons on the shirt don't quite look even, so I unfold and try again. As I'm folding the suit for the third time, Ronald and Bruce come back in.

"How would you like to talk to Officer Justice?" asks Bruce. "He's really excited to talk to you."

"I'm sort of busy." I don't like the crooked way the collar sits, so I start folding the suit again.

"We'll fold those and hold on to them for you," says Ronald.

"No, I'll do it." The more I try to get the folds to look good, the more of a mess I make of them. Ronald and Bruce are breaking my concentration.

"But you need to talk to Officer Justice now," says Bruce.

"Leave me alone." I unfold the suit so hard that I pop one of the buttons off the shirt. I flap out the shirt and try to get it to fold even.

"Thor," says Bruce, "the better you behave yourself, the easier it will be to get you out of here soon."

"I don't care."

"You will care," says Ronald.

"No, I won't."

Bruce grabs the shirt. I try to hold onto it, but he yanks, and the shirt flies out of my hands with a ripping noise.

"You tore it."

"Let's go," says Ronald, and the cops are on either side of me, pulling me off the bench and leading me forcefully out of the little room. I don't want to go with them, so I try to make my feet heavy, but every time I drag my feet, they shove me ahead and tighten their grips. I hear myself screaming at them, but I don't get any kind of response. They keep shoving and frowning, and the more I scream, the tighter they hold me.

Ronald and Bruce march me down a damp stone corridor lined with heavy-duty metal doors. At the end of the hallway, there's a small red door. Ronald opens the door and pushes me through, and I find myself in a white-tiled room with dull orange lighting and a fold-up metal table in the middle. A mammoth man in a cop outfit is standing at the table, going through a folder full of papers. When he sees me come into the room, his smile pushes his cheeks up into his eyes, and I don't like him. The man rubs a huge hand over his stubbly chin and then comes around the table to shake my hand.

"I'm Officer Louie Justice," says the man in a loud, deep voice. "It's a pleasure to meet you, Mister Gunderson."

I look behind me to Bruce and Ronald, but if they notice me looking at them, they don't make any sign of it.

"I'll handle everything from here," says Officer Justice to Bruce and Ronald.

"Thank you, sir," says Bruce.

"Go easy on him, sir," says Ronald. "He's a good kid."

"I'm not a kid," I mumble under my breath so that nobody can hear.

"Go easy on him?" says Officer Justice, spreading his arms apart wide. "We're just going to have a chat. We're going to be great friends," he says to me with a phony wink, and gestures at a folding chair in front of the table.

I look at Bruce and Ronald again, but they back out of the room without saying anything more. The door shuts with a cold, echoing slam. I shiver and stare at the cracked concrete floor. A circular orange stain takes up part of the floor nearby, and I step onto it to see if it is bigger than my foot. It is.

"Have a seat," says Officer Justice.

"No, thanks."

"Oh, Thor," says Officer Justice, like we've been friends my whole life. He grasps both my shoulders and, nicely but surely, guides me down into the folding chair. "I'm eager to be your friend, you know that?"

I think he wants an answer, but I'm not sure.

"We're both on the same side, you know?" says Officer Justice. "Everybody says you're a good guy, and I try to be a good guy, too, in my way." Officer Justice touches his chest with both hands as he circles around me, and I hate him.

"I think we both only want what's right, am I correct?" he says.

I stare up at him. With me sitting and him standing, his mountainous body looks like a solid wall of blue fabric and gold buttons.

"Thor," says Officer Justice, and he bends down so his hard blue eyes are staring right into mine. "It's hard to be friends when you won't talk to me."

"Sorry," I say, hoping that this will make him stop staring at me. It doesn't work—he keeps his eyes locked on mine and, even though he's smiling, his eyes look mean.

"Thanks for that," he says, trying to sound happy. "I appreciate it. I really do."

I shift around on the folding chair, and it squeaks under my weight. The air in the room is damp and tastes like cardboard.

"I appreciate," continues Officer Justice, finally turning his glare away from me, "that you are willing to communicate with me. That means a great deal, you know?"

He again clutches my shoulders and his stare is worse than ever. I close my eyes, but then realize it makes me look like a coward, so I open my eyes again and try to stare Officer Justice down.

"So, how about I pull up a chair?" Officer Justice says. He lets go of me and drags over a folding chair from against the wall. He puts the chair right in front of me and eases himself into it, like he's afraid he'll break it if he sits down too fast.

"How about I sit right here, and you tell me where you ran off to after you laid waste to Mister Bogale Gojjam's business enterprise?"

Officer Justice leans forward in his chair so his forehead is only a few inches away from mine. His warm breath hits my face. I don't answer. I wrinkle my forehead. I make my eyes as mean as I can. I try to make my breath hit Officer Justice's face as hard as his breath hits mine.

One of Officer Justice's giant hands snares my chin and starts to squeeze. I feel my cheeks caving together. I ball my hands into fists and try to not feel any pain. Officer Justice keeps squeezing, and I wonder if maybe my jaw will shatter. My eyes fill up with tears, but I'm not going to make any noise.

"Are you aware that we have a copy of an extremely sensitive document that was discovered in your room?" Officer Justice asks. "Are you aware that this extremely sensitive document indicates to me that you were central in the planned arson of the Rasta-Raunt?"

I think about the Big, Big Anvil. I think about the waves out at the beach, lapping softly on the sunny coast. I think about lemonade. I think about the days when Mom and Dad and me were happy and together. The pressure on my face doesn't let up.

"Are you aware that we have reports of you threatening an employee at the rental agency and making off with a stolen automobile?"

Officer Justice is wearing a thick gold ring, which presses painfully on my cheekbone. I think about Barbara. I try not to think about Barbara. I think about Barbara.

"Are you aware we have evidence of you having trafficked stolen cultural artifacts?"

I gurgle with surprise, and Officer Justice immediately lets go of my face. My hands fly up to my cheeks and start massaging the feeling back into them. I feel myself starting to blush, and I wish I hadn't made any noise.

"Didn't think we knew about that one, huh?" says Officer Justice, like he's my friend and he just caught me out in something embarrassing.

"I don't know."

"You don't know?" Officer Justice chuckles and smacks my knee. "Well, I'll tell you who *do* know. The people of France. The people of France know. The people of France are hopping mad. It's like somebody tinkled in their collective brie."

"What about the people of France?"

"So you're into game-playing now? You're into the concept of obfuscation?"

"Sure, yeah. What happened to France?"

"'What happened to France?' he asks," Officer Justice says, forcing out a fake guffaw. His wide face fills my whole vision, and his breath smells like stale coffee. "Obfuscation it is, then?"

"Sure," I say with a shrug. "It's that."

"Good," says Officer Justice, smacking my knee again. "Good. Well, my friend, if you don't care to lay bare the nature of your malfeasance, then permit me. Does the name 'Tintoretto' ring a bell?"

"No," I blurt out, then, "wait—yes. He painted *Chronos*." The thought of that old, lonely man in the painting makes my skin shrink.

"He painted *Chronos*, indeed, as well as *The Annunciation of the Virgin*, and numerous other works with which I don't intend to concern myself today. My interest in Tintoretto ends with the two plundered works you recently unburied and carelessly foisted onto an unsuspecting Swiss art dealer."

"Plundered?" The word seems like a bad one, and I feel my face flushing with anger at Mr. Hans.

"Plundered indeed, my friend—sacked from a prominent Breton gallery by Nazi forces in the summer of 1940 and, from that time, unknown to their rightful owners until last night, when they were traced to a receipt of sale in your hand. In short, Thor," he says with a terrible wink, "between grand theft auto, premeditated arson, and high treason— trafficking in the spoils of a long-dead war—I would say that, if you haven't already found a religion that appeals to you, now is the time to begin the hunt."

With force I didn't know I had, I'm on my feet and flipping over the table. Officer Justice's papers fly every which way. I grab Officer Justice by both shoulders and try to shake him.

"That was Mister Hans! That was Mister Hans! I don't know anything about Nazi paintings!"

Officer Justice flies to his feet and wrenches my arm behind my back. Tears flood into my eyes as he grinds my arm further up along my back. My shoulder is going to pop out of place.

"Assaulting an officer of law," he says, with a calmness that drives me into frenzy, makes me thrash and kick, "is not an ideal way to suggest your innocence."

"It was Mister Hans! I hate him! I hate him, and I hate you!" I want to say something terrible, something cruel and hurtful and terrible, but I don't know words mean enough to express how full I am with anger, so I just keep screaming, "I hate him! I hate him!" as Officer Justice yanks me out of the room, shoves me down the hall, and gives my arm one last twist before he flings me into a stone-walled room as small as the front foyer at A Panini for Your Thoughts.

A heavy metal door slams shut behind me, but I'm too furious to take stock of my surroundings, so I rush to the door and pound at it and pound at it and pound at it.

"Let me out!" I scream, and continue to pound, ripping up my knuckles on the hard metal door. "Let me out! Let me out! Let me out!"

But Officer Justice is gone, and it's just me and the door.

But I don't care.

So I keep pounding and yelling until I can't pound and yell anymore. And when I can't pound and yell anymore, I slump down to the floor, make myself as small as I can, and try to shut off my brain.

***

Some time later, a trap door opens up and a plate of grey mashed potatoes gets shoved through. I fling the mashed potatoes at the wall like a snowball. Later, the trap door opens again. Somebody asks for my plate, but I don't hand it through. Whoever is on the other side of the door starts hollering at me. Some big men come in my room, take the plate, and shove me around. The door's closed again, and I'm alone.

***

I'm shouting and shouting that I need to pee, but if anybody on the other side of my door hears me, they don't care. I notice I have a mossy toilet in the corner of my cell, along with a cracked sink and a rusty bunk bed with thin, smelly mattresses. I keep yelling, but my bladder is so swollen I don't think I can wait any longer. I walk to the corner but, instead of peeing into the toilet, I pee all over the floor and the base of the sink. I feel good about it for a minute but then realize nobody's around to see, so whoever I wanted to annoy won't even know what I did.

***

I want more mashed potatoes or something else to throw. I try to lift up the bunk bed, but it's bolted to the ground.

***

I kill another spider and figure I should probably keep track of how many bugs I've killed. So far, two. There's nothing for me to keep a tally with, so I have to remember. Two.

***

Three.

***

Four and five. I think they were maybe mating, but whatever they were doing together, they're not doing it anymore.

***

Do I forgive Alan? I don't. Do I forgive Dad? I do. Do I forgive Mr. Hans? I don't. Do I forgive Barbara? Do I forgive Barbara? Do I forgive Barbara?

***

I'm lying on the bottom mattress, which smells like wet dog. I flip onto my back. I flip onto my front. I roll over to one side, and then to the other. In some places, I feel lumps; in others, the mattress is so thin I can feel the wires of the bed frame underneath it. My pillow is stiff and reeks like moldy old eggs. I close my eyes. Something, somewhere is dripping. I open my eyes. Drip. Drip. I close my eyes. Drip.

***

"Time for exercise!" says some guy who's standing in my doorway.
    I roll my eyes up to look at his face. His mouth is huge and his blonde hair is slicked down and parted tidily. It takes too much energy for me to keep looking up at him, so I let my eyes roll back down to look at the

floor.

"Come on, buckshot!" he tells me as he steps up to the bunk and puts a soft hand on my shoulder. "Don't you want your exercise? Don't you feel well?"

Would it take more energy to answer his question or to just go with him?

"Let's go get some sunshine," he says. "You'll feel better after exercise."

I take a deep breath and pull myself up into a sitting position.

"That's the way, buckshot," he says. Even without looking right at his face, I can see this guy's huge, white smile. "That's the way."

I reach out and take hold of his arm in both of my hands. He pulls me off the mattress and then drapes one of his arms around my shoulders. With his other hand, he clips a pair of handcuffs onto my wrists. The metal is cold and heavy on my skin.

"A formality," he says, as he guides me out and into the corridor. I see other guys in handcuffs and orange outfits being guided around by other men. Something about the sight of so many people makes me tired and sad, so I lean a little more weight on my guide. He smells clean, like orange-spiced cologne.

"You're new here," he says. "My name's Don Christian. I've heard you didn't get on too well with Officer Justice, but that's okay. I'm the one who's going to look after you, and I believe in giving everybody a chance. Just between you and me, Officer Justice sometimes brings out the worst in people. Do you know what I mean?"

Don Christian leads me out onto a large gravelly lawn full of rusty metal gym equipment and fellows in orange suits. I don't want to talk—I just want to keep on listening to Don Christian—but Don Christian doesn't seem to be expecting me to say anything, anyway.

"You get fifteen minutes out here today," he says, unclicking my handcuffs. I immediately start rubbing the warmth back into my wrists. "If you behave yourself, like I know you will, then you'll get more and more time every day. How's that sound?"

I rub my eyes. Sunlight seems brighter than I remember it being. I look at all the guys in orange outfits running around, throwing balls to each other, and smoking cigarettes by the chain-link fence. I don't want to be with them. I want to stay with Don Christian and listen to him talk.

Don Christian throws his head back and laughs happily. He rubs his knuckles between my shoulder blades and points out at the yard.

"Go on, buckshot!" he says. "Go have a good time. Go get some exercise. You'll feel better; I swear it!"

Don Christian gives me a light shove, and I wander out into the gravel yard like I'm in a dream. Nobody seems to pay much notice to me, and I don't pay much notice to anybody in particular. I don't know anybody, and all their faces blur together for me. The best thing to do is not get in anybody's way, so I make my way to the fence, keeping my distance from the smokers, and sit down on the ground. The sun is too bright for my eyes, so I stare at the gravel. I pick up a handful of pebbles and let them rain down through my fingers. Another handful, another rainfall.

"Thor!" says a familiar voice.

"Yeah," I say, without looking up.

"Of all the most flummoxing coincidences in the history of God's holy earth," says the voice. A body sits next to me, and a man's hand is on my knee.

"Yeah," I say.

"Oh, for the love of Christ's crown of thorns, would it kill you to bowl me over a tad more with a warmhearted appreciation for the reunion of old friends?" The person sitting next to me is Alan, of course.

With effort, I pull my head up so I can look Alan in the face. He looks thinner than I remember, his cheeks sunken in and his eyes wide and fearful. He smiles at me, but his smile seems panicked and crazy. This is a guy I once knew and thought was my buddy.

"I'm just not in the mood right now," I say.

"Oh, imprisonment," says Alan, and he laughs in a higher-pitched voice than I've ever heard him use. He giggles and giggles and I start to think about gathering up enough strength to walk away. "Imprisonment has a way of corroding people's moods. Not mine, of course. I'm having a blast." Alan explodes into giggles again and stuffs his hands against his mouth like he's trying to push his laughter back into his body.

"That was a joke," he says, nodding at me ferociously. "You're allowed to laugh."

"It's not funny," I say. Alan grips onto my knee again, harder. His fingernails are nibbled down all the way to the pink.

"You know," says Alan, "two days ago, I was furious with you. If I'd seen you then, there's no accounting for what I might have done. It's a good thing I didn't see you. Leaving your battle plans lying around in your room for anybody to see? Pretty foolish, Crafthor. *Pretty foolish.*"

Alan giggles again. I grab his wrist to force his hand off my knee, but he keeps a firm hold on me like holding on to my knee is the only thing keeping him sane.

"But that was the past, Thor," he says, leaning his head onto my shoulder. I shake him off. Feeling him touch me makes my skin crawl. *"That was the past.* A few days of compulsory reflection have done wonders for my mental acuity, and I've realized this: I'd still be locked up in this, ahmmm, reformatory, even if the police had never found your battle plans. I trusted the Germans not to double-cross me, and the Germans double-crossed me, and you were just as much a pawn as I was. So, in short," Alan says, trying again to lean his head on my shoulder. I push his face away harder than I did before, but Alan just smiles at me. "In short, Thor, I forgive you."

I feel a hot flash of anger in my chest.

"I'm the good guy," I say, quiet and angry. "You're the bad guy. They locked me up. Leave me alone."

I drop my chin to my chest so I don't have to look at Alan. If I see Alan's face again, I don't think I'm going to be able to keep my anger stuffed into my chest.

"Oh, Thor," says Alan, putting his awful arm over my shoulders. I squirm, but Alan doesn't move his arm. "We're both the good guys. We're two good guys who got told a lot of lies by the guys who aren't good. If the world were just, they'd set us free and they'd lock up the guys who deserve to be here. They'd lock up Tony Rigatoni—well, Anton Richter ... that's his name, you know? And they'd lock up Hans Hess. And they'd set us free."

Curiosity edges in on my anger.

"How do you know about Mister Hans?"

"How do I know about Hans Hess?" Alan giggles again, like I asked a stupid question. He pulls his arm tighter around me, and I latch onto it and wrench it off my shoulders. "Hans Hess is the brains, Thor! Hans Hess is the *man at the top*. Hans Hess is the CEO of the Sauerkraut Kitchen. Hans Hess is worth billions. Hans Hess is worth trillions. Hans Hess has built up an empire of capital off the ruin of others."

"Hans Hess lied to me about *Chronos*!" I yell. Blood runs into my face and I hear it pounding through my ears.

"You've met Hans Hess?"

When I don't respond, he keeps talking. "Well, Hans Hess has lied to a lot of people about a lot of things. Us good guys who stay honest? We get locked up—which is not a complaint, not in the slightest conceivable interpretation a complaint because, you know, it really is pleasant here. Reposeful. But, it's all my way of saying we, the honest folks, get locked up, while the inveterate liars and scoundrels—they are untouchable."

"Hans Hess should get locked up," I say, sort of to Alan, sort of to myself. I look out at the orange guys wrestling each other out on the exercise yard, and that sharp orange color keeps bleeding into everything else. My hands are orange. The sky.

"It's true, it's true," says Alan, giggling, his voice going higher still. "Hans Hess *should* get locked up!" Alan presses his lips against my ears and starts whispering fast. "But Hans Hess won't get locked up, you know? Hans Hess owns this prison." He pulls his lips away from my ear and screams out for the whole world to hear, "Hans Hess owns the entire federal justice system!" Alan laughs and laughs and laughs.

I realize I've got my neck tensed, and I'm holding my head up stiff. My shoulders are so tight I've got them hiked almost to my ears.

"Don't tell me," I say.

Alan leaps to his feet and starts giving me shoves on the shoulder.

"Oh, Thor, but it's just the truth!" Alan shoves me hard and I flinch.

"Don't tell me."

Alan springs to one side of me and then to the other, as if he can't decide where he likes to be. He puts his head over my right shoulder and then over my left. He's talking and laughing, but all I can see is that bright orange color all around me.

"Hans Hess bought up the police," Alan says to my right ear.

"Hans Hess pays Officer Justice a commission so that Officer Justice discovers only what Hans Hess wants Officer Justice to discover." To my left ear.

Back to my right, louder: "Hans Hess owns one of Saturn's moons."

Again to my left, almost shouting: "Hans Hess has no fingerprints."

"Hans Hess owns a home deep under the earth's crust, shingled with goldbrick and protected by a uniformed coterie of moles!"

And then something else about Hans Hess.

And then something else about Hans Hess.

And then nothing else about Hans Hess, because Alan is flat on his back on the gravel, his lips and my fist covered in blood.

And then nothing else about Hans Hess, because Don Christian is tearing my arms out of their sockets, chaining my wrists behind my back, and slamming me into the fence again and again.

And then Alan's voice, watery and muffled through swollen lips — "I'm still your friend, Thor! I forgive you, Thor, I do!" — getting further and further away as I'm hauled across the exercise yard, past orange stares and orange faces and orange laughter and everything orange.

And then a punch to my guts, shoving all my breath out from underneath my ribs, and another, and then one on my face, then my side, then my other side, then my face again, and Bruce's face orange, and Ronald's, and Don Christian's.

And then the floor of my room, and my door banged shut, and I'm alone again, every part of my body feeling bruised and done for.

***

It's later. Slowly, slowly, slowly, I can crawl to my mattress.

***

Someone's humming. It's me. The tune is Mr. Hans's German song, which I guess I remember after all. I try to change the tune, but it comes back to that German song. I stop humming.

I'm humming again. That German song.

***

More potatoes. They hurt as they go down my throat. I leave half.

***

Shapes in my bruises. A boat. A house. A happy family. Barbara, right there, on my skin. I cover her up with my orange outfit. She tries to talk to me, but I tell her, "No, no-no-no-no-no."

I peek again at my bruise. A car. A tree. A fountain.

***

"You've got a visitor if you can behave," says Don Christian from the door. I press my hands against my eyes, which feel like they're throbbing.

"Okay."

"Can you behave, or should I send her away?"

"Okay." The word scratches my throat.

"How are you feeling?"

I pull myself up onto my elbows. As I move, pounding echoes in my head. My face feels split open and tender. My lips are swollen. My headache hammers at a part of my head just behind the bridge of my nose.

"Fine," I say. I ease my feet off the bed and slide into a sitting position.

"You'll be feeling a lot better in a few days. But you need to rest. Are you sure you're ready for a visitor?"

"Either way, I don't care." Holding on to the edge of my bed for support, I push myself up onto my feet. I'm dizzy for a second, so I close my eyes and massage my forehead.

"Okay," says Don Christian, coming to my elbow to help me walk to the door. "I think you'll be happy to see her."

"Her?" I pause and take a deep breath in, which hurts when it presses against my ribs. "Is it some woman with beautiful red hair?"

"No," says Don Christian. "She's grey-haired and pretty slight. It'll do you some good to see her, buckshot."

I balance my arm on Don Christian's and let him do most of the walking out through the corridor and into a room with a big see-through panel looking out into another room. People in orange outfits are sitting by the panel and talking on telephones. People in clothes that aren't orange are walking around in the room I can see through the window, and a lot of them are talking on black telephones, too. I scan out over the crowd in the other room, and there's Mom, done up in her nicest green dress, twisting a phone cord nervously around her fingers. When I see her, she sees me, and presses her palms flat against the window. Her mouth is stretched out from crying, and she tries to twist up her crying mouth into a smiling mouth, but she just keeps on crying. My heart feels cold and knotted up into my throat. I stand still, wobbling a bit on my feet, but Don Christian gives my elbow a squeeze.

"It's okay," he says. "She's just happy to see you, I bet. It can be hard for people to see the people they care about in trouble."

"Yeah," I say, and steady myself against Don Christian. He helps me walk to the window and ease onto a stool next to a black telephone. I press my hands against the glass panel to say hello to Mom, and she puts her face into her hands so I don't have to watch her crying.

"You've got ten minutes, buckshot," says Don Christian, "but I'm sure she'll be back again."

Don Christian backs away, and I watch Mom through the glass. I can see the bones of her shoulders through her dress as she cries into her hands. Her skin looks thin and yellowy, and she's even smaller than I remember.

Mom peeks up, wipes her eyes on the back of her wrist, and picks up her phone. I pick up my phone and can hear Mom breathing.

"You're hurt, Thorrie," Mom says, putting her fingers up to her own face, on the spots where my face is hurt. I look down at my hands, ashamed of how I must look.

"Not too bad," I say.

"You're all bruised." She takes her fingers off her face and presses them up to the glass, like she can cure me that way.

"It doesn't hurt." Between the pain in my throat and the tangle in my heart, it's hard to get the words out. Mom opens her mouth to say something, then stops.

"They say you've been fighting," she says, after a moment.

"I'm sorry."

"Why would you, Thorrie?"

"I don't know."

"Oh, baby." Mom looks away and starts knotting the phone cord into a figure eight. "I know it must seem bad now, but your father and I never taught you to fight. Why would you?"

"I'm sorry."

"Your father says you came at him when you were at the house. Is that true?" Mom's voice quivers as she talks, and I want to lie to her and tell her there's some explanation for everything and we're all just having this big misunderstanding.

"I'm sorry."

"Oh, Thorrie," says Mom, and then she falls silent. We look at each other through the panel, and when my cheeks feel wet I know I'm crying.

"I just want it all to be okay again," I've said before I even realize I'm talking. "I didn't understand about the invasion, and I didn't understand about Mister Hans, and I didn't understand about Barbara, and now it's too late. The money's gone, and Barbara's gone, and I just don't care what happens anymore, and it'll never be okay."

"Shhhh," Mom says. Her forehead wrinkles up and I know I'm giving her pain. "Don't say that, Thorrie. It's never too late to fix what's gone wrong."

"I'm sorry I'm making you so sad, Mom." I push my knuckles together and watch them turn white. "You're probably just about sick of me."

"*Thor*," says Mom, so loud and strong I look up at her. "I am not sick of you, but I am sick of this nonsense. I love you very much, and so does your father, and it's about time you learned that life is hard and you can't wait around for good things to happen, but you need to be strong, and you need to be smart, and y—"

"Mom, I—"

"Do *not* tell me 'Mom.' I don't want to hear anything out of you, Thorrie. I don't want to hear about how hard it is and how many good reasons you have for this or that, because there is no reason to go around fighting or smashing up restaurants, and I don't think there's anything possible you or anyone else can say that's going to change my mind on that. So don't tell me 'Mom' anything."

"But, Mom," I say, and then stop, because she's right. There *is* nothing to say. "Where's Dad?"

"Thor," says Mom, and a smile—a real one—flickers up from the corners of her mouth. "Your father loves you so much, but it's hard for him. You disappointed him. And, I hate to say it, but one of these days you'll understand that the harder you love, the harder the disappointment."

"I know, Mom," I say. And I realize now that no matter how bad she hurt me, the only wish I have for Barbara is that she can get far, far away with that money and can be happy, and that no police ever catches her out they way they caught me out. I wish I had some way to tell her that.

"Your father and I will do everything we can for you, Thor," says Mom, "but you need to do everything you can do for yourself, too, okay? Do you promise me you will?"

"Sure, Mom."

"Let's think about getting you back to your cell, buckshot," says Don Christian, suddenly with his hand on my shoulder. I look up at him and see him looking down at me. He wants me to be good. He wants me to go through this prison thing and come out a better person, and I think somewhere, deep down, he thinks that's possible.

"Okay," I say to him. "Can I say goodbye to Mom?"

"By all means," says Don Christian.

"Goodbye, Mom," I say into the phone. "I love you so much, and I love Dad."

"I'll be back to see you, Thor. And I'll try to get your father to come along. We'll do what we can for lawyers, but you know we don't have the money. Just don't give up, Thorrie, and I won't either. We'll see our way to the end of this."

Mom hangs up the phone, but stays sitting with her hand resting on the receiver as Don Christian helps me stand and walks me back out to the corridor.

Don Christian leads me back to my room and, when we get to the door, asks, "Do you need help getting back into bed?"

"I'll stay standing."

"Okay. Was it good to see your mother?"

I smile a little and nod.

"Good," says Don Christian, and smiles back as he shuts the door and locks me into my small stone room.

***

Days go by, and weeks go by, and my bruises start to heal up. Sometimes I am extremely sad; other times, I am not as sad. Mom comes back to see me a few times. Dad is never with her, but she keeps saying she will bring him. Before she leaves, every time, she makes me promise that I will not give up. I am not always sure what she means, but I always promise her, because it makes her happier. I do not see Alan again, and Don Christian informs me he's been taken away to some other place for people with very particular problems. Mandy-Mandy visits once with the twins. They bring a plate of pesto, but Don Christian will not let me have it. Mandy-Mandy tells me there is no more A Panini for Your Thoughts. There's only the Sauerkraut Kitchen. I ask her what she's heard about Alan, and she hasn't heard anything. I ask her what she's heard about Barbara, and she hasn't heard anything about her either.

I have to sit in a lot of rooms and get asked a lot of questions by a lot of men. Sometimes they yell at me. Sometimes they throw punches. I try to do what they ask me to and, then, if they get violent, protect my face. Sometimes I get mad back, but I try not to. Officer Justice tells me I'm going on trial for treason and if I'm found guilty, it could mean a lifetime of prison, or deportation. He tells me that this thing with Tintoretto is very important. I try again and again to tell him about Mr. Hans, but Officer Justice doesn't care about Mr. Hans, and Don Christian doesn't care about Mr. Hans, and nobody here seems to care about Mr. Hans.

The longer I stay in jail, the more I wonder when I will be allowed to leave. I ask Don Christian every time he comes to take me to exercise or to the room where I talk to Mom. Every time, he says there's no way to know and it all depends on this trial, but the better decisions I make, the sooner I'll be able to leave. So, some days it's hard, and some days it's not as hard, but I do what I can. The future is unclear and a little scary, and I find it's best to just shut myself off from thinking about what might happen. I try to wake up each morning and make the best decisions I can, without thinking about how much I have to feel sick about, and hope that, somehow, life will get better instead of getting worse.

About the Author

Nick Sansone holds an MFA in fiction from the University of Massachusetts and is the author of the novel *Shooting Angels*. His short fiction has appeared in a large number of journals, including *PANK*, *Pear Noir!*, *Bartleby Snopes*, *NANO Fiction*, *Word Riot*, *Denver Syntax*, and *The Los Angeles Review*. His work has been nominated for the Pushcart Prize and the AWP Intro Journal Award. Learn more at his website: http://nicksansone.yolasite.com.

www.ingramcontent.com/pod-product-compliance
Lightning Source LLC
Chambersburg PA
CBHW051647260626
47170CB00004B/1383